P.S.
I
still
love
you

## Also by Jenny Han

*Shug*

*The Summer I Turned Pretty*

*It's Not Summer Without You*

*We'll Always Have Summer*

*To All the Boys I've Loved Before*

## Cowritten with Siobhan Vivian

*Burn for Burn*

*Fire with Fire*

*Ashes to Ashes*

# P.S. I still love you

## JENNY HAN

SIMON & SCHUSTER BFYR

New York    London    Toronto    Sydney    New Delhi

An imprint of Simon & Schuster Children's Publishing Division

1230 Avenue of the Americas, New York, New York 10020

For information about special discounts for bulk purchases, please contact Simon & Schuster
Special Sales at 1-866-506-1949 or business@simonandschuster.com.

The Simon & Schuster Speakers Bureau can bring authors to your live event. For
more information or to book an event, contact the Simon & Schuster Speakers Bureau
at 1-866-248-3049 or visit our website at www.simonspeakers.com.

Book design by Lucy Ruth Cummins

The text for this book is set in Bembo Std.

Manufactured in the United States of America

2 4 6 8 10 9 7 5 3 1

CIP data for this book is available from the Library of Congress.

ISBN 978-1-4424-2673-3

ISBN 978-1-4424-2675-7 (eBook)

For Logan. I've only just met you
and already I love you.

P.S.

I still love you

She was glad that the cosy house, and Pa and Ma and the fire-light and the music, were now. They could not be forgotten, she thought, because now is now. It can never be a long time ago.

—LAURA INGALLS WILDER, *Little House in the Big Woods*


Time is the longest distance between two places.

—TENNESSEE WILLIAMS, *The Glass Menagerie*

Dear Peter,

I miss you. It's only been five days but I miss you like it's been five years. Maybe because I don't know if this is just it, if you and I will ever talk again. I mean I'm sure we'll say hi in chem class, or in the hallways, but will it ever be like it was? That's what makes me sad. I felt like I could say anything to you. I think you felt the same way. I hope you did.

So I'm just going to say anything to you right now, while I'm still feeling brave. What happened between us in the hot tub scared me. I know it was just a day in the life of Peter for you, but for me it meant a lot more, and that's what scared me. Not just what people were saying about it, and me, but that it happened at all. How easy it was, how much I liked it. I got scared and I took it out on you and for that I'm truly sorry.

And at the recital party, I'm sorry I didn't defend you to Josh. I should have. I know I owed you that much. I owed you that much and more. I still can't believe you came, and that you brought those fruitcake cookies. You looked cute in your sweater, by the way. I'm not saying that to butter you up. I mean it.

Sometimes I like you so much I can't stand it. It fills up inside me, all the way to the brim, and I feel like I could overflow. I like you so much I don't know what to do with it. My heart beats so fast when I know I'm going to see you again. And then, when you look at me the way you do, I feel like the luckiest girl in the world.

Those things Josh said about you, they weren't true. You haven't brought me down. Just the opposite. You've brought me out. You gave me my first love story, Peter. Please just don't let it be over yet.

Love,

Lara Jean

# 1

KITTY'S BEEN A LITTLE COMPLAINER ALL
morning, and I suspect both Margot and Daddy are suf-
fering from New Year's Eve hangovers. And me? I've got
hearts in my eyes and a letter that's burning a hole in my
coat pocket.

As we're putting on our shoes, Kitty's still trying to weasel
her way out of wearing a hanbok to Aunt Carrie and Uncle
Victor's. "Look at the sleeves! They're three-quarter length
on me!"

Unconvincingly Daddy says, "They're supposed to be that
way."

Kitty points to me and Margot. "Then why do theirs fit?"
she demands. Our grandma bought the hanboks for us the last
time she was in Korea. Margot's hanbok has a yellow jacket and
apple-green skirt. Mine is hot pink with an ivory-white jacket
and a long hot-pink bow with flowers embroidered down the
front. The skirt is voluminous, full like a bell, and it falls all the
way to the floor. Unlike Kitty's, which hits right at her ankles.

"It's not our fault you grow like a weed," I say, fussing with
my bow. The bow is the hardest thing to get right. I had to
watch a YouTube video multiple times to figure it out, and it
still looks lopsided and sad.

"My skirt's too short too," she grumps, lifting the bottom.

The real truth is, Kitty hates wearing a hanbok because you have to walk delicately in it and hold the skirt closed with one hand or the whole thing comes open.

"All of the other cousins will be wearing them, and it will make Grandma happy," Daddy says, rubbing his temples. "Case closed."

In the car Kitty keeps saying "I hate New Year's Day," and it puts everyone but me in a sour mood. Margot is already in a semi-sour mood because she had to wake up at the crack of dawn to get home from her friend's cabin in time. There's also the matter of that maybe hangover. Nothing could sour my mood, though, because I'm not even in this car. I'm somewhere else entirely, thinking about my letter to Peter, wondering if it was heartfelt enough, and how and when I'm going to give it to him, and what he'll say, and what it will mean. Should I drop it in his mailbox? Leave it in his locker? When I see him again, will he smile at me, make a joke of it to lighten the mood? Or will he pretend he never saw it, to spare us both? I think that would be worse. I have to keep reminding myself that, despite everything, Peter is kind and he is easygoing and he won't be cruel no matter what. Of that much I can be sure.

"What are you thinking so hard about?" Kitty asks me.

I barely hear her.

"Hello?"

I close my eyes and pretend to be asleep, and all I see is Peter's face. I don't know what I want from him exactly, what I'm ready for—if it's boyfriend-girlfriend heavy-duty serious love, or if it's what we had before, just fun and some here-and-there kisses, or if it's something in between, but I do know I can't get his Handsome Boy face out of my mind. The way he smirks when he says my name, how when he's near me I forget to breathe sometimes.

Of course, when we get to Aunt Carrie and Uncle Victor's, none of the other cousins are wearing hanboks, and Kitty practically turns purple with the effort of not yelling at Daddy. Margot and I give him some side-eye too. It's not particularly comfortable to sit around in a hanbok all day. But then Grandma gives me an approving smile, which makes up for it.

As we take off our shoes and coats at the front door, I whisper to Kitty, "Maybe the adults will give us more money for dressing up."

"You girls look so cute," Aunt Carrie said as she hugs us. "Haven refused to wear hers!"

Haven rolls her eyes at her mom. "I love your haircut," she says to Margot. Haven and I are only a few months apart, but she thinks she's so much older than me. She's always trying to get in with Margot.

We get the bowing out of the way first. In Korean culture, you bow to your elders on New Year's Day and wish them luck in the new year, and in return they give you money. The order goes oldest to youngest, so as the oldest adult, Grandma sits down on the couch first, and Aunt Carrie and Uncle Victor bow first, then Daddy, all the way down the line to Kitty, who is youngest. When it's Daddy's turn to sit on the couch and receive his bows, there's an empty couch cushion next to him as there has been every New Year's Day since Mommy died. It gives me an achy feeling in my chest to see him sitting there alone, smiling gamely, handing out ten-dollar bills. Grandma catches my eye pointedly and I know she's thinking the same thing. When it's my turn to bow, I kneel, hands folded in front of my forehead, and I vow that I will not see Daddy alone on that couch again next year.

We get ten dollars from Aunt Carrie and Uncle Victor, ten from Daddy, ten from Aunt Min and Uncle Sam, who aren't our real aunt and uncle but second cousins (or is it cousins once removed? They're Mommy's cousins, anyway), and twenty from Grandma! We didn't get more for wearing hanboks, but all in all a good take. Last year the aunts and uncles were only doing five apiece.

Next we do rice cake soup for good luck. Aunt Carrie also made black-eyed pea cakes and insists we try at least one, though no one wants to. The twins, Harry and Leon—our third cousins? Cousins twice removed?—refuse to eat the soup or the black-eyed pea cakes and are eating chicken nuggets in the TV room. There isn't enough room at the dining table, so Kitty and I eat on stools at the kitchen island. We can hear everyone laughing from over here.

As I begin to eat my soup, I make a wish. *Please, please let things work out with me and Peter.*

"Why do I get a smaller bowl of soup than everyone else?" Kitty whispers to me.

"Because you're the littlest."

"Why don't we get our own bowl of kimchi?"

"Because Aunt Carrie thinks we don't like it because we're not full Korean."

"Go ask for some," Kitty whispers.

So I do, but mainly because I want some too.

While the adults drink coffee, Margot, Haven, and I go up to Haven's room and Kitty tags along. Usually she plays with the twins, but this time she picks up Aunt Carrie's Yorkie, Smitty, and follows us upstairs like one of the girls.

Haven has indie rock band posters on her walls; most I've never heard of. She's always rotating them out. There's a new one, a letterpressed Belle and Sebastian. It looks like denim. "This is cool," I say.

"I was just about to switch that one out," Haven says. "You can have it if you want."

"That's all right," I tell her. I know she's only offering it to feel above me, as is her way.

"I'll take it," Kitty says, and Haven's face pulls into a frown for a second, but Kitty's already peeling it off the wall. "Thanks, Haven."

Margot and I look at each other and try not to smile. Haven's never had much patience for Kitty, and the feeling is infinitely mutual.

"Margot, have you been to any shows since you've been in Scotland?" Haven asks. She plops down on her bed and opens up her laptop.

"Not really," Margot says. "I've been so busy with classes."

Margot's not much of a live-music person anyway. She's looking at her phone; the skirt of her hanbok is fanned around her. She's the only one of us Song girls still fully clothed. I've taken off my jacket, so I'm just in the slip and skirt, and Kitty's taken off both the jacket and the skirt and is just wearing an undershirt and bloomers.

I sit down on the bed next to Haven so she can show me pictures from their vacation to Bermuda on Instagram. As she's scrolling through her feed, a picture from the ski trip pops up. Haven's in the Charlottesville Youth Orchestra, so she knows people from a lot of different schools, including mine.

I can't help but sigh a little when I see it—a picture of a bunch of us on the bus the last morning. Peter has his arm around me, he's whispering something in my ear. I wish I remembered what.

All surprised, Haven looks up and says, "Oh, hey, that's you, Lara Jean. What's this from?"

"The school ski trip."

"Is that your boyfriend?" Haven asks me, and I can tell she's impressed and trying not to show it.

I wish I could say yes. But—

Kitty scampers over to us and looks over our shoulders. "Yes, and he's the hottest guy you've ever seen in your life, Haven." She says it like a challenge. Margot, who was scrolling on her phone, looks up and giggles.

"Well, that's not exactly true," I hedge. I mean, he's the hottest guy I've ever seen in *my* life, but I don't know what kind of people Haven goes to school with.

"No, Kitty's right, he's hot," Haven admits. "Like, how did you get him? No offense. I just thought you were the non-dating type."

I frown. The non-dating type? What kind of type is that? A little mushroom who sits at home in a semidark room growing moss?

"Lara Jean dates plenty," Margot says loyally.

I blush. I date never, Peter barely even counts, but I'm glad for the lie.

"What's his name?" Haven asks me.

"Peter. Peter Kavinsky." Even saying his name is a remembered pleasure, something to savor, like a piece of chocolate dissolving on my tongue.

*"Ohh,"* she says. "I thought he dated that pretty blond girl. What's her name? Jenna? Weren't you guys best friends when you were little?"

I feel a pang in my heart. "Her name is Genevieve. We used to be friends, not anymore. And she and Peter have been broken up for a while."

"So then how long have you and Peter been together?" Haven asks me. She has a dubious look in her eye, like she 90 percent believes me but there's still that niggling 10 percent that has doubt.

"We started hanging out in September." At least that much is true. "We're not together right now; we're kind of on a break. . . . But I'm . . . optimistic."

Kitty pokes my cheek, makes a dimple with her pinky. "You're smiling," she says, and she's smiling too. She cuddles closer to me. "Make up with him today, okay? I want Peter back."

"It's not that simple," I say, though maybe it could be?

"Sure it's that simple. He still likes you a lot—just tell him you still like him, too, and boom. You're back together and it'll be like you never kicked him out of our house."

Haven's eyes go even wider. "Lara Jean, *you* broke up with *him*?"

"Geez, is it so hard to believe?" I narrow my eyes at her, and Haven opens and then wisely closes her mouth.

She takes another look at the picture of Peter. Then she gets up to go to the bathroom, and as she closes the door, she says, "All I can say is, if that boy was my boyfriend, I'd never let him go."

My whole body tingles when she says those words.

I once had that exact same thought about Josh, and look at me now: It's like a million years have gone by and he's just a memory to me. I don't want it to be like that with Peter. The farawayness of old feelings, like even when you try with all your might, you can barely make out his face when you close your eyes. No matter what, I always want to remember his face.

When it's time to go, I'm putting on my coat and Peter's letter falls out of my pocket. Margot picks it up. "Another letter?"

I blush. In a rush I say, "I haven't figured out when I should give it to him, if I should leave it in his mailbox, or if I should actually mail it? Or face to face? Gogo, what do you think?"

"You should just talk to him," Margot says. "Go right now.

Daddy will drop you off. You go to his house, you give him the letter, and then you see what he says."

My heart pumps wildly at the thought. Right now? Just go over there, without calling first, without a plan? "I don't know," I hedge. "I feel like I should think it over more."

Margot opens her mouth to respond, but then Kitty comes up behind us and says, "Enough with the letters. Just go get him back."

"Don't let it be too late," Margot says, and I know she's not just talking about me and Peter.

I've been tiptoeing around the subject of Josh because of everything that's happened with us. I mean, Margot's forgiven me, but there's no sense in rocking the boat. So these past couple of days I've stayed silently supportive and hoped that was enough. But Margot leaves for Scotland again in less than a week. The thought of her leaving without at least talking to Josh doesn't feel right to me. We've all been friends for so long. I know Josh and I will mend things, because we're neighbors, and that's how it goes with people you see a lot. They mend, almost on their own. But not so for Margot and Josh, with her so far away. If they don't talk now, the scar will only harden over time, it will calcify, and then they'll be like strangers who never loved each other, which is the saddest thought of all.

While Kitty's putting on her boots, I whisper to Margot, "If I talk to Peter, you should talk to Josh. Don't go back to Scotland and leave things like this with him."

"We'll see," she says, but I see the hope that flares in her eyes, and it gives me hope too.

# 2

*MARGOT AND KITTY ARE BOTH ASLEEP IN THE* backseat. Kitty's got her head in Margot's lap; Margot's sleeping with her head back and her mouth wide open. Daddy is listening to NPR with a faint smile on his face. Everyone's so peaceful, and my heart is thumping a million beats a minute just in anticipation of what I'm about to do.

I'm doing it now, this very night. Before we're back at school, before all the gears shift back to normal and Peter and I are nothing more than a memory. Like snow globes, you shake them up, and for a moment everything is upside down and glitter everywhere and it's just like magic—but then it all settles and goes back to where it's supposed to be. Things have a way of settling back. I can't go back.

I time it so that we are one stoplight from Peter's neighborhood when I ask Daddy to drop me off. He must hear the intensity in my voice, the *necessity*, because he doesn't ask any questions, he just says yes.

When we pull up to Peter's house, the lights are on and his car is in the driveway; so is his mom's minivan. The sun is just going down, early because it's winter. Across the street, Peter's neighbors still have their holiday lights up. Today's probably the last day for that, seeing as how it's a new year. New year, new start.

I can feel the veins in my wrists pulsing, and I'm nervous, I'm so nervous. I run out of the car and ring the doorbell. When I hear footsteps from inside, I wave Daddy off, and he backs out of the driveway. Kitty's awake now, and she's got her face up against the back window, grinning hard. She sends me a thumbs-up and I wave back.

Peter opens the door. My heart jumps like a Mexican jumping bean in my chest. He's wearing a button-down I've never seen before, plaid. It must have been a Christmas present. His hair is mussed on top, like he's been lying down. He doesn't look so very surprised to see me. "Hey." He eyes my skirt, which is poofing out from under my winter coat like a ball gown. "Why are you so dressed up?"

"It's for New Year's." Maybe I should've gone home and changed first. At least then I would feel like me, standing at this boy's door, proverbial hat in hand. "So, hey, how was your Christmas?"

"Good." He takes his time, four whole seconds, before he asks, "How was yours?"

"Great. We got a new puppy. His name is Jamie Fox-Pickle." Not even a trace of a smile from Peter. He's cold; I didn't expect him to be cold. Maybe not even cold. Maybe just indifferent. "Can I talk to you for a second?"

Peter shrugs, which seems like a yes, but he doesn't invite me in. I have this sudden sick-to-my-stomach fear that Genevieve is inside—which quickly dissipates when I remember that if she *were* inside, he wouldn't be out here with me. He leaves the door ajar as he puts on sneakers and a coat, and then steps onto the porch. He closes the door behind him and sits down on the steps. I sit next to him, smoothing my skirt around me. "So, what's up?" he says, like I'm taking up his precious time.

This isn't right. Not what I expected at all.

But what, exactly, did I expect from Peter? I'd give him the letter, and he'd read it, and then he'd love me? He'd take me in his arms; we'd kiss passionately, but just kissing, just innocent. Then what? We'd date? How long until he grew bored of me, missed Genevieve, wanted more than I was prepared to give, bedroomwise and also just lifewise? Someone like him could never be content staying at home and watching a movie on the couch. This is Peter Kavinsky we're talking about, after all.

I take so long swept up in my fast-forward reverie that he says it again, just slightly less cold this time. "What, Lara Jean?" He looks at me like he's waiting for something, and suddenly I'm afraid to give it.

I tighten my fist around the letter, shove it into my coat pocket. My hands are freezing. I don't have any gloves or hat; I should probably just go home. "I just came to say . . . to say I'm sorry for the way things turned out. And . . . I hope we can still be friends, and happy new year."

His eyes narrow at this. "'Happy new year'?" he repeats. "That's what you came here to say? Sorry and *happy new year*?"

"And I hope we can still be friends," I add, biting my lip.

"You hope we can still be friends," he repeats, and there is a note of sarcasm in his voice that I don't understand or like.

"That's what I said." I start to stand up. I was hoping he'd give me a ride home, but now I don't want to ask. But it's so cold outside. Maybe if I hint. . . . Blowing on my hands, I say, "Well, I'm gonna head home."

"Wait a minute. Let's go back to the apology part. What are you apologizing for, exactly? For kicking me out of your house, or for thinking I'm a dirtbag who would go around telling people we had sex when we didn't?"

A lump forms in my throat. When he puts it that way, it really does sound terrible. "Both of those things. I'm sorry for both of those things."

Peter cocks his head to the side, his eyebrows raised. "And what else?"

I bristle. *What else?* "There is no 'what else.' That's it." Thank God I didn't give him the letter, if this is how he's going to be. It's not like I'm the only one with stuff to apologize for.

"Hey, you're the one who came here talking about 'I'm sorry' and 'let's be friends.' You don't get to force me into accepting your half-assed apology."

"Well, I wish you a happy new year anyway." Now I'm the one being sarcastic, and it sure is satisfying. "Have a nice life. Auld lang syne and all that."

"Fine. Bye."

I turn to go. I was so hopeful this morning, I had such stars in my eyes imagining how this was all going to go. God, what a jerk Peter is. Good riddance to him!

"Wait a minute."

Hope leaps into my heart like Jamie Fox-Pickle leaps into my bed—swift and unbidden. But I turn back around, like *Ugh, what do you want now*, so he doesn't see it.

"What's that you've got crumpled up in your pocket?"

My hand flies down to my pocket. "That? Oh, it's nothing. It's junk mail. It was on the ground by your mailbox. No worries, I'll recycle it for you."

"Give it to me and I'll recycle it right now," he says, holding out his hand.

"No, I said I'll do it." I reach down to stuff the letter deeper into my coat pocket, and Peter tries to snatch it out of my hand. I twist away from him wildly and hold on tight. He shrugs, and I relax and let out a small sigh of relief, and then he lunges forward and plucks it away from me.

I pant, "Give it back, Peter!"

Blithely he says, "Tampering with US mail is a federal offense." Then he looks down at the envelope. "This is to me. From you." I make a desperate grab for the envelope, and it takes him by surprise. We wrestle for it; I've got the corner of it in my grip, but he's not letting go. "Stop, you're going to rip it!" he yells, prying it out of my grasp.

I try to grab harder, but it's too late. He has it.

Peter holds the envelope above my head and tears it open and begins to read. It's torturous standing there in front of him, waiting—for what, I don't know. More humiliation? I should probably just go. He's such a slow reader.

When he's finally done, he asks, "Why weren't you going to give me this? Why were you just going to leave?"

"Because, I don't know, you didn't seem so glad to see me. . . ." My voice trails off lamely.

"It's called playing hard to get! I've been waiting for you to call me, you dummy. It's been six days."

I suck in my breath. "Oh!"

"'Oh.'" He pulls me by the lapels of my coat, closer to him, close enough to kiss. He's so close I can see the puffs his breath makes. So close I could count his eyelashes if I wanted. In a low voice he says, "So then . . . you still like me?"

"Yeah," I whisper. "I mean, sort of." My heartbeat is going quick-quick-quick. I'm giddy. Is this a dream? If so, let me never wake up.

Peter gives me a look like *Get real, you know you like me.* I do, I do. Then, softly, he says, "Do you believe me that I didn't tell people we had sex on the ski trip?"

"Yes."

"Okay." He inhales. "Did . . . did anything happen with you and Sanderson after I left your house that night?" He's jealous! The very thought of it warms me up like hot soup. I start to tell him no way, but he quickly says, "Wait. Don't tell me. I don't want to know."

"No," I say, firmly so he knows I mean it. He nods but doesn't say anything.

Then he leans in, and I close my eyes, heart thrumming in my chest like hummingbird wings. We've technically only kissed four times, and only one of those times was for real. I'd like to just get right to it, so I can stop being nervous.

But Peter doesn't kiss me, not the way I expect. He kisses me on my left cheek, and then my right; his breath is warm. And then nothing. My eyes fly open. Is this a literal kiss-off? Why isn't he kissing me properly? "What are you doing?" I whisper.

"Building the anticipation."

Quickly I say, "Let's just kiss."

He angles his head, and his cheek brushes against mine, which is when the front door opens, and it's Peter's younger brother, Owen, standing there with his arms crossed. I spring away from Peter like I just found out he has some incurable infectious disease. "Mom wants you guys to come in and have some cider," he says, smirking.

"In a minute," Peter says, pulling me back.

"She said right now," Owen says.

Oh my God. I throw a panicky look at Peter. "I should probably get going before my dad starts to worry. . . ."

He nudges me toward the door with his chin. "Just come inside for a minute, and then I'll take you home." As I step inside, he takes off my coat and says in a low voice, "Were you really going to walk all the way home in that fancy dress? In the cold?"

"No, I was going to guilt you into driving me," I whisper back.

"What's with your outfit?" Owen says to me.

"It's what Korean people wear on New Year's Day," I tell him.

Peter's mom steps out of the kitchen with two steaming

mugs. She's wearing a long cashmere cardigan that's loosely belted around her waist, and cream cable-knit slippers. "It's stunning," she says. "You look gorgeous. So colorful."

"Thank you," I say, feeling embarrassed over the fuss.

The three of us sit down in the family room; Owen escapes to the kitchen. I still feel flushed from the almost kiss and from the fact that Peter's mom probably knows what we were up to. I wonder, too, what she knows about what's been going on with us, how much he's told her, if anything.

"How was your Christmas, Lara Jean?" his mom asks me.

I blow into my mug. "It was really nice. My dad bought my little sister a puppy, and we've just been fighting over who gets to hold him. And my older sister's still home from college, so that's been nice too. How was your holiday, Mrs. Kavinsky?"

"Oh, it was nice. Quiet." She points to her slippers. "Owen got me these. How did the holiday party go? Did your sisters like the fruitcake cookies Peter baked? Honestly, I can't stand them."

Surprised, I look over at Peter, who is suddenly busy scrolling on his phone. "I thought you said your mom made them."

His mom smiles a proud kind of smile. "Oh no, he did it all by himself. He was very determined."

"They tasted like garbage!" Owen yells from the kitchen.

His mom laughs again, and then things are silent. My mind is racing, trying to think up potential conversation pieces. New Year's resolutions, maybe? The snowstorm we're supposed to get next week? Peter's no help at all; he's look-ing at his phone again.

She stands up. "It was nice to see you, Lara Jean. Peter, don't keep her out too late."

"I won't." To me he says, "I'll be right back; I'm just gonna get my keys."

When he's gone, I say, "I'm sorry for dropping in like this on New Year's Day. I hope I wasn't interrupting anything."

"You're welcome here anytime." She leans forward and puts her hand on my knee. With a meaningful look she says, "Just be easy with his heart is all I ask."

My stomach does a dip. Did Peter tell her what happened between us?

She gives my knee a pat and stands up. "Good night, Lara Jean."

"Good night," I echo.

Despite her kind smile, I feel like I've just gotten in trouble. There was a hint of reproach in her voice—I know I heard it. *Don't mess with my son* is what she was saying. Was Peter very upset by what happened between us? He didn't make it out like he was. Annoyed, maybe a little hurt. Certainly not hurt enough to talk to his mom about it. But maybe he and his mom are really close. I hate to think I may have already made a bad impression, before Peter and I have even gotten going.

It's pitch black out, not many stars in the sky. I think maybe it'll snow again soon. At my house, all the lights are on downstairs, and Margot's bedroom light is on upstairs. Across the street I can see Ms. Rothschild's little Christmas tree lit up in the window.

Peter and I are warm and cozy in his car. Heat billows out the vents. I ask him, "Did you tell your mom about how we broke up?"

"No. Because we never broke up," he says, turning the heat down.

"We didn't?"

He laughs. "No, because we were never really together, remember?"

*Are we together now?* is what I'm wondering, but I don't ask, because he puts his arm around me and tilts my head up to his, and I'm nervous again. "Don't be nervous," he says.

I give him a quick kiss to prove I'm not.

"Kiss me like you missed me," he says, and his voice goes husky.

"I did," I say. "My letter told you I did."

"Yeah, but—"

I kiss him before he can finish. Properly. Like I mean it. He kisses back like he means it too. Like it's been four hundred years. And then I'm not thinking anymore and I'm just lost in the kissing.

# 3

AFTER PETER DROPS ME OFF, I RUN INSIDE to tell Margot and Kitty everything, and I feel like a purse bulging with gold coins. I can't wait to spill.

Kitty's lying on the couch, watching TV with Jamie Fox-Pickle in her lap, and she scrambles up when I come through the door. In a hushed voice she says, "Gogo's crying."

My enthusiasm dries up instantly. "What! Why?"

"I think she went over to Josh's and they had a talk and it wasn't good. You should go check on her."

Oh no. This isn't how it was supposed to go for them. They were supposed to get back together, like Peter and me.

Kitty settles back on the couch, remote in hand, her sisterly duty fulfilled. "How did it go with Peter?"

"Great," I say. "Really great." The smile comes to my face without me even intending it, and I quickly wipe it away, out of respect for Margot.

I go to the kitchen and make Margot a cup of Night-Night tea, two tablespoons of honey, like Mommy used to make us for bedtime. For a second I contemplate adding a splash of whiskey because I saw it on a Victorian show on PBS—the maids would put whiskey in the lady of the manor's hot beverage to calm her nerves. I know Margot drinks at college, but she already has a hangover, and besides, I doubt Daddy would be into it. So I just put the tea, sans whiskey, in my favorite mug, and I send Kitty upstairs with it. I tell her to act adorable. I say she should first give Margot the tea and then snuggle with her for at least five minutes. Which Kitty balks at, because Kitty only cuddles if there's something in it for her, and also because I know it frightens her to see Margot upset. "I'll just bring her Jamie to cuddle with," Kitty says.

Selfish!

When I go to Margot's room with a piece of buttered cinnamon toast, Kitty's nowhere in sight and neither is Jamie. Margot's curled up on her side, crying. "It's really over, Lara Jean," she whispers. "It's been over, but now I know it's over for good. I th-thought that if I wanted to get back together, he would too, but he d-doesn't." I curl up next to her, my forehead pressed to her back. I can feel every breath she takes. She weeps into her pillow, and I scratch her shoulder blades the way she likes. The thing to know about Margot is she never cries, so seeing her cry sets my world, and this house, off its axis. Everything feels tilted somehow. "He says that long distance is too h-hard, that I was right to break up with him in the first place. I missed him so much, and it seems like he didn't miss me at all."

I bite my lip guiltily. I was the one who encouraged her to talk to Josh. This is partly my fault. "Margot, he did miss you. He missed you like crazy. I would look out the window during French class, and I would see him outside on the bleachers eating his lunch alone. It was depressing."

She sniffles. "Did he really?"

*"Yes."* I don't understand what's the matter with Josh. He acted like he was so in love with her; he practically went into a depression when she was gone. And now this?

Sighing, she says, "I think . . . I think I just still really love him."

"You do?" *Love.* Margot said "love." I don't think I've ever heard her say she loved Josh before. Maybe "in love," but never "love."

Margot wipes her eyes with her sheet. "The whole reason I broke up with him was so I wouldn't be that girl crying over her boyfriend, and now that's exactly what I am. It's pathetic."

"You're the least pathetic person I know, Gogo," I tell her.

Margot stops sniffling and rolls around so we're lying face to face. Frowning at me, she says, "I didn't say *I* was pathetic. I said crying over a boy was."

"Oh," I say. "Well, I still don't think it's pathetic to cry over someone. It just means you care about them deeply and you're sad."

"I've been crying so much I feel like my eyes look like . . . like shriveled-up raisins. Do they?" Margot squints at me.

"They *are* swollen," I admit. "Your eyes just aren't used to crying. I have an idea!" I leap out of bed and run downstairs to the kitchen. I fill a cereal bowl with ice and two silver spoons and come running back. "Lie back down," I instruct, and Margot obeys. "Close your eyes." I put a spoon over each eye.

"Does this really work?"

"I saw it in a magazine."

When the spoons warm up against her skin, I dip them back into the ice and back onto her face, over and over again. She asks me to tell her what happened with Peter, so I do, but I leave out all the kissing because it feels in poor taste in light of her own heartbreak. She sits up and says, "You don't have to pretend to like Peter just to spare my feelings." Margot swallows painfully, like she has a sore throat. "If any part of you still likes Josh . . . if he likes you . . ." I gasp in horror. I open my mouth to deny it, to say that it feels like forever ago already, but she silences me with her hand. "It would be really hard, but I wouldn't want to stand in the way of that, you know? I mean it, Lara Jean. You can tell me."

I'm so relieved, so grateful she's bringing it up. I rush to say, "Oh my gosh, I don't like Josh, Gogo. Not like that. Not at all. And he doesn't like me like that either. I think . . . I think we were both just missing you. Peter's the one I like." Under the blanket I find Margot's hand and link my pinky with hers. "Sister swear."

She swallows hard. "Then I guess there's no secret reason for him not wanting to get back together. I guess it's as simple as he just doesn't want to be with me anymore."

"No, it's as simple as you're in Scotland and he's in Virginia and it's too hard. You were wise to break it off when you did. Wise and brave and right."

Doubt creeps across her face like dark shadows, and then she shakes her head and her expression clears. "Enough about me and Josh. We're yesterday's news. Tell me more about Peter. Please, it'll make me feel better." She lies back down, and I put the spoons back on her eyes.

"Well, tonight at first he was very cool with me, very blasé blasé—"

"No, go all the way back to the beginning."

So I go back further: I tell her about our pretend relationship, the hot tub, everything. She keeps taking the spoons off so she can look at me as I tell her. But before long her eyes do look less puffy. And I feel lighter—giddy, even. I've kept all these things secret from her for months, and now she knows everything that's happened since she's been gone, and I feel so close to her again. You can't be close to someone, not truly, with secrets in between you.

Margot clears her throat. She hesitates and then asks, "So, how does he kiss?"

I'm blushing. I tap my fingers on my lips before I say, "He kisses like . . . like it could be his job."

Margot giggles and lifts the spoons off her eyes. "Like a male prostitute?"

I grab one of the spoons and tap her on the forehead with it like a gong.

"Ow!" She snatches for the other spoon, but I'm too quick and I've got them both. We're both laughing like crazy as I try to get in another gong on her forehead.

"Margot . . . did it hurt when you had sex?" I'm careful not to say Josh's name. It's strange, because Margot and I have never talked about sex before in any kind of real way, because neither of us had a point of reference. But now she does and I don't, and I want to know what she knows.

"Umm. I mean, the first couple of times, a little." Now she's the one who's blushing. "Lara Jean, I can't talk about this with you. It's too weird. Can't you just ask Chris?"

"No, I want to hear it from you. Please, Gogo. You have to tell me everything about it so I'll know. I don't want to look like a fool when I do it the first time."

"It's not like Josh and I had sex hundreds of times! I'm not an expert. He's the only person I've done it with. But if you're thinking about having sex with Peter, make sure you're careful and you use a condom and everything." I nod quickly. This is when she'll get to the good stuff. "And just be really sure, as sure as you *can* be. And make sure he knows to be really gentle and caring with you, so it's special and it's something you can look back on with good feelings."

"Got it. So, like, how long did it last from start to finish?"

"Not that long. Don't forget, it was Josh's first time too." She sounds wistful. Now I feel wistful too. Peter's done it with Genevieve so many times, he's probably an expert by now. I'll probably even have an orgasm my first time out. Which is great, but it might've been nice if we both didn't know what we were doing instead of just me.

"You don't regret it, do you?"

"No. I don't think so. I think I'll always be glad it was with Josh. No matter how it's turned out." This is a relief to me, that even now, with eyes red from crying, Margot still doesn't regret having loved Josh.

★ ★ ★

I sleep in her room that night like old times, huddled beside her under her quilt. Margot's room is coldest, because it's above the garage. I listen as the heat clicks off and on.

In the dark next to me she says, "I'm going to date a bunch of Scottish guys when I get back to school. When else will I have another opportunity like that, right?"

I giggle and roll over so we're face-to-face. "No, wait— don't date a bunch of Scottish guys. Date one from England, one from Ireland, one from Scotland. And Wales! A tour of the British Empire!"

"Well, I *am* going to school to study anthropology," Margot says, and we giggle some more. "You know the saddest part? Josh and I will never be friends like we were before. Not after all this. That part's just over now. He was my best friend."

I give her fake-wounded eyes to lighten the mood, so she won't start crying again. "Hey, I thought I was your best friend!"

"You're not my best friend. You're my sister, and that's more."

It *is* more.

"Josh and I started out so easy, so fun, and now we're like strangers. I'll never have that person back, who I knew better than anyone and who knew me so well."

I feel a pinch in my heart. When she says it that way, it's so sad. "You could become friends again, after some time has passed." But it wouldn't be the same, I know that. You'd always be mourning what once was. It would always be a little bit . . . less.

"But it won't be like before."

"No," I agree. "I suppose it won't." Strangely, I think of Genevieve, of who we used to be to each other. Ours was the kind of friendship that makes sense as a kid but not so much now that we're older. I suppose you can't hold on to old things just for the sake of holding on.

It's the end of an era, it seems. No more Margot and Josh. This time for real. It's real because Margot is crying, and I can hear it in her voice that it's over, and this time we both know it. Things have changed.

"Don't let it happen to you, Lara Jean. Don't get too serious to where things can't go back. Be in love with Peter if you want, but be careful with your heart. Things feel like they'll be forever, but they aren't. Love can go away, or people can, without even meaning to. Nothing is guaranteed."

Gulp. "I promise I'll be careful." But I'm not sure I even know what that means. How can I be careful when I already like him so much?

# 4

MARGOT'S OFF SHOPPING FOR NEW BOOTS
with her friend Casey, Daddy's at work, and Kitty and
I are lazing about watching TV when my phone buzzes
next to me. It's a text from Peter. Movie tonight? I text
back yes, exclamation point. Then I delete the exclamation point for sounding too eager. Though without the
exclamation point, the yes seems completely unenthused.
I settle on a smiley face and press send before I can obsess
over it further.

"Who are you texting with?" Kitty is sprawled out on the
living room floor, spooning pudding into her mouth. Jamie
tries to steal a lick, but she shakes her head and scolds, "You
know you can't have chocolate!"

"I was texting with Peter. You know, that might not even
be real chocolate. It might be imitation. Check the label."

Of all of us, Kitty is firmest with Jamie. She doesn't immediately pick him up when he's crying to be held; she sprays
him in the face with a water bottle when he's naughty. All
tricks she's learning from our across-the-street neighbor Ms.
Rothschild, who it turns out is kind of a dog whisperer. She
used to have three dogs, but when she and her husband got
divorced, she got to keep Simone the golden retriever, and
he got custody of the other two.

"Is Peter your boyfriend again?" Kitty asks me.

"Um. I'm not sure." After what Margot said last night about taking things slow and being careful with my heart and not going to a point of no return, maybe it's good to exist in a place of unsureness for a while. Also, it's hard to redefine something that never had a clear definition in the first place. We were two people pretending to like each other, pretending to be a couple, so now what are we? And how might it have unfolded if we'd started liking each other without the pretense? Would we ever have been a couple? I guess we'll never know.

"What do you mean, you're not sure?" Kitty presses. "Shouldn't you know if you're somebody's girlfriend or not?"

"We haven't discussed it yet. I mean, not explicitly."

Kitty switches the channel. "You should look into that."

I roll on my side and prop myself up on my elbow. "But would that change anything? I mean, we like each other. What's the difference between that and the label? What would change?" Kitty doesn't answer. "Hello?"

"Sorry, can you say that again at the commercial break? I'm trying to watch my show."

I throw a pillow at her head. "I would be better off discussing these things with Jamie." I clap my hands. "C'mere, Jamie!"

Jamie lifts his head to look at me and then lies back down again, nestled against Kitty's side, still hoping for pudding, I'm sure.

In the car last night Peter didn't seem troubled by the

status of our relationship. He seemed happy and carefree as always. I'm definitely a person who worries too much over every little thing. I could do with a bit more of Peter's roll-with-it philosophy in my life.

"Wanna help me pick out what to wear to the movies with Peter tonight?" I ask Kitty.

"Can I come too?"

"No!" Kitty starts to pout and I amend: "Maybe next time."

"Fine. Show me two options and I'll tell you which is the better one."

I dart upstairs to my room and start going through my closet. This will be our actual first date, I want to wow him a bit. Unfortunately, Peter's already seen me in my good outfits, so the only thing to do is go for Margot's closet. She has a cream sweater dress she brought back from Scotland that I can put with tights and my little brown boots. There's also her periwinkle Fair Isle sweater I've been admiring; I can wear it with my yellow skirt and a yellow ribbon in my hair, which I'll curl, because Peter once told me he liked it curled.

"Kitty!" I scream. "Come up and look at my two options!"

"On the commercial break!" she screams back.

In the meantime I text Margot:

Can I borrow your fair isle sweater or
your cream sweater dress??

Oui.

*JENNY HAN*

Kitty votes for the Fair Isle sweater, saying I look like I'm wearing an ice-skating outfit, which I like the sound of. "You can wear it if we go ice skating," she says. "You, me, and Peter."

I laugh. "All right."

# 5

*PETER AND I ARE STANDING IN LINE FOR POP-*
corn at the movies. Even just this mundane thing feels like
the best mundane thing that's ever happened to me. I check
my pocket to make sure I've still got my ticket stub. This I'll
want to save.

Gazing up at Peter, I whisper, "This is my first date." I feel
like the nerdy girl in the movie who lands the coolest guy
in school, and I don't mind one bit. Not one bit.

"How can this be your first date when we've gone out
plenty of times?"

"It's my first *real* date. Those other times were just pretend;
this is the real thing."

He frowns. "Oh, wait, is this real? I didn't realize that."

I move to slug him in the shoulder, and he laughs and
grabs my hand and links my fingers with his. It feels like my
heart is beating right through my hand. It's the first time
we've held hands for real, and it feels different from those
fake times. Like electric currents, in a good way. The best
way.

We're moving up in the line, and I realize I'm nervous,
which is strange, because this is Peter. But he's also a different Peter, and I'm a different Lara Jean, because this is a date,
an actual date. Just to make conversation, I ask, "So, when

you go to the movies are you more of a chocolate kind of candy or a gummy kind of candy?"

"Neither. All I want is popcorn."

"Then we're doomed! You're neither, and I'm either or all of the above." We get to the cashier and I start fishing around for my wallet.

Peter laughs. "You think I'm going to make a girl pay on her first date?" He puffs out his chest and says to the cashier, "Can we have one medium popcorn with butter, and can you layer the butter? And a Sour Patch Kids and a box of Milk Duds. And one small Cherry Coke."

"How did you know that was what I wanted?"

"I pay a lot better attention than you think, Covey." Peter slings his arm around my shoulders with a self-satisfied smirk, and he accidentally hits my right boob.

"Ow!"

He laughs an embarrassed laugh. "Whoops. Sorry. Are you okay?"

I give him a hard elbow to the side, and he's still laughing as we walk into the theater—which is when we see Genevieve and Emily coming out of the ladies' room. The last time I saw Genevieve, she was telling everyone on the ski trip bus how Peter and I had sex in the hot tub. I feel a strong surge of panic, of fight or flight.

Peter slows down for a second, and I'm not sure what's going to happen. Do we have to go over and say hi? Do we keep walking? His arm tightens around me, and I can feel Peter's hesitance too. He's torn.

Genevieve solves it for everyone. She walks into the theater like she didn't see us. The same theater we're going into. I don't look at Peter, and he doesn't say anything either. I guess we're just going to pretend like she isn't here? He steers me through the same set of doors and picks our seats, far left toward the back. Genevieve and Emily are sitting in the middle. I see her blond head, the back of her dove gray dress coat. I make myself look away. If Gen turns around, I don't want to be caught staring.

We sit down, and I'm taking off my coat and getting comfy in my seat when Peter's phone buzzes. He pulls it out of his pocket and then puts it away, and I know it was Gen, but I feel like I can't ask. Her presence has punctured the night. Two vampire bite marks right into it.

The lights dim, and Peter puts his arm back around me. Is he going to keep it there the whole movie, I wonder. I feel stiff, and I try to even my breathing. He whispers in my ear, "Relax, Covey."

I'm trying, but it's sort of impossible to relax on command under these circumstances. Peter gives my shoulder a squeeze, and he leans in and nuzzles my neck. "You smell nice," he says in a low voice.

I laugh, a touch too loudly, and the man sitting in front of us whips around in his seat and glares at me. Chastened, I say to Peter, "Sorry, I'm really ticklish."

"No worries," he says, keeping his arm around me.

I smile and nod, but now I'm wondering—is he expecting that we're going to do stuff during the movie? Is that why he picked seats in the back when there were still free seats in the middle? Panic is rising inside me. Genevieve is here! And other people too! I might have made out with him in a hot tub, but there wasn't anyone around to see. Also, I kind of just want to watch the movie. I lean forward to take a sip of soda, but really it's just so I can subtly move away from him.

After the movie we have an unspoken understanding to hustle out so we don't run into Genevieve again. The two of us bolt out of the theater like the devil is on our heels—which, I suppose, she sort of is. Peter's hungry, but I'm too full from all the junk to eat a real dinner, so I suggest we just go to the diner and I'll share his fries. But Peter says, "I feel like we should go to a real restaurant since this is your first date."

"I never knew you had such a romantic side." I say it like it's a joke, but I mean it.

"Get used to it," he boasts. "I know how to treat a girl."

He takes me to Biscuit Soul Food—his favorite restaurant, he says. I watch him scarf down fried chicken with hot honey and Tabasco drizzled on top, and I wonder how many times Genevieve has sat and watched him do the very same thing. Our town isn't that big. There aren't many places we can go that he hasn't already been with Genevieve. When I get up to go to the bathroom, I suddenly wonder if he's texting her back, but I make myself push this thought out of my mind tout de suite. So what if he does text back? They're still friends. He's allowed. I'm not going to let Gen ruin this night for me. I want to be right here, in this moment, just the two of us on our first date.

I sit back down, and Peter's finished his fried chicken and he has a pile of dirty napkins in front of him. He has a habit of wiping his fingers every time he takes a bite. There's honey on his cheek, and a bit of breading is stuck to it, but I don't tell him, because I think it's funny.

"So how was your first date?" Peter asks me, stretching back in his chair. "Tell it to me like it wasn't me that took you."

"I liked it when you knew what kinds of movie theater snacks I like." He nods encouragingly. "And . . . I liked the movie."

"Yeah, I got that. You kept shushing me and pointing at the screen."

"That man in front of us was getting mad." I hesitate. I'm not sure if I should say this next thing I want to say, the thing I've been thinking all night. "I don't know . . . is it just me, or . . ."

He leans in closer, now he's listening. "What?"

I take a deep breath. "Is it . . . a little weird? I mean, first we were fake, and then we weren't, and then we had a fight, and now here we are and you're eating fried chicken. It's like we did everything in the wrong order, and it's good, but it's . . . still kind of upside down." *And also were you trying to feel me up during the movie?*

"I guess it's a little weird," he admits.

I sip my sweet tea, relieved that he doesn't think I'm the weird one for bringing up all the weirdness.

He grins at me. "Maybe what we need is a new contract."

I can't tell if he's joking or if he's serious, so I play along. "What would go in the contract?"

"Off the top of my head . . . I guess I'd have to call you every night before I went to bed. You'd agree to come to all my lacrosse games. Some practices, too. I'd have to come to your house for dinner. You'd have to come to parties with me."

I make a face at the parties part. "Let's just do the things we want to do. Like before." Suddenly I hear Margot's voice in my head. "Let's . . . let's have fun."

He nods, and now he's the one who looks relieved. "Yeah!"

I like that he doesn't take things too seriously. In other people that could be annoying, but not him. It's one of his best qualities, I think. That and his face. I could stare at his face all day long. I sip sweet tea out of my straw and look at him. A contract might actually be good for us. It could help us to head problems off at the pass and keep us accountable. I think Margot would be proud of me for this.

I pull a little notebook out of my purse and a pen. I write *Lara Jean and Peter's New Contract* on the top of the page.

Line one I write, *Peter will be on time.*

Peter cranes his neck to read upside down. "Wait, does that say, 'Peter will be on time'?"

"If you say you're going to be somewhere, then be there."

Peter scowls. "I didn't show up *one time* and you hold a grudge—"

"But you're always late."

"That's not the same as not showing up!"

"Being late all the time shows a lack of respect for the person who's waiting for you."

"I respect you! I respect you more than any girl I know!"

I point at him. "'Girl'? Just 'girl'? What boy do you respect more than me?"

Peter throws his head back and groans so loudly it's a roar. I reach across the table, over the food, and grab him by the collar and kiss him before we can fight again. Though I have to say, it's this kind of fighting, the bickering kind, not the hurt-feelings kind, that makes us feel like *us* for the first time all night.

This is what we decide on.

Peter will not be more than five minutes late.

Lara Jean will not make Peter do crafts of any kind.

Peter doesn't have to call Lara Jean before he goes to bed at night, but he can if he feels like it.

Lara Jean will only go to parties if she feels like it.

Peter will give Lara Jean rides whenever she wants.

Lara Jean and Peter will always tell each other the truth.

There's one thing I want to add to the contract, but I'm nervous to broach the subject now that things are going smoothly.

*Peter can still be friends with Genevieve, as long as he is up front with Lara Jean about it.*

Or maybe it's *Peter will not lie to Lara Jean about Genevieve.* But that's redundant, because we already have the rule about always telling each other the truth. A rule like that wouldn't be the truth anyway. What I really want to say is *Peter will always pick Lara Jean over Genevieve.* But I can't say that. Of course I can't. I don't know a ton about dating or guys, but I do know that jealous insecurity is a real turnoff.

So I bite my tongue; I don't say what I'm thinking. There's only one thing, one really important thing I want to be sure of.

"Peter?"

"Yeah?"

"I don't want us to ever break each other's hearts."

Peter laughs easily; he cups my cheek in his hand. "Are you planning on breaking my heart, Covey?"

"No. And I'm sure you're not planning on breaking mine. Nobody ever plans it."

"Then put that in the contract. Peter and Lara Jean promise not to break each other's hearts."

I beam at him, relieved as anything, and then I write it down. *Lara Jean and Peter will not break each other's hearts.*

# 6

*THE DAY BEFORE WE GO BACK TO SCHOOL,* Kitty and I are lying in my bed watching pet videos on my computer. Our puppy, Jamie Fox-Pickle, is curled up in a ball at the foot of the bed. Kitty wrapped him up in her nubby old baby blanket so only his face is peeking out. He's dreaming—I can tell by the way he shudders and shakes every so often. I can't tell if it's a good dream or a bad dream.

"Do you think we should start doing videos of Jamie?" Kitty asks me. "He's cute enough, right?"

"He's definitely got the look, but he doesn't have any discernible talent or quirky thing about him." As soon as I say the word "quirky," I think of Peter and how he once said I was "cute in a quirky way." I wonder if that's still how he sees me. I've heard people say that the more you like someone, the more you think they are beautiful even if you didn't think so in the beginning.

"Jamie does that thing where he prances around like a baby deer," Kitty reminds me.

"Hm. I wouldn't exactly call that a 'thing.' It's not the same as leaping into cardboard boxes or playing the piano or having a really grumpy face."

"Ms. Rothschild will help me train him. She thinks he has the right personality for tricks." Kitty clicks on the next video, a dog that howls when you play Michael Jackson's "Thriller." Kitty and I crack up and we watch it again.

After a video of a woman whose cat wraps itself around her face like a scarf, I say, "Wait a minute—did you do your homework?"

"All I had to do was read a book."

"So did you read it?"

"Mostly," Kitty hedges, snuggling in closer to me.

"You've had all of Christmas break to read it, Kitty!" I really wish Kitty were more of a reader like Margot and me. She much prefers TV. I click stop on the video and snap my computer shut with a flourish. "No more pet videos for you. You go finish your book." I start to shove her out of the bed, and Kitty grabs on to my leg.

"Sweet my sister, cast me not away!" Proudly she says, "That's Shakespeare. *Romeo and Juliet*, in case you haven't read it."

"Don't act high and mighty like you were reading Shakespeare. I saw you watching the movie on TV the other day."

"Who cares if I read it or I saw the movie? The message is still the same." Kitty crawls back up by me.

I pat her hair. "So what's the message?"

"Don't kill yourself over a boy."

"Or a girl."

"Or a girl," she agrees. She opens up my computer. "One more cat video and then I'll go read."

My phone buzzes, a text from Chris.

Check Anonybitch's instagram NOW.

Anonybitch is an anonymous Instagram account that puts up scandalous pictures and videos of people hooking up and getting drunk at parties around town. No one knows who runs the account; they just send in the content. There was a picture of a girl from another high school that went viral last year—she was flashing a cop car. I heard she got expelled from school for it.

My phone buzzes again.

NOW!

"Hold on, Kitty, let me check something first," I say, pausing the video. As I type in the address, I say, "If you want to stay in here, close your eyes until I tell you to open them."

Kitty obeys.

At the top of Anonybitch's feed, there is a video of a boy and a girl making out in a hot tub. Anonybitch is particularly famous for her hot tub videos. She tags them #rubadub. This one's a little grainy, like it was zoomed in from far away. I click play. The girl is sitting in the boy's lap, her body draped over his, legs hooked around his waist, arms around his neck. She's wearing a red nightgown, and it billows in the water like a full sail. The back of her head obscures the boy. Her hair is long, and the ends dip into the hot tub like calligraphy brushes in ink. The boy runs his hands down her spine like she is a cello and he is playing her.

I'm so entranced I don't notice at first that Kitty is watching with me. Both of our heads are tilted, trying to suss out what it is we're looking at. "You shouldn't be looking at this," I say.

"Are they doing it?" she asks.

"It's hard to say because of her nightgown." But maybe?

Then the girl touches the boy's cheek, and there is something about the movement, the way she touches him like she is reading braille. Something familiar. The back of my neck goes icy cold, and I am hit with a *gust* of awareness, of humiliating recognition.

That girl is me. Me and Peter, in the hot tub on the ski trip.

Oh my God.

I scream.

Margot comes racing in, wearing one of those Korean beauty masks on her face with slits for eyes, nose, and mouth. "What? *What?*"

I try to cover the computer screen with my hand, but she pushes it out of the way, and then she lets out a scream too. Her mask falls off. "Oh my God! Is that you?"

*Oh my God oh my God oh my God.*

"Don't let Kitty see!" I shout.

Kitty's wide-eyed. "Lara Jean, I thought you were a goody-goody."

"I am!" I scream.

Margot gulps. "That . . . that looks like . . ."

"I know. Don't say it."

"Don't worry, Lara Jean," Kitty soothes. "I've seen worse on regular TV, not even HBO."

"Kitty, go to your room!" Margot yells. Kitty whimpers and clings closer to me.

I can't believe what I am seeing. The caption reads *Goody two shoes Lara Jean having full-on sex with Kavinsky in the hot tub. Do condoms work underwater? Guess we'll find out soon enough. ;)* The comments are a lot of wide-eyed emojis and *lol*s. Someone named Veronica Chen wrote, *What a slut! Is she Asian??* I don't even know who Veronica Chen is!

"Who could have done this to me?" I wail, pressing my hands to my cheeks. "I can't feel my face. Is my face still my face?"

"Who the hell is Anonybitch?" Margot demands.

"No one knows," I say, and the roaring in my ears is so loud I can hardly hear my own voice. "People just re-gram her. Or him. Am I talking really loud right now?" I'm in shock. Now I can't feel my hands or feet. I'm gonna faint. Is this happening? Is this my life?

"We have to get this taken down right now. Is there a help line for inappropriate content? We have to report this!" Margot's grabbing the computer from me. She clicks the REPORT INAPPROPRIATE tab. Scanning the comments on the page, she seethes, "People are absolute jerks! We might have to call a lawyer. This won't get taken down right away."

"No!" I scream. "I don't want Daddy to see!"

"Lara Jean, this is serious. You don't want colleges to google you and have this video come up! Or, like, future employers—"

"Gogo! You're making me feel so much worse right

now!" I grab my phone. Peter. He'll know what to do. It's five o'clock, which means he's still at lacrosse practice. I can't even call him right now. I text instead:

Call me ASAP.

Then I hear Daddy's voice calling up the staircase. "These potatoes won't mash themselves! Who's helping me?"

Oh my God. Now I have to sit at dinner and look my dad in the face, knowing that this video exists. This can't be my life.

Margot and Kitty look at each other, then back at me. "Nobody says a word to Daddy!" I hiss at them. "That means you, Kitty!"

She gives me a hurt look. "I know when to keep my mouth shut."

"Sorry, sorry," I mumble. My heart is pounding so hard it's giving me a headache. I can't even think straight.

At dinner, my stomach is churning and I can barely get down a bite of potatoes. Luckily, I have Margot and Kitty to run interference and keep a steady chatter going so I don't have to talk. I just push the food around on my plate and sneak Jamie Fox-Pickle bites under the table. As soon as everyone else is done eating, I sprint upstairs and look at my phone. Still nothing from Peter. Just more texts from Chris and one from Haven:

OMG is this you??!

I don't know who the girl in the video is. I don't recognize me in it. It's not how I see myself at all. It's like some other person who has nothing to do with me. I'm not someone who climbs into hot tubs with boys and sits in their laps and kisses them passionately with a wet nightgown clinging to them. But I was that night. The video just doesn't tell the whole truth.

I keep telling myself it's not like we're really having sex in the video. It's not like I'm naked. It just *feels* like I'm naked in the video. And all I can think is, everybody at school has seen that video, a video of me in one of the most intimate and truly romantic moments of my life. And not only that, but someone recorded it. Someone was there. That memory was supposed to only be mine and Peter's, but now it turns out there was some random Peeping Tom in the woods there with us. It's not just ours anymore. It feels tawdry now. It certainly looks that way. In the moment I felt free, and adventurous, maybe even sexy. I don't know that I've ever felt sexy in my whole life. And now I just want to not exist.

I'm lying in bed staring up at the ceiling, phone at my side. Margot and Kitty have forbidden me from looking at the video. They tried to take my phone away, but I told them I need it for when Peter calls. Then I snuck a look at the video, and so far there are over a hundred comments, none good.

Kitty's playing with Jamie Fox-Pickle on the floor and Margot's emailing Instagram customer service when Chris knocks on my window. Margot unlocks it for her, and Chris climbs inside, shivering and pink-cheeked. "Is she okay?"

"I think she's in shock," Kitty says.

"I'm not in shock," I say. But maybe I am. Maybe this is shock. It's a queer, surreal sort of feeling, like I'm numb, but also all my senses feel heightened.

Margot says to Chris, "Why can't you come in through the front door like a normal person?"

"Nobody answered." Chris yanks off her boots and sits down on the floor next to Kitty. Petting Jamie, she says, "Okay, first of all, you can barely tell it's you. And second of all, it's really hot, so there's nothing to be ashamed of. I mean, you look great."

Margot makes a disgusted sound. "That's so beside the point I don't even know where to begin."

"I'm just being honest! Objectively, it sucks, but also objectively, Lara Jean looks awesome in it."

Crawling under my quilt, I say, "I thought you could barely even tell it was me! I knew I shouldn't have gone on that ski trip. I hate hot tubs. Why would I willingly get into a hot tub?"

"Hey, be glad you were in your pajamas," Chris says. "You could have been nude!"

My head pops out from under the quilt and I glare at her. "I would never be nude!"

Chris snorts. "Never nude. Did you know that's a real thing? Some people call themselves never-nudes and they wear clothes at all times, even in the shower. Like, jean shorts."

I turn on my side, away from Chris.

The weight of my bed shifts as Margot climbs in. "It's

going to be fine," she says, peeling back the blanket. "We'll get them to take the video down."

"It won't matter," I say. "Everyone's already seen it. They all think I'm a slut."

Chris's eyes go narrow. "So are you saying that if a girl has sex in a hot tub, that makes her a slut?"

"No! That's not what I'm saying; that's what other people are saying."

"Then what *are* you saying?" she demands.

I look at Kitty, who's braiding Chris's hair in microbraids. She's being extra quiet so we forget she's here and don't kick her out. "I think that as long as you're ready and it's what you want to do and you're protecting yourself, then it's okay and you should do what you want to do."

Margot says, "Society is far too caught up in shaming a woman for enjoying sex and applauding a man. I mean, all of the comments are about how Lara Jean is a slut, but nobody's saying anything about Peter, and he's right there with her. It's a ridiculous double standard."

I hadn't thought of that.

Chris looks down at her phone. "Like, three different people just texted the video to me as we were sitting here."

I let out a sob and Margot says, "Chris, that's not helping. At all." To me she says, "If people say anything, just be really blasé, like it's beneath you."

"Or just, like, lean into it," Chris says.

From behind her Kitty says, "Nobody will say anything to

Lara Jean because she's Peter's girl. That means she's under his protection, like on *The Sopranos*."

Aghast, Margot says, "Oh my God, you've seen *The Sopranos*? How have you seen *The Sopranos*? It's not even on TV anymore."

"I watched it on demand. I'm on season three."

"Kitty! Stop watching it!" She shuts her eyes and shakes her head. "Never mind. That's not what's important right now. We'll talk about it later. Kitty, Lara Jean doesn't need a boy to protect her."

"No, Kitty has a good point," Chris says. "It's not about the fact that Peter's a guy. Well, not completely. It's about the fact that he's popular and she isn't. That's where the protection comes into play. No offense, LJ."

"None taken," I say. It's slightly insulting, but it's also true, and now isn't the time for me to get my feelings hurt about something so miniscule in comparison to a would-be sex tape.

"What did Kavinsky say about it?" Chris asks me.

"Nothing yet. He's still at lacrosse practice."

My phone immediately starts to buzz, and the three of us look at each other, wide-eyed. Margot picks it up and looks at it. "It's Peter!" She hot-potatoes the phone to me. "Let's give them some privacy," she says, nudging Chris. Chris shrugs her off.

I ignore both of them and answer the phone. "Hello." My voice comes out thin as a reed.

Peter starts talking fast. "Okay, I've seen the video, and the first thing I'm going to say to you is don't freak out."

He's breathing hard; it sounds like he's running.

"Don't freak out? How can I not? This is terrible. Do you know what they're all saying about me in the comments? That I'm a slut. They think we're having sex in that video, Peter."

"Never read the comments, Covey! That's the first rule of—"

"If you say 'Fight Club' to me right now, I will hang up on you."

"Sorry. Okay, I know it sucks but—"

"It doesn't 'suck.' It's a literal nightmare. My most private moment, for everybody to see. I'm completely humiliated. The things people are saying—" My voice breaks. Kitty and Margot and Chris are all looking at me with sad eyes, which makes me feel even sadder.

"Don't cry, Lara Jean. Please don't cry. I promise you I'm going to fix this. I'm going to get whoever runs Anonybitch to take it down."

"How? We don't even know who they are! And besides, I bet our whole school's seen it by now. Teachers, too. I know for a fact that teachers look at Anonybitch. I was in the faculty lounge once and I overheard Mr. Filipe and Ms. Ryan saying how bad it makes our school look. And what about college admissions boards and our future employers?"

Peter guffaws. "Future employers? Covey, I've seen much worse. Hell, I've seen worse pictures of *me* on there. Remember that picture of me with my head in a toilet bowl, and I'm naked?"

I shudder. "I never saw that picture. Besides, that's you; that's not me. I don't do that kind of stuff."

"Just trust me, okay? I promise I'll take care of it."

I nod, even though I know he can't see me. Peter is powerful. If anyone could fix such a thing, it would be him.

"Listen, I've gotta go. Coach is gonna kick my ass if he sees me on the phone. I'll call you tonight, okay? Don't go to sleep."

I don't want to hang up. I wish we could talk longer. "Okay," I whisper.

When I hang up, Margot, Chris, and Kitty are all three staring at me.

"Well?" Chris says.

"He says he'll take care of it."

Smugly Kitty says, "I told you so."

"What does that even mean, 'he'll take care of it'?" Margot asks. "He hasn't exactly proven himself to be responsible."

"It's not his fault," Kitty and I say at the same time.

"Oh, I know exactly who's responsible for this," Chris proclaims. "My she-devil cousin."

This knocks the wind out of me. "What? Why?"

She gives me an incredulous look. "Because you took her man!"

"Genevieve's the one who cheated on Peter. That's why they broke up. It wasn't because of me!"

"Like that matters!" Chris shakes her head. "Come on, Lara Jean. Remember what she did to Jamila Singh? Telling everyone that her family had an Indonesian slave just because she had the balls to date Peter after they broke up? I'm just saying, I wouldn't put a bitch move like this past her."

On the ski trip, Genevieve said she knew about the kiss, which has to mean that Peter told her about it at some point in their relationship—though I doubt he told her that he was the one who kissed me and not the other way around! Even so, I find it hard to believe that she could do something so cruel to me. Jamila Singh and Genevieve never liked each other. But Gen and I were best friends once. Sure, we haven't talked much the last few years, but Gen was always loyal to her friends.

It had to have been one of the guys hanging out in the rec room, or maybe . . . I don't know. Maybe anyone!

"I've never trusted her," Margot says. Then she says to Chris, "No offense. I know she's your cousin."

Chris snorts. "Why would I be offended? I can't stand her."

"I'm pretty sure she's the one who scraped up the side of Grandma's car with her bike," Margot says. "Remember, Lara Jean?"

It was actually Chris, but I don't say so. Chris starts biting her nails and giving me panicky eyes and I say, "I don't think Genevieve was the one who posted the video. It could've been anybody who happened to see us that night."

Margot puts her arm around me. "Don't worry, Lara Jean. We'll get them to take the video down. You're underage."

"Pull it up again," I say. Kitty cues it up and pushes play. I feel the same sinking feeling in my stomach every time

I watch it. I close my eyes so I don't have to. Thank God the only things you can hear are the sounds of the woods and the hot tub water bubbling. "Is it . . . is it as bad as I'm remembering? I mean, does it really look like we're having sex? Be honest." I open my eyes.

Margot's peering at it, head tilted. "No, it really doesn't. It just looks like . . ."

"Like a hot makeout," Chris supplies.

"Right," Margot agrees. "Just a hot makeout."

"You guys swear?"

In unison they say, "We swear."

"Kitty?" I ask.

She bites her lip. "It looks like sex to me, but I'm the only one here besides you who's never had sex, so what do I know?" Margot lets out a gasp. "Sorry, I read your diary." Margot swats at her, and Kitty crawls away fast like a crab.

I take a deep breath. "Okay. I can live with that. I mean, who cares about a hot makeout, right? That's just part of life, right? And you can barely even see my face? You'd have to really know me to know it was me. My full name isn't on here anywhere, just Lara Jean. There must be a ton of Lara Jeans, right? Right?"

Margot gives me an impressed nod. "I've never seen any-body move through the five stages of grief that fast. You really do have an incredible bounce-back."

"Thank you," I say, feeling a little proud.

But then in the dark, when my sisters and Chris have left and Peter and I have said our good nights and he has assured me for the millionth time that everything will be fine, I look at Instagram again, at all the comments. And I am mortified.

I asked Peter who he thought could have done it; he said he didn't know. Probably just some horny pathetic guy, he said. I don't ask the thing I'm still thinking about, the thing that's still stuck in my craw. Was it Genevieve? Could she really hate me so much that she'd want to hurt me that badly?

I remember the day we exchanged friendship bracelets. "This proves that we're best friends," she said to me. "We're closer with each other than with anyone else."

"What about Allie?" I asked. We'd always been a trio, though Genevieve had taken to spending more time at my house, mainly because Allie's mom was strict about boys coming over and being on the Internet.

"Allie's okay but I like you better," she'd said, and I had felt guilty but honored. Genevieve liked me best. We were close, closer than with anyone else. The bracelets were proof. How cheaply I was bought then, with just a bracelet made out of string.

# 7

*THE NEXT MORNING I DRESS FOR SCHOOL*
with special care. Chris said I should lean into it, which
would mean a look-at-me kind of outfit. Margot said I
should be above it all, which means something mature
like a pencil skirt or maybe my green corduroy blazer.
But my instinct is to blend, blend, blend. Big sweater that's
more like a blanket. Leggings, Margot's brown boots. If I
could wear a baseball cap to school, I would, but no hats
allowed.

I make myself a bowl of Cheerios with sliced banana on
top, but I can only force down a few bites. I'm too nervous.
Margot notices and slips a cashew bar in my bag for later.
I'm lucky that she's still here to take such good care of me.
She'll be heading back to Scotland tomorrow.

Daddy feels my forehead. "Are you sick? You barely had
any dinner last night either."

I shake my head. "Probably just cramps. My period's coming soon." I have only to say the magic word, "period," and
I know he won't push it further.

"Ah," he says with a sage nod. "After you get some food
in your stomach, take two ibuprofen so you have it in your
system."

"Got it," I say. I feel bad for the lie, but it's a tiny one, and it's for his own good. He can never know about that video, not ever.

Peter pulls up in front of our house right on time for once. He's really sticking to our contract. Margot walks me to the door and says, "Just hold your head up high, all right? You haven't done anything wrong."

As soon as I get in the car, Peter leans over and kisses me on the mouth, which still feels surprising somehow. I'm taken off guard, so I accidentally cough into his mouth a little. "Sorry," I say.

"No worries," he says, smooth as ever. He places his arm on the back of my seat as he puts the car in reverse; then he tosses me his phone. "Check Anonybitch."

I open up his Instagram and go to Anonybitch's page. I see the entry that was below ours, a picture of a passed-out guy with penises permanent-markered all over his face. It's the top of the feed now. I gasp. The hot tub video is gone! "Peter, how did you do this?"

Peter grins a peacocky kind of grin. "I messaged Anonybitch last night and told them to take that shit down or we're suing. I told them how my uncle is a lawyer and you and I are both underage." He gives my knee a squeeze.

"Is your uncle really a lawyer?"

"No. He owns a pizza parlor in New Jersey." We both laugh, and it feels like such a relief. "Listen, don't worry about anything today. If anybody says anything, I'll kick their ass."

"I just wish I knew who did it. I could've sworn we were alone that night."

Peter shakes his head. "It's not like we did anything so wrong! I mean, who cares if we made out in a damn hot tub? Who cares if we had sex in it?" I frown and he quickly says, "I know, I know. You don't want people thinking we did something when we didn't. We definitely didn't, and that's what I told that bitch Anonybitch."

"It's different for guys and girls, Peter."

"I know. Don't be mad. I'm going to find out who did this." He looks straight ahead, so serious and unlike himself; his profile is almost noble for all its good intent.

Oh, Peter, why do you have to be so handsome! If you weren't so handsome I never would have gotten in that hot tub with you. It's all your fault. Except it isn't. I'm the one who took off my shoes and socks and got in. I wanted it too. I just appreciate that he's taking it as seriously as he is, writing emails on our behalf. I know this is the kind of thing that Genevieve wouldn't care about; she never had a problem with PDAs or being the center of attention. But I care, I care a lot.

He turns his head and looks at me, studying my eyes, my face. "You don't regret it, do you, Lara Jean?"

I shake my head. "No, I don't." He smiles at me so sweetly I can't help but smile back. "Thanks for getting them to take the video down for me."

"Us," Peter corrects. "I did it for us." He links our fingers together. "It's you and me, kid."

I tighten my fingers around his. If we just hold on tight enough, it will all be okay.

★ ★ ★

When we walk down the hall together, girls whisper. Boys snicker. One guy from the lacrosse team runs up and tries to high-five Peter, who swats him away with a growl.

Lucas comes up to me when I'm alone at my locker trading out my books. "I'm not going to mince words," he says. "I'm just going to ask. Is the girl in the video really you?"

I take deep, calming breath. "It's me."

Lucas lets out a low whistle. "Damn."

"Yeah."

"So . . . did you guys . . ."

"No, we definitely did not. We *are* not."

"Why not?"

I'm embarrassed by the question, though I know there's no reason for me to be. It's just that I've never been in a position to talk about my sex life before, because who would ever have thought to ask me anything? "We aren't because we aren't. There's no big reason behind it, other than I'm not ready yet and I don't know if he is either. We haven't even talked about it."

"Well, it's not like he's a virgin. Not by any stretch of the imagination." Lucas makes his cerulean blue angel eyes go wide for emphasis. "I know you're innocent, Lara Jean, but Kavinsky definitely isn't. I'm saying this to you as a guy."

"I don't see what that has to do with me," I say, even though I've wondered and worried about this myself. Peter and I had a conversation about this once, about whether a guy and a girl who'd dated for a long time were automatically having sex, but I don't remember if he ever said what his take on it was. I should have listened harder. "Look, just because he and Genevieve did it like . . . like wild rabbits or whatever—" Lucas snickers at this, and I pinch him. "Just because they did it doesn't mean we automatically are, or that he automatically even wants to." Does it?

"He definitely wants to."

Gulp. "Well, too bad, so sad, if that's the case. But honestly, I don't think it is." In this very moment I decide that Peter and I will be the relationship equivalent of a brisket. Slow and low. We will heat up for each other over time. Confidently I say, "What Peter and I have is completely different than what he and Genevieve were. Or had. Whatever. The point is, you shouldn't compare relationships, okay?" Never mind the fact that I've been doing that constantly in my head.

In French class, I hear Emily Nussbaum whisper to Genevieve, "If it turns out she's preggo, do you think Kavinsky will pay for the abortion?"

Genevieve whispers back, "No way. He's too cheap. Maybe half." And everyone laughs.

My face burns in mortification. I want to scream at them, *We didn't have sex! We are brisket!* But that would only give them more satisfaction, to know they're getting a rise out of me. That's what Margot would say anyway. So I hold my chin up even higher, as high as I can, so high my neck hurts.

Maybe Gen did do it. Maybe she really does hate me that much.

Ms. Davenport grabs me on my way to my next class. She

puts her arm around me and says, "Lara Jean, how are you holding up?"

I know she doesn't care about me, not really. She just wants gossip. She's the biggest gossip of all the teachers, maybe even the students. Well, I'm not going to be faculty-lounge fodder. "I'm great," I say sunnily. Chin up, chin up.

"I saw the video," she whispers, eyes darting around to see if anyone's listening. "Of you and Peter in the hot tub."

My jaw is clenched so tight my teeth hurt.

"You must be really upset about the comments, and I don't blame you." Ms. Davenport really needs to get a life if all she's doing over her winter break is looking at high school kids' Instagrams! "Kids can be very cruel. Trust me, I know this from personal experience. I'm not that much older than you guys."

"I'm really fine, but thanks for checking in." Nothing to see here, folks. Keep it moving.

Ms. Davenport's lower lip pushes out. "Well, if you need to talk to someone, you know I'm here for you. Let me be a resource. Come hang out with me anytime; I'll write you a note."

"Thank you, Ms. Davenport." I slither out of from under her arm.

Mrs. Duvall, the guidance/college counselor stops me on my way to English. "Lara Jean," she begins, then falters. "You're such a bright, talented girl. You're not the type of girl to get caught up in these sorts of things. I'd hate to see you go down a wrong path."

I can feel tears coming up the back of my throat, pushing their way to the surface. I respect Mrs. Duvall. I want her to think well of me. All I can do is nod.

She tips my chin up tenderly. Her perfume smells like dried rose petals. She's an older woman; she's worked at the school forever. Mrs. Duvall really cares about the students. She is the one kids come back and say hi to when they're home from college for winter break. "Now is the time to buckle down and get serious about your future, not high school drama. Don't give colleges a reason to turn you down, okay?"

Again I nod.

"Good girl," she says. "I know you're better than that."

The words echo in my ears: *Better than that.* Better than what? Than who?

During lunch, I escape to the girls' bathroom so I don't have to speak to anybody. And of course there Genevieve is, standing in front of the mirror, dabbing on lip balm. Her eyes meet mine in the mirror. "Hi there." It's the way she says it—*hi there.* So smug, so sure of herself.

"Was it you?" My voice echoes against the walls.

Genevieve's hand goes still. Then she recovers, and screws the top back on her lip balm. "Was *what* me?"

"Did you send that video to Anonybitch?"

"No," she scoffs. Her mouth turns up to the right, the smallest of quivers. That's when I know she's lying. I've seen her lie to her mom enough times to know her tell. Even though I suspected it, maybe even knew it deep down, this confirmation takes my breath away.

"I know we're not friends anymore, but we used to be. You know my sisters, my dad. You know me. You knew how much this would hurt me." I clench my fists to keep from crying. "How could you do something like this?"

"Lara Jean, I'm sorry this happened to you, but it honestly wasn't me." She gives me a pseudosympathetic shrug, and there it is again: The corner of her mouth turns up.

"It was you. I know it was. Once Peter finds out . . ."

She raises one eyebrow. "He'll what? Kick my ass?"

I'm so angry my hands shake. "No, because you're a girl. But he won't forgive you either. I'm glad you did it if it proves to him what kind of person you really are."

"He knows exactly what kind of person I am. And you know what? He still loves me more than he'll ever like you. You'll see." With that she turns on her heel and walks away.

This is when it dawns on me. She's jealous. Of me. She can't stand that Peter's with me and not her. Well, she just played herself, because once Peter finds out she's the one who did this to us, he'll never look at her the same way again.

When school lets out, I race to the parking lot, where Peter is in his car waiting for me with the heat on. As soon as I open the passenger side door, I gasp out, "It was Genevieve!" I scramble inside. "She's the one who sent the video to Anony-bitch. She just admitted it to me!"

Soberly he asks me, "She said she took the video? She said those exact words?"

"Well . . . no." What were her exact words? I walked away feeling like she'd confessed, but now that I'm going over it in my head, she never out-and-out admitted it. "She didn't admit it per se, but she practically did. Also, she did that thing with her mouth!" I turn up the corner of my mouth. "See? That's her tell!"

He raises an eyebrow. "Come on, Covey."

"Peter!"

"Okay, okay. I'll talk to her." He starts the car.

I'm pretty sure I know the answer to this question, but I have to ask. "Have any teachers said anything to you about the video? Maybe Coach White?"

"No. Why? Has anyone said anything to you?"

This is what Margot was talking about, this double standard. Boys will be boys, but girls are supposed to be careful: of our bodies, of our futures, of all the ways people judge us. Abruptly I ask him, "When are you going to talk to Genevieve?"

"I'll go over there tonight."

"You're going over to her house?" I repeat.

"Well, yeah. I have to see her face to know whether she's lying or not. I'll check out this 'tell' you're so excited about."

Peter's starving, so we stop and get hamburgers and milkshakes on the way. When I finally get home, Margot and Kitty are waiting for me. "Tell us everything," Margot says, handing me a cup of cocoa. I check to see if she's put mini marshmallows inside, and she has.

"Did Peter fix it?" Kitty wants to know.

"Yes! He got Anonybitch to take the video down. He told them how he has an uncle who's a top lawyer, when in actuality he owns a pizza parlor in New Jersey."

Margot smiles at this. Then her face gets serious. "Were people horrible at school?"

Blithely I say, "Nah, it wasn't bad at all." I feel a swell of pride for putting on a brave face in front of my sisters. "But I'm pretty sure I know who did it."

In unison they say, *"Who?"*

"Genevieve, just like Chris said. I confronted her in the bathroom and she denied it, but then she did that thing she does with her mouth when she's lying." I demonstrate for them. "Gogo, do you remember that thing?"

"I think so!" she says, but I can tell she doesn't. "What did Peter say when you told him it was Genevieve? He believed you, right?"

"Not exactly," I hedge, blowing on my hot cocoa. "I mean, he says he's going to talk to her and get down to the bottom of it."

Margot frowns. "He should have your back no matter what."

"He does, Gogo!" I grab her hand and link my fingers through hers. "This is what he did. He said, 'It's you and me, kid.' It was really romantic!"

She giggles. "You're hopeless. Don't ever change."

"I wish you weren't leaving tomorrow," I sigh. I'm homesick for her already. Margot being here, making judgments and doling out sage advice, makes me feel secure. It gives me strength.

"Lara Jean, you've got this," she says, and I listen hard, look hard for any doubt or falseness in her, any hint that she's only saying it to bolster me. But there is none. Only confidence.

# 8

*IT'S MARGOT'S LAST DINNER BEFORE SHE* leaves for Scotland tomorrow. Daddy makes Korean short ribs and potatoes au gratin from scratch. He even bakes a lemon cake. He says, "It's been so gray and cold; I think we're all due a little sunshine by way of lemon cake." Then he puts an arm around my waist and pats my side, and though he isn't asking, I know he knows there's something up with me that's a lot bigger than my period.

We've barely had a chance to put our forks to our lips before Daddy's asking, "Does this galbi jjim taste like Grandma's?"

"Basically," I say. Daddy's mouth turns down and I quickly add, "I mean, it might even be better."

"I tenderized the meat the way she said," Daddy says. "But it's not falling right off the bone the way hers does, you know? You shouldn't even need a knife to eat galbi jjim if it's prepared correctly." Margot was sawing away at a piece of meat with her steak knife, and she stops short. "The first time I ever had it was with your mom. She took me to a Korean restaurant on our first date and ordered everything for us in Korean and told me about each dish. I was so in awe of her that night. My one regret is that you girls didn't keep up with Korean school." The corners of his mouth turn down for just a moment, and then he's smiling again. "Eat up, girls."

"Daddy, UVA has a Korean language program," I say. "If I get in, I'm definitely going to take Korean."

"Your mom would've loved that," he says, and he gets that sad look in his eyes again.

Swiftly Margot says, "The galbi jjim is delicious, Daddy. They don't have good Korean food in Scotland."

"Pack some seaweed to take back with you," Daddy suggests. "And some of that ginseng tea Grandma brought us back from Korea. You should take the rice cooker too."

Kitty frowns. "Then how will *we* have rice?"

"We can buy a new one." Dreamily he says, "What I'd really love to do is take a family vacation there. How great would that be? Your mom always wanted to take you girls on a trip to Korea. You still have a lot of family there."

"Could Grandma come with us?" Kitty asks. She keeps sneaking bites of meat to Jamie, who sits on his hind legs, looking at us with hopeful eyes.

Daddy nearly chokes on a bite of potatoes. "That's a great idea," he manages. "She'd be a good tour guide."

Margot and I exchange a little smile. Grandma would drive Daddy crazy after a week. What I'm excited about is the shopping. "Oh my gosh, just think of all the stationery," I say. "And clothes. And hair pins. BB cream. I should make a list."

"Daddy, you could take a Korean cooking class," Margot suggests.

"Yeah! Let's think about it for the summer," Daddy says. He's already getting excited, I can tell. "Depending on everyone's schedules, of course. Margot, you're going to be here all summer, right?" That's what she was saying last week.

She looks down at her plate. "I'm not sure. Nothing's been decided yet." Daddy looks puzzled, and Kitty and I exchange a look. For sure this has to do with Josh, and I don't blame her. "There's a chance I could get an internship at the Royal Anthropological Institute in London."

"But I thought you said you wanted to go back to work at Montpelier," Daddy says, his forehead creased in confusion.

"I'm still figuring things out. Like I said, I haven't decided anything yet."

Kitty interjects. "If you do the royal internship, would you get to meet any royal people?"

I roll my eyes, and Margot throws her a grateful look and says, "I doubt it, Kitten, but you never know."

"What about you, Lara Jean?" Kitty asks, innocent and round-eyed. "Aren't you supposed to be doing stuff this summer to look good for colleges?"

I shoot her a dirty look. "I've got plenty of time to figure things out." Under the table I pinch her hard, and she yelps.

"You were supposed to be looking for an internship for this spring," Margot reminds me. "I'm telling you, Lara Jean, if you don't act fast, all the good internships will be gone. Also have you emailed Noni yet about SAT tutoring? See if she's doing summer school or if she's going home for the summer."

"All right, all right. I will."

"I might be able to get you a job at the hospital gift shop," Daddy offers. "We could ride to work together, have lunch together. It would be fun hanging out all day with your old man!"

"Daddy, don't you have any friends at work?" Kitty asks. "Do you sit by yourself at lunch?"

"Well, no, not every day. Sometimes I suppose I do eat alone at my desk, but that's because I don't have much time to eat. If Lara Jean worked at the gift shop, I'd make time, though." He taps his chopsticks on his plate absentmindedly. "There might also be a job for her at the McDonald's, but I'd have to see."

Kitty pipes up, "Hey, if you got a job at McDonald's, I bet they'd let you eat fries as much as you want."

I frown. I can see a preview into my summer, and I'm not liking what I'm seeing. "I don't want to work at McDonald's. And no offense, Daddy, but I don't want to work at the gift shop, either." I think fast. "I've been thinking about doing something more official at Belleview. Maybe I could be the activities director's intern. Or assistant. Margot, which sounds more impressive?"

"Assistant activities director," Margot says.

"That does sound more professional," I agree. "I've got a lot of ideas. Maybe I'll stop by this week and pitch them to Janette."

"Like what?" Daddy asks me.

"A scrapbooking class," I improvise. "They have so many pictures and tokens and things that they've collected, I think it'd be good to bind it all up in a book so nothing gets lost." Suddenly I'm on a roll. "And then maybe we could have a little exhibit, with all of the scrapbooks on display, and people can flip through them and see their life stories. I could make cheese puffs, there could be white wine . . ."

"That's an *amazing* idea," Margot says with an approving nod.

"Really great," Daddy enthuses. "Obviously no white wine for you, but the cheese puffs, definitely!"

"Oh, Daddy," we all chorus, because he loves it when we do that, when he gets to be the cheesy dad (pun intended!) and we all groan like we're exasperated and say "Oh, Daddy."

When we're doing the dishes, Margot tells me I should follow up with the Belleview idea for sure. "They need someone like you to take charge of things," she says, sudsing up the Dutch oven. "Fresh energy, new ideas. People can get burned out working at a retirement home. Janette will be relieved to have an extra set of hands."

I mostly said all that stuff about Belleview to get everybody off my back, but now I'm thinking I really should talk to Janette.

When I go back upstairs, I have a missed call from Peter. I call him back, and I can hear the TV on in the background. "Did you talk to her?" I hope hope hope he believes me now.

"I talked to her."

My heart thuds. "And? Did she admit it?"

"No."

"No." I let out a breath. Okay. That was to be expected, I guess. Gen isn't the type to lie down in the street and die. She's a fighter. "Well, she can say whatever she wants, but I know it was her."

"You can't get all that from a look, Covey."

"It's not just a look. I know her. She used to be my best friend. I know how she thinks."

"I know her better than you, and I'm telling you, I don't think it was her. Trust me."

He does know her better; of course he does. But girl to girl, ex–best friend to ex–best friend, I know it was her. I don't care how many years it's been. There are things a girl knows in her gut, her bones. "I trust *you*. I don't trust *her*. This is all her plan, Peter."

There's a long silence, and I hear my last words ringing in my ears, and they sound crazy, even to me.

His voice is heavy with patience as he says, "She's stressed out with family stuff right now; she doesn't even have time to plot against you, Covey."

Family stuff? Could that be? I feel a pang of guilt as I remember how Chris mentioned that their grandma broke her hip and the families were discussing whether or not to put her into a home. Genevieve was always close to her grandma; she said she was the favorite out of all the grand-children because she looked just like her—i.e., gorgeous.

Or maybe it's her parents. Genevieve used to worry about them getting divorced.

Or maybe it's all a lie. It's on the very tip of my tongue to say, and then he says, wearily, "My mom's calling me down-stairs. Can we talk about this more tomorrow?"

"Sure," I say.

I mean, I guess it could be anything. Peter's right. Maybe I knew her well once, but not anymore. Peter is the one who knows her best now. And besides, isn't this the way one loses boyfriends, by acting paranoid and jealous and insecure? I'm fairly certain this is not a good look on me.

After we hang up I resolve to put the video behind me once and for all. What's done is done. I have a boyfriend, a possible new job (unpaid, I'm sure, but still), and my studies to think about. I can't let this bring me down. Besides, you can't even see my face in the video.

# 9

*THE NEXT MORNING BEFORE SCHOOL, WE'RE* packing up the car so Daddy can take Margot to the airport, and I keep looking up at Josh's bedroom window, wondering if he'll come down and say good-bye. It's the least he can do. But his lights are off, so he must still be asleep.

Ms. Rothschild comes out with her dog while Margot's saying her good-byes to Jamie Fox-Pickle. As soon as he sees her, he leaps out of Margot's arms and makes a run for it across the street. Daddy chases after him. Jamie is barking and jumping all over Ms. Rothschild's poor old dog Simone, who ignores him. Jamie is so excited he pees on Ms. Rothschild's green Hunter boots, and Daddy's apologizing, but she's laughing. "It'll wash right off," I hear her say. She looks pretty, her brown hair is in a high ponytail, and she's in yoga pants and a puffy bomber jacket that I think Genevieve has.

"Hurry, Daddy!" Margot calls out. "I need to be at the airport three hours early."

"Three's a bit much," I say. "Two hours is plenty." We watch as Daddy tries to scoop up Jamie and Jamie tries to wriggle away. Ms. Rothschild snatches him up with one arm and plants a kiss on his head.

"With international flights you're supposed to be at the

airport three hours early. I have bags to check, Lara Jean."

Kitty doesn't say anything; she's just gazing across the street at all the dog drama.

When Daddy returns with a squirming Jamie in his arms, he says, "We'd better get out of here before Jamie causes any more trouble." We three hug each other fiercely, and Margot whispers to me to be strong, and I nod, and then she and Daddy are gone for the airport.

It's still early, earlier than we would've woken up on a school morning, so I make Kitty and me banana pancakes. She's still lost in thought. Twice I have to ask her if she wants one pancake or two. I make a few extra and wrap them in aluminum foil to share with Peter on the way to school. I do the dishes; I even send Janette over at Belleview a feeler email, and she writes back right away. Margot's replacement quit a month ago, so it's perfect timing, she says. Come in on Saturday and we'll talk about your responsibilities.

I feel like finally, I've gotten it together: I've hit my stride. I can do this.

So when I walk into school that cold January morning, holding Peter's hand, full on banana pancakes, with a new job and wearing Margot's Fair Isle sweater she left behind, I am feeling good. Great, even.

Peter wants to stop in the computer lab to print out his English paper, so that's our first stop. He logs in, and I gasp out loud when I see the wallpaper.

Someone has taken a still of the hot tub video, of me in Peter's lap in my red flannel nightgown, skirt hitched

*JENNY HAN*

up around my thighs, and across the top it reads HOT HOT TUB SEX. And on the bottom—YOU'RE DOING IT WRONG.

"What the hell?" Peter mutters, looking around the computer lab. Nobody looks up. He goes to the next computer—same picture, different caption. SHE DOESN'T KNOW ABOUT SHRINKAGE on top. HE'S HAPPY WITH WHAT HE CAN GET across the bottom.

We are a meme.

Over the next couple of days, the picture shows up all over the place. On other people's Instagrams, on their Facebook walls.

There's one with a dancing shark photoshopped in. Another one where our heads have been replaced by cat heads.

And then one that just says AMISH BIKINI.

Peter's lacrosse friends think it's hilarious, but they swear they don't have anything to do with it. At the lunch table Gabe protests, "I don't even know how to use Photoshop!"

Peter stuffs half his sandwich into his mouth. "Fine, then who's doing it? Jeff Bardugo? Carter?"

"Dude, I don't know," Darrell says. "It's a meme. A lot of people could be throwing their hat in the ring."

"You have to admit, the cat-head one was pretty funny," Gabe says. Then he turns to me and says, "My bad, Large."

I stay quiet. The cat heads *were* kind of funny. But overall it is not. Peter tried to laugh the first one off, but now we are a few days in and I can tell it's bothering him. He isn't used to being the butt of the joke. I suppose I'm not either, but only because I'm not used to people paying this much attention to anything I'm doing. But ever since I've been with Peter, people are, and I wish they weren't.

# 10

*THAT AFTERNOON, WE HAVE A JUNIOR CLASS* assembly in the auditorium. Our class president, Reena Patel, is onstage giving a PowerPoint presentation on the state of the union—how much money we've fund-raised for prom, the proposal for senior class trip. I'm sitting low in my seat, relieved for the respite, where people aren't looking at me, whispering and making judgments.

She clicks on the last slide, and that's when it happens. "Me So Horny" blasts out of the speakers and my video, mine and Peter's, flashes on the projector screen. Someone has taken the video from Anonybitch's Instagram and put their own soundtrack to it. They've edited it too, so I bop up and down on Peter's lap at triple speed to the beat.

*Oh no no no no. Please, no.*

Everything happens at once. People are shrieking and laughing and pointing and going "Oooh!" Mr. Vasquez is jumping up to unplug the projector, and then Peter's running onstage, grabbing the microphone out of a stunned Reena's hand.

"Whoever did that is a piece of garbage. And not that it's anybody's fucking business, but Lara Jean and I did not have sex in the hot tub."

My ears are ringing, and people are twisting around in

their seats to look at me and then shifting back around to look at Peter.

"All we did was kiss, so fuck off!" Mr. Vasquez, the junior class advisor, is trying to grab the mic back from Peter, but Peter manages to maintain control of it. He holds the mic up high and yells out, "I'm gonna find whoever did this and kick their ass!" In the scuffle, he drops the mic. People are cheering and laughing. Peter's being frog-marched off the stage, and he frantically looks out into the audience. He's looking for me.

The assembly breaks up then, and everyone starts filing out the doors, but I stay low in my seat. Chris comes and finds me, face alight. She grabs me by the shoulders. "Ummm, that was crazy! He freaking dropped the F bomb twice!"

I am still in a state of shock, maybe. A video of me and Peter hot and heavy was just on the projector screen, and everyone saw. Mr. Vasquez, seventy-year-old Mr. Glebe who doesn't even know what Instagram is. The only passionate kiss of my life and everybody saw.

Chris shakes my shoulders. "Lara Jean! Are you okay?" I nod mutely, and she releases me. "He's kicking whoever did it's ass? I'd love to see that!" She snorts and throws her head back like a wild pony. "I mean, the boy's an idiot if he thinks for one second it wasn't Gen who posted that video. Like, wow, those are some serious blinders, y'know?" Chris stops short and examines my face. "Are you sure you're okay?"

"Everybody saw us."

"Yeah . . . that sucked. I'm sure that was Gen's handiwork.

She must've gotten one of her little minions to sneak it onto Reena's PowerPoint." Chris shakes her head in disgust. "She's such a bitch. I'm glad Peter set the record straight, though. Like, I hate to give him credit, but that was an act of chivalry. No guy has ever set the record straight for me."

I know she's thinking of that boy from freshman year, the one who told everyone that Chris had sex with him in the locker room. And I'm thinking of Mrs. Duvall, of what she said before. She would probably lump Chris in with the party girls, the girls who sleep around, the girls who aren't "better than that." She would be wrong. We're all the same.

After school, I'm walking out of class when my phone buzzes in my purse. It's Peter.

I'm out on parole. Meet me at my car!

I race to the parking lot, where Peter is in his car waiting for me with the heat on. Grinning at me, he says, "Aren't you going to kiss your man? I just got released from prison."

"Peter! This isn't a joke. Are you suspended?"

He smirks. "Nah. I sweet-talked my way out of it. Principal Lochlan loves me. Still, I could've been. If it had been anybody else . . ."

Oh, Peter. "Please don't brag to me right now."

"When I came out of Lochlan's office, there were a bunch of sophomore girls waiting for me to give me a standing O. They were like, 'Kavinsky, you're so romantic.'" He hoots, and I give him a look. He pulls me to his side. "Hey, they know I'm taken. There's only one girl I want to see in an Amish bikini."

I laugh; I can't help it. Peter loves attention, and I hate to be another girl who gives it to him, but he makes it really hard sometimes. Besides, it *was* kind of romantic.

He plants a kiss on my cheek, nuzzles against my face. "Didn't I tell you I would take care of it, Covey?"

"You did," I admit, patting his hair.

"So did I do a good job?"

"You did." That's all it takes for him to be happy, me telling him that he did a good job. He's smiley all the way home. But I'm still thinking about it.

I beg off the lacrosse party I was supposed to go to with Peter tonight. I say it's because I have to prepare for my meeting with Janette tomorrow, but we both know it's more than that. He could call me on it, remind me that we promised to always tell the truth to each other, but he doesn't. He knows me well enough to know that I just need to burrow in my little hobbit hole for a while, and when I'm ready, I'll come out again and be all right.

That night I bake chai sugar cookies with cinnamon-eggnog icing—they're like a hug in your mouth. Baking calms me; it's stabilizing. It's what I do when I don't want to think about anything hard. It is an activity that requires very little from you— you just follow the directions, and then at the end you have created something. From ingredients to an actual dessert. It's like magic. Poof, deliciousness.

After midnight, I've set the cookies on the cooling rack and put on my cat pajamas, and I'm climbing into bed to read when there's a knock at my window. I think it's Chris, and I go to the window to check and see if I've locked it, but it's not—it's Peter! I push the window up. "Oh my God, Peter! What are you doing here?" I whisper, my heart pounding. "My dad's home!"

Peter climbs in. He's wearing a navy beanie on his head and a thermal with a puffy vest. Taking off the hat, he grins and says, "Shh. You're gonna wake him up."

I run to my door and lock it. "Peter! You can't be here!" I am equal parts panicky and excited. I don't know if a boy has ever been in my room before, not since Josh, and that was ages ago.

He's already taking off his shoes. "Just let me stay for a few minutes."

I cross my arms because I'm not wearing a bra and say, "If it's only a few minutes, why are you taking off your shoes?"

He dodges this question. Plopping down on my bed, he says, "Hey, why aren't you wearing your Amish bikini? It's so hot." I move to slap him upside the head, and he grabs my waist and hugs me to him. He buries his head in my stomach like a little boy. His voice muffled, he says, "I'm sorry all this is happening because of me."

I touch the top of his head; his hair feels soft and silky against my fingers. "It's okay, Peter. I know it's not your fault." I glance at my moonbeam alarm clock. "You can stay for fifteen minutes, but then you have to go." Peter nods and releases me. I sink down on the bed next to him and put my head on his shoulder. I hope the minutes go slow. "How was the party?"

"Boring without you."

"Liar."

He laughs an easy kind of laugh. "What did you bake tonight?"

"How do you know I baked?"

Peter breathes me in. "You smell like sugar and butter."

"Chai sugar cookies with eggnog icing."

"Can I take some with me?"

I nod, and we lean our backs against the wall. He slides his arm around me, safe and secure. "Twelve minutes left," I say into his shoulder, and I feel rather than see him smile.

"Then let's make it good." We start to kiss, and I've definitely never kissed a boy in my bed before. This is brand-new. I doubt I'll ever be able to think of my bed the same way again. Between kisses he says, "How much time do I have left?"

I glance over at my clock. "Seven minutes." Maybe I should tack on an extra five . . .

"Can we lie down, then?" he suggests.

I shove him in the shoulder. "Peter!"

"I just want to hold you for a little bit! If I was going to try to do more, I'd need more than seven minutes, trust me."

So we lie down, my back to his chest, him curved around me, his arms slung around mine. He snuggles his chin into the hollow between my neck and my shoulder. It might be my favorite thing we've ever done. I like it so much I have to keep reminding myself to be vigilant that we don't fall asleep. I want to close my eyes but I keep them trained on my clock.

"Spooning's the freaking best," he sighs, and I wish he didn't say it, because it makes me think of how many times he must have held Genevieve just like this.

At the fifteen-minute mark, I sit up so fast he jumps. I clap him on the shoulder. "Time to go, buddy."

His mouth falls into a sulk. "Come on, Covey!"

I shake my head, resolute.

*If you hadn't made me think of Genevieve, I would've given you five minutes more.*

After I send Peter off with a bag of cookies, I lie back down and close my eyes and imagine his arms are still around me, and that's how I fall asleep.

# *11*

*I GO TO JANETTE'S OFFICE AT BELLEVIEW*
the next day, armed with my notebook and my pen. "I had
an idea for a craft class. 'Scrapbooking to the Oldies.'" Janette
nods at me and I continue. "I can teach the residents how
to scrapbook, and we'll go through all their old photos and
mementos and listen to oldies."

"That sounds great," she says.

"So I could run that class and also I could take on Friday
night cocktail hour?"

Janette takes a bite of her tuna-fish sandwich and swallows. "We might cut the cocktail hour altogether."

"Cut it?" I repeat in disbelief.

She shrugs. "Attendance has been waning ever since we
started offering a computer class. The residents have figured
out Netflix. It's a whole new world out there."

"What if we made it more of an event? Like, more special?"

"We don't really have the budget for anything fancy, Lara
Jean. I'm sure Margot's told you how we have to make do
around here. Our budget's tiny."

"No, no, it could be really DIY stuff. Just simple little
touches will make all the difference. Like we could make
a jacket mandatory for the men. And couldn't we borrow

glassware from the dining room instead of using plastic cups?" Janette is still listening, so I keep on going. "Why serve peanuts right out of the can, when we can put them in a nice bowl, right?"

"Peanuts taste like peanuts no matter the receptacle."

"They'd taste more elegant served out of a crystal bowl."

I've said too much. Janette is thinking this all sounds like too much trouble, I can tell. She says, "We don't have crystal bowls, Lara Jean."

"I'm sure I can scrounge one up at home," I assure her.

"It sounds like a lot of work for every Friday night."

"Well—maybe it could just be once a month. That would make it feel even more special. Why don't we take a little hiatus and bring it back in full force in a month or so?" I suggest. "We can give people a chance to miss it. Build the anticipation and then really do it right." Janette nods a begrudging nod, and before she can change her mind I say, "Think of me as your assistant, Janette. Leave it all to me. I'll take care of everything."

She shrugs. "Have at it."

Chris and I are hanging out in my room that afternoon when Peter calls. "I'm driving by your house," he says. "Wanna do something?"

"No!" Chris shouts into the phone. "She's busy."

He groans into my ear.

"Sorry," I tell him. "Chris is over."

He says he'll call me later, and I've barely set down the

phone when Chris grouses, "Please don't become one of those girls who gets in a relationship and goes MIA."

I'm very familiar with "those girls," because Chris disappears every time she meets a new guy. Before I can remind her of this, she goes on. "And don't be one of those lax groupies either. I fucking hate those groupies. Like, can't they find a better thing to be a groupie for? Like a band? Oh my God, I would be so good at being a groupie for an actual, important band. Like being a muse, you know?"

"What happened to that idea about you starting your own band?"

Chris shrugs. "The guy who plays bass fucked up his hand skateboarding and then nobody felt like it anymore. Hey, do you want to drive to DC tomorrow night and see this band Felt Tip? Frank's borrowing his dad's van, so there's probably room."

I have no idea who Frank is, and Chris has probably only known him for all of two minutes. She always says people's names like I should already know who they are. "I can't—tomorrow's a school night."

She makes a face. "See, that's exactly what I'm talking about. You're already becoming one of 'those girls.'"

"That has nothing to do with it, Chris. A, my dad would never let me go to DC on a school night. B, I don't know who Frank is, and I'm not riding in the back of his van. C, I have a feeling Felt Tip is not my kind of music. *Is* it my kind of music?"

"No," she admits. "Fine, but the next thing I ask you to do, you have to say yes. None of this A–B–C 'here are all of the reasons why' bullshit."

"All right," I agree, though my stomach does a little lurch, because with Chris you never know what you're getting yourself into. Though, also knowing Chris, she's already forgotten about it.

We settle onto the floor and get down to the business of manis. Chris grabs one of my gold nail pens and starts painting tiny stars on her thumbnail. I'm doing a lavender base and dark purple flowers with marigold centers. "Chris, will you do my initials on my right hand?" I hold up my hand for her. "Starting with the ring finger down to my thumb. *LJSC.*"

"Fancy font or basic?"

I give her a look. "Come on. Who are you talking to here?" At the same time we both say, "Fancy."

Chris is good with doing script. So good, in fact, that as I'm admiring her handiwork, I say, "Hey, I have an idea. What if we started doing manicures at Belleview? The residents would love that."

"For how much?"

"For free! You could think of it like community service but not mandatory. Out of the goodness of your heart. Some of the residents can't cut their own nails very well. Their hands get really gnarled. Toes, too. The nails get thick and . . ." I trail off when I see the disgusted look on her face. "Maybe we could have a tip jar."

"I'm not going to cut old people's toenails for free. I'm

not doing it for less than fifty bucks a set at the very least. I've seen my grandpa's feet; his toenails are like eagle talons." She gets back to my thumb, giving me a beautiful cursive *C* with a flourish. "Done. God, I'm good." She throws her head back and yells, "Kitty! Get your booty in here!"

Kitty comes running into my room. "What? I was in the middle of something."

"'I was in the middle of something,'" Chris mimics. "If you go get me a Diet Coke, I'll do your nails for you like I did Lara Jean's." I display my hands lavishly like a hand model. Chris counts with her fingers. "Kitty Covey fits perfectly."

Kitty bounds off, and I call after her, "Bring me a soda too!"

"With ice!" Chris screams. Then she sighs a wistful sigh. "I wish I had a little sister. I would be amazing at bossing her around."

"Kitty doesn't usually listen so well. It's only because she looks up to you."

"She does, doesn't she?" Chris picks at a fuzzy on her sock, smiling to herself.

Kitty used to look up to Genevieve, too. She was sort of in awe of her. "Hey," I say suddenly. "How's your grandma?"

"She's all right. She's pretty tough."

"And how's . . . the rest of your family? Everything all right?"

Chris shrugs. "Sure. Everything's fine."

Hmm. If Chris doesn't know, how bad could things be

with Genevieve's family? Either not that bad or, more likely, just another one of Genevieve's deceptions. Even when we were little she lied a lot, whether it was to get out of trouble with her mom, in which case she'd blame me, or to gain sympathy from adults.

Chris peers at me. "What are you thinking about so hard? Are you still stressing over your sex tape?"

"It's not a sex tape if you're not having sex in it!"

"Calm down, Lara Jean. I'm sure Peter's grandstanding did the trick and people will leave it alone. They'll be on to the next thing."

"I hope you're right," I say.

"Trust me, there'll be someone or something new to obsess over by next week."

It turns out that Chris is right, that people have moved on to the next thing. On Tuesday, a sophomore boy named Clark is caught masturbating in the boys locker room, and it's all everyone can talk about. Lucky me!

# 12

ACCORDING TO STORMY, THERE ARE TWO
kinds of girls in this world. The kind who breaks hearts and
the kind who gets her heart broken. One guess as to which
kind of girl Stormy is.

I'm sitting cross-legged on Stormy's velvet fainting couch,
going through a big shoe box of mostly black-and-white
photos. She's agreed to join my scrapbooking class, and we're
getting a head start organizing. I have several piles going.
Stormy: the early years; her teenagehood; her first, second,
and fourth weddings—no pictures from her third wedding,
because they eloped.

"*I* am a heartbreaker, but *you*, Lara Jean, are a girl who gets
her heart broken." She lifts her eyebrows at me for emphasis.
I think she forgot to pencil them in today.

I mull this over. I don't want to be a girl who gets her
heart broken, but I also don't really want to break boys'
hearts. "Stormy, did you have a lot of boyfriends in high
school?"

"Oh, sure. Dozens. That's how we did it in my day.
Drive-in on Friday with Burt and cotillion with Sam on
Saturday. We kept our options open. A girl didn't settle down
unless she was supremely, supremely sure."

"Sure that she liked him?"

"Sure that she wanted to *marry* him. Otherwise what was the point in ending all the fun?"

I pick up a picture of Stormy in a sea-foam formal gown, strapless with a full skirt. She looks like she could be Grace Kelly's sneaky cousin, with her pale blond hair and the lift of her brow. There's a boy standing next to her, and he isn't very tall or particularly handsome, but there's something about him. A glint in his eye. "Stormy, how old were you in this one?"

Stormy peers at it. "Sixteen or seventeen. About your age."

"Who's the boy?"

Stormy takes a closer look, her face wrinkling like a dried apricot. She taps her red fingernail on the picture. "Walter! We all called him Walt. He was a real charmer."

"Was he your boyfriend?"

"No, he was just a boy I saw from time to time." She waggles her pale eyebrows at me. "We went skinny-dipping out by the lake, and we got caught by the police. It was quite the *scandale*. I got to ride home in a police car in nothing but a blanket."

"And so . . . did people gossip about you?"

*"Bien sûr."*

"I've had a little bit of a *scandale* of my own," I say. Then I tell her about the hot tub, and the video, and all the fallout. I have to explain to her what a meme is. She is delighted; she's practically vibrating from the salaciousness of it all.

"Excellent!" she crows. "I'm so relieved you have some bite to you. A girl with a reputation is so much more interesting than a Goody Two-shoes."

"Stormy, this is on the Internet. The Internet is forever. It's not just gossip at school. And also, I kind of *am* a Goody Two-shoes."

"No, your sister Margaret's the Goody Two-shoes."

"Margot," I correct.

"Well, she certainly seems like a Margaret. I mean, really, every Friday night at a nursing home! I'd have slit my wrists if I was a teenage girl spending all my beauty years at a damn nursing home. Excuse my French, darling." She fluffs up the pillow behind her. "Oldest children are always high-achieving bores. My son Stanley is a frightful bore. He's the worst. He's a podiatrist, for God's sake! I suppose it's my fault for naming him Stanley. Not that I had any say in it. My mother-in-law insisted we name him after her dead husband. Good Lord, she was a crone." Stormy takes a sip of her iced tea. "Middle children are supposed to have fun, you know. You and I, we have that in common. I was glad you hadn't been coming around as much. I was hoping you were getting into trouble. Sounds like I was right. Although you might've come around a *bit* more."

Stormy's terrific at making a person feel guilty. She's mastered the art of the injured sniff.

"Now that I've got a proper job here, I'll be around a lot more often."

"Well, not too often." She perks up. "But next time bring that boy of yours. We could use some fresh blood around here. Give the place a jolt. Is he handsome?"

"Yes, he's very handsome." The handsomest of all the handsome boys.

Stormy claps her hands together. "Then you *must* bring him by. Give me advance notice, though, so I look my absolute best. Who else have you got waiting in the wings?"

I laugh. "No one! I told you, I have a boyfriend."

"Hmm." That's all she says, just "hmm." Then, "I have a grandson who could be about your age. He's still in high school, anyhow. Maybe I'll tell him to come by and see you. It's good for a girl to have options." I wonder what a grandson of Stormy's might be like—probably a real player, just like Stormy. I open my mouth to say no thank you, but she waves me off with a *shh*. "When we're done with my scrapbook, I'm going to transcribe my memoirs to you, and you'll type them up for me on the computer. I'm thinking of calling it *The Eye of the Storm*. Or *Stormy Weather*." Stormy starts to hum. "Stormy weather," she sings. "Since my man and I ain't together . . . keeps rainin' all the time. . . ." She stops short. "We should have a cabaret night! Picture it, Lara Jean. You in a tuxedo. Me in a slinky red dress draped over the piano. It'll give Mr. Morales a heart attack."

I giggle. "Let's not give him a heart attack. Maybe just a tremor."

She shrugs and goes on singing, adding a shimmy to her hips. "Stormy weather . . ."

She'll go off on a singing jag if I don't redirect her. "Stormy, tell me about where you were when John F. Kennedy died."

"It was a Friday. I was baking a pineapple upside-down cake for my bridge club. I put it in the oven and then I saw the news and I forgot all about the cake and nearly burned the house down. We had to have the kitchen repainted because of all the soot." She fusses with her hair. "He was a saint, that man. A prince. If I'd met him in my heyday, we really could've had some fun. You know, I flirted with a Kennedy once at an airport. He sidled up to me at the bar and bought me a very dry gin martini. Airports used to be so very much more glamorous. People got dressed up to travel. Young people on airplanes these days, they wear those horrible sheepskin boots and pajama pants and it's an *eyesore*. I wouldn't go out for the *mail* dressed like that."

"Which Kennedy?" I ask.

"Hmm? Oh, I don't know. He had the Kennedy chin, anyway."

I bite my lip to keep from smiling. Stormy and her escapades. "Can I have your pineapple upside-down cake recipe?"

"Sure, darling. It's just yellow box cake with Del Monte pineapple and brown sugar and a maraschino cherry on top. Just make sure you get the *rings* and not the *chunks*."

This cake sounds horrible. I try to nod in a diplomatic way, but Stormy is onto me. Crossly she says, "Do you think I had time to sit around baking cakes from scratch like some boring old housewife?"

"You could never be boring," I say on cue, because it's true and because I know it's what she wants to hear.

"You could do with a little less baking and a little more living life." She's being prickly, and she's never prickly with me. "Youth is truly wasted on the young." She frowns. "My legs ache. Get me some Tylenol PM, would you?"

I leap up, eager to be in her good graces again. "Where do you keep it?"

"In the kitchen drawer by the sink."

I rummage around, but I don't see it. Just batteries, talcum powder, a stack of McDonald's napkins, sugar packets, a black banana. Covertly, I throw the banana in the trash. "Stormy, I don't see your Tylenol PM in here. Is there anywhere else it could be?"

"Forget it," she snaps, coming up behind me and pushing me to the side. "I'll find it myself."

"Do you want me to put on some tea?" Stormy is old; that's why she's acting this way. She doesn't mean to be harsh. I know she doesn't mean it.

"Tea is for old ladies. I want a cocktail."

"Coming right up," I say.

# *13*

*MY SCRAPBOOKING TO THE OLDIES CLASS* has officially begun. I won't deny that I'm disappointed with the turnout. So far it's just Stormy, Alicia Ito, who is sprightly and put-together—short, buffed nails, pixie cut—and wily Mr. Morales, who I think has a crush on Stormy. Or Alicia. It's hard to know definitively, because he flirts with everyone, but they both have full pages in the scrapbook he's working on. He's decided to title it "The Good Old Days." He's decorated Stormy's page with music notes and piano keys and a picture of the two of them dancing on Disco Night last year. Alicia's page he's still working on, but his focal point is a picture of her sitting on a bench in the courtyard, gazing off into space, and he's affixed some flower stickers around it. Very romantic.

I haven't got much of a budget, so I've brought my own supplies. I've also instructed the three of them to collect scraps from magazines and other little bobbles and buttons. Stormy's a pack rat like me, so she has all kinds of treasures. Lace from her kids' christening gowns, a matchbook from the motel where she met her husband ("Don't ask," she said), old ticket stubs to a cabaret she went to in Paris. (I piped up, "In 1920s Paris? Did you ever meet Hemingway?" and she cut me with her eyes and said she obviously wasn't *that* old and I needed a history lesson.) Alicia's style is more minimalist and clean. With my black felt tip calligraphy pen, she writes descriptions in Japanese underneath each picture.

"What does it say here?" I ask, pointing to a description below a picture of Alicia and her husband, Phil, at Niagara Falls, holding hands and wearing yellow plastic ponchos.

Alicia smiles. "It says 'the time we got caught in the rain.'"

So Alicia's a romantic too. "You must miss him a lot." Phil died a year ago. I only met him a couple of times, back when I'd help out Margot with Friday cocktail hour. Phil had dementia, and he didn't talk much. He'd sit in his wheelchair in the common room and just smile at people. Alicia never left his side.

"I miss him every day," she says, tearing up.

Stormy jostles her way between us, green glitter pen tucked behind her ear, and says, "Alicia, you need to jazz up your pages more." She flicks a sheet of umbrella stickers Alicia's way.

"No, thank you," Alicia says stiffly, flicking the page back at Stormy. "You and I have different styles."

Stormy's eyes narrow at this.

I quickly go over to the speakers and turn up the volume to lighten the mood. Stormy dances over to me and sings, "Johnny Angel, Johnny Angel. You're an angel to me." We put our heads together and chorus, "I dream of him and me and how it's gonna be . . ."

When Alicia goes to the bathroom, Stormy says, "Ugh, what a bore."

"I don't think she's a bore," I say.

Stormy points at me with her hot-pink manicured nail. "Don't you dare go liking her better than me just because you're both Asian."

Hanging around a retirement home, I've gotten used to the vaguely racist things old people say. At least Stormy doesn't use the word "Oriental" anymore. "I like you both equally," I tell her.

"There's no such thing," she sniffs. "No one can ever like anyone exactly the same."

"Don't you love your kids the same?"

"Of course not."

"I thought parents didn't have favorites?"

"Of course they do. My favorite's my youngest, Kent, because he's a mama's boy. He visits with me every Sunday."

Loyally I say, "Well, I don't think my parents had favorites." I say it because it seems like the right thing to say, but is it true? I mean, if somebody put a gun to my head and said I had to choose, who would I say was Daddy's favorite? Margot, probably. They're the most alike. She's genuinely into documentaries and bird-watching, just like him. Kitty's the baby, which automatically gives her an edge. Where does that leave me, the middle Song girl? Maybe I was Mommy's favorite. I wish I could know for sure. I'd ask Daddy, but I doubt he'd tell the truth. Margot might.

I'd never be able to pick between Margot and Kitty. But if, say, they were both drowning and I could only throw one a life jacket, it would probably have to be Kitty. Margot would never forgive me otherwise. Kitty's both of ours to care for.

The thought of ever losing Kitty puts me in a kinder, more contemplative mood, and so that night after she's asleep, I bake off a tray of snickerdoodles, her favorite cookie. I have bags of cookie dough in the freezer, frozen into perfect cylindrical balls so that when any of us gets a taste for cookies, we can have them in twenty minutes flat. She'll have a nice surprise when she opens her lunch bag tomorrow.

I let Jamie have a cookie too, even though I know I shouldn't. But he keeps looking up at me with sorrowful puppy eyes and I can't resist.

# 14

"*WHAT ARE YOU DAYDREAMING ABOUT?*"
Peter taps my forehead with his spoon to get my attention.
We are at Starbucks doing homework after school.

I dump two raw sugar packets into my plastic cup and stir
it all up with my straw. I take a long sip, and sugar granules
crunch satisfyingly against my teeth. "I was thinking about
how it would be neat if people our age could be in love
like it's the 1950s." Right away I wish I didn't say "in love,"
because Peter's never said anything about being in love with
me, but it's too late, the words are already out of my mouth,
so I just press on and hope he didn't catch it. "In the 50s,
people just dated, and it was as easy as that. Like one night
Burt might take you to a drive-in movie, and the next night
Walter might take you to a sock hop or something."

Bemused, he says, "What the hell is a sock hop?"

"It's like a dance, like in *Grease*." Peter looks back at me
blankly. "You've never seen *Grease*? It was on TV last night.
Never mind. The point is, back then you weren't somebody's
girl until you had a pin."

"A pin?" Peter repeats.

"Yes, a fellow would give a girl his fraternity pin, and it
meant they were going steady. But you weren't official until
you had the pin."

"But I'm not in a fraternity. I don't even know what a fraternity pin looks like."

"Exactly," I say.

"Wait—are you saying you want a pin or you don't want a pin?"

"I'm not saying it either way. I'm just saying, don't you think there was something cool in the way it used to be? It's old-fashioned, but it's almost . . ." What's Margot always saying? "Postfeminist."

"Wait. So do you want to go on dates with other guys?" He doesn't sound upset, necessarily, just confused.

"No! I just . . . I'm just making an observation. I think it would be cool to bring back casual dating. There's something sweet about it, don't you think? My sister told me she wishes she didn't let things get so heavy with her and Josh. You said yourself how you hated how serious it got with Genevieve. If we break up, I don't want things to ever get so bad that we can't be in the same room together. I want to still be friends no matter what."

Peter dismisses this. "With me and Gen, it's complicated because of who Gen is. It's not like with me and you. You're . . . different."

I can feel my face get all flush again. I try not to sound too eager as I say, "Like different how?" I know I'm digging for a compliment, but I don't care.

"You're easy to be with. You don't make me get all crazy and worked up; you're . . ." Peter's voice trails off as he looks at my face. "What? What did I say?"

My whole body feels tight and stiff. No girl wants to hear what he just said. No girl. A girl *wants* to get a boy crazy and worked up—isn't that part of being in love?

"I mean that in a good way, Lara Jean. Are you mad? Don't be mad." He rubs his face tiredly.

I hesitate. Peter and I tell each other the truth; that's how it's been since the beginning. I'd like it to stay that way, on both sides. But then I catch the sudden worry in his eyes, the uncertainty, and it's not something I'm used to seeing on him. I don't like to see it. We've only been back together a couple of weeks, and I don't want to start a new fight when I know he didn't mean any harm. I hear myself say, "No, I'm not mad," and just like that, I'm not anymore. After all, I'm the one who was worrying about going too far too fast with Peter. Maybe it's a good thing he doesn't get crazy and worked up over me.

The clouds in his face clear away instantly, and he is sunny and bright again. That's the Peter I know. He gulps at his tea. "See, that's what I mean, Lara Jean. That's why I like you. You just get it."

"Thank you."

"You're welcome."

# 15

*EARLY MORNING BEFORE SCHOOL, JOSH IS* chiseling ice off his windshield when I run out to my car. Daddy's already scraped the ice off mine and started the engine and turned on the heat. By the looks of Josh's car, he's not going to make it to school on time.

We've hardly seen Josh since Christmas; after all the strangeness with me and then the breakup with Margot, he's been a ghost in this house. He leaves a little earlier for school now, comes home a little later. He never reached out to me when all the video stuff happened either, though part of me was relieved for that. I didn't want to hear I told you so from Josh about how he was right about Peter.

I back out my driveway, and at the last second I open the window and lean toward it. "Do you want a ride?" I call out to Josh.

His eyes widen in surprise. "Yeah. Sure." He throws his ice scraper into his car and grabs his backpack, then comes running over. Climbing in, he says, "Thanks, Lara Jean." He warms his hands on the heating vents.

We make our way out of the neighborhood, and I'm driving carefully, because the roads are icy from the night before.

"You've gotten really good at driving," Josh says.

"Thanks." I *have* been practicing, on my own and with Peter. I still get nervous sometimes, but each time I get in the car and drive, it's a little bit less, because now I know I can do it. You only know you can do something if you keep on doing it.

We're a few minutes from school when Josh asks, "When are we going to talk again? Just tell me so I have a general idea."

"We're talking right now, aren't we?"

"You know what I mean. What happened with me and Margot was between us—can't you and I still be friends like we were before?"

"Josh, of course we'll still be friends. But you and Margot have been broken up less than a month."

"No, we broke up in August. She decided she wanted to get back together three weeks ago, and I said no."

I sigh. "Why did you say no, though? Was it just the distance?"

Josh sighs too. "Relationships are hard work. You'll see. After you've been in it with Kavinsky longer, you'll see what I'm talking about."

"Oh my God, you're such a know-it-all. The biggest know-it-all I ever met, besides my sister."

"Which one?"

I can feel a giggle bubbling up inside of me, which I push down. "Both. They're both know-it-alls."

"One more thing." He hesitates, then keeps going. "I was wrong about Kavinsky. The way he's handled this whole video thing, I can tell he's a good guy."

"Thanks, Joshy. He really is."

He nods, and there is a comfortable quiet between us, and I'm glad for the bad weather we had last night, glad for the ice on his windshield this morning.

# 16

*AFTER SCHOOL THE NEXT DAY I'M SITTING ON* a bench, waiting for Peter out front, when Genevieve walks out the double doors on her phone. "If you don't tell her, I will. I swear I'll do it."

My heart stills. Who is she talking to? Not Peter.

Her friends Emily and Judith burst out the doors then, and she abruptly hangs up. "Where the hell have you bitches been?" she snaps.

They exchange a look. "Gen, chill out," Emily says, and I can tell she is walking that tightrope, a little bit feisty but careful not to further incur her wrath. "We still have plenty of time to shop."

Genevieve notices me then, and her peevish expression disappears. Waving, she says, "Hey, Lara Jean. Are you waiting for Kavinsky?"

I nod, and blow on my fingers just to have something to do. Also, it's cold.

"That boy's always running late. Tell him I'll call him later tonight, okay?"

I nod without thinking, and the girls walk away, arms linked.

Why did I nod? What is wrong with me? Why can't I ever come up with a good comeback? I'm still berating myself when Peter appears. He slides onto the bench beside me and slings his arm around my shoulders. Then he ruffles the top of my head the way I've seen him to do to Kitty. "What up, Covey."

"Thanks for making me wait for you outside in the cold," I say, pressing my freezing fingers on his neck.

Peter yelps and jumps away from me. "You could've waited inside!"

He has a point. That's not what I'm mad about anyway. "Gen says to tell you she'll call you later tonight."

He rolls his eyes. "She's such a shit stirrer. Don't let her get to you, Covey. She's just jealous." Standing up, he offers me his hands, which I accept begrudgingly. "Let me take you for a hot chocolate to warm up your poor frozen body."

"We'll see," I say.

In the car, he keeps sneaking peeks at me, checking to see if I'm still annoyed. I don't keep up my chilly routine for much longer, though; it takes up too much energy. I let him buy me a hot chocolate and I even share it with him. But I tell him he can't have any of the marshmallows.

That night my phone buzzes on my nightstand, and I know without looking that it's Peter looking for more reassurance. I take off my headphones and pick it up. "Hi."

"What are you doing?" His voice is low; I can tell he's lying down.

"My homework. What about you?"

"I'm in bed. I just called to say good night." There's a pause. "Hey, how come you never call me to say good night?"

"I don't know. I guess I never thought of it. Do you want me to?"

"Well. You don't *have* to—I just wondered why not."

"I thought you hated the whole 'last call' thing. Remember? You put it in the contract. You said that Genevieve insisted that she be your last call every night, and it was annoying."

He groans. "Can we please not talk about her? Also, why is your memory so good? You remember everything."

"It's my gift and my curse." I highlight a paragraph and try to balance the phone on my shoulder, but it keeps slipping. "So wait, do you want me to call you every night or not?"

"Ugh, just forget it."

"Ugh, fine," I say, and I can hear him smiling through the phone.

"Bye."

"Bye."

"Wait—can you bring me one of those yogurt drinks for lunch?"

"Say please."

"Please."

"Say pretty please."

"Bye."

"Byeeee."

It takes me another two hours to finish my homework, but when I fall asleep that night, I fall asleep smiling.

# 17

*I THINK MY DAD IS ON A DATE. TONIGHT HE* said he had plans with a friend, and he shaved and put on a nice button-down shirt and not one of his ratty sweaters. He was in a hurry to leave, so I didn't ask who the friend was. Someone from the hospital, probably. Daddy doesn't exactly have wide social circles. He's shy. Whoever it is, this sounds like a good thing.

As soon as he leaves, I turn to Kitty, who is lying on the couch watching TV and licking the sour off sour gummies. Jamie lies asleep next to her. "Kitty, do you think Daddy's—"

"On a date? Duh."

"And you're okay with it?"

"Sure. Though I'd rather it was with someone I knew and already liked."

"What if he got married again? Would you be okay with that?"

"Sure. So you can quit making your concerned-big-sister face at me, all right?"

I try to smooth my face out like a blank sheet of paper. Serenely I say, "So you're saying you're okay with Daddy getting married again."

"It's just a date, Lara Jean. People don't get married off of one measly date."

"But they do off of a lot of dates."

A flash of worry crosses her face, and then she says, "We'll just wait and see. There's no point in getting all revved up yet."

I wouldn't say I'm revved up, exactly, but I am curious. When I told Grandma I wouldn't mind if Daddy dated, I meant it, but I do want to know that she's good enough for him, whoever she is. I change the subject. "What do you want for your birthday?" I ask her.

"I've got a list going," she says. "A new collar for Jamie. Leather. With spikes. A treadmill."

"A treadmill!"

"Yeah, I want to teach Jamie how to walk on one."

"I doubt Daddy will go for a treadmill, Kitty. They're really expensive, and besides, where would we even put it?"

"Okay fine. Scratch the treadmill. I also want night-vision goggles."

"You should cc Margot on that."

"What kinds of special things can I get only from Scotland?" she asks.

"Genuine Scottish shortbread. A tartan kilt. What else . . . golf balls. Loch Ness monster paraphernalia."

"What's paraphernalia?"

"A stuffed Loch Ness monster. A Loch Ness T-shirt. Maybe a glow-in-the-dark poster."

"Stop right there. That's a good idea. I'm gonna add that to my list."

After Kitty goes to bed, I clean up the kitchen—I even scrub the stove with a Brillo pad and organize the refrigerator—so that I can give Daddy the third degree the second he gets home. I'm refilling the flour canister when Daddy walks through the door. Casually I say, "How was your date?"

He frowns in confusion. "Date? I went to the symphony with my colleague Marjorie. Her husband came down with the flu, and she didn't want the ticket to go to waste."

I deflate. "Oh."

Humming, he pours himself a glass of water and says, "I should go to the symphony more often. Any interest, Lara Jean?"

"Um . . . maybe," I say.

I make myself a stack of snickerdoodles, and I run up to my room and sit down at my desk. Munching on one, I open up my computer and type in "dating for dads," and lo and behold I find a dating site for single parents.

I start drafting a profile. First things first, he'll need a profile pic. I start going through the photos of him on my computer. There are hardly any of him alone. I finally settle on two, which I bookmark: one from last summer at the beach—a full-length shot, because that's one of the tips on the website—and one of him from this past Christmas, wearing that Scandinavian sweater we got him. He's carving a roast chicken, and he looks daddish in a wholesome coffee-commercial way but still vital. The dim dining room light makes him look hardly wrinkled at all, just some crinkles around the eyes. Which reminds me: I should get on him about wearing sunscreen every day. A men's skin-care kit could be a good Father's Day gift. I make a note of it in my Reminders.

Daddy is only in his early forties. That's still plenty young enough to meet someone and fall in love, maybe two or three times over, even.

# 18

*WHEN KITTY WAS BORN, I SAID SHE LOOKED* like a kitten and not a Katherine, so that's the name that stuck. After we came home from visiting her and Mommy at the hospital, Margot and I made a HAPPY BIRTHDAY, KITTEN banner to make the time go faster. We got out all the paints and craft supplies, and Grandma got annoyed because there was a big mess to clean in the kitchen, colors dripping all over the floor, handprints everywhere. We have a picture of Mommy standing underneath the sign holding Kitty that very first day, eyes tired but bright. Happy.

It's our tradition to put the sign on Kitty's door so it's the first thing she sees when she wakes up. I get up really early and hang the sign with care, so the edges don't bend or rip. For breakfast I make her a muenster-cheese omelet. With a ketchup bottle I squeeze out a cat face with a heart around it. We have a "celebrations drawer," which is birthday candles, paper hats, tablecloths, emergency birthday cards. I take out the paper hats and put one on my head, jauntily to the side. I set one each by Kitty and Daddy's plate, and I put one on Jamie Fox-Pickle too. He is not into it, but I'm able to get a picture before he knocks the hat off.

Daddy's prepared Kitty's favorite lunch to take to school.

A Brie sandwich and chips, plus a red velvet cupcake with cream cheese frosting.

Kitty delights in the place settings and in her cat face omelet. She claps and laughs like a hyena when the rubber band on Daddy's hat snaps, and the hat springs off his head. Truly, there's no happier birthday girl than our Kitty.

"Can I wear your sweater with the daisies on it?" she asks me, her mouth full of omelet.

I glance at the clock. "I'll go get it, but you have to eat fast." He'll be here any minute.

When it's time to leave, we put on our shoes, kiss Daddy good-bye, and tumble out the front door. Waiting for us on the street in front of his car is Peter with a bouquet of cellophane-wrapped pink carnations. "Happy birthday, kid," he says.

Kitty's eyes bulge. "Are those for me?"

He laughs. "Who else would they be for? Hurry and get in the car."

Kitty turns to me, her eyes bright, her smile as wide as her face. I'm smiling too. "Are you coming too, Lara Jean?"

I shake my head. "No, there's only room for two."

"You're my only girl today, kid," Peter says, and Kitty runs to him and snatches the flowers out of his hand. Gallantly, he opens the door for her. He shuts it and turns and winks at me. "Don't be jealous, Covey."

I've never liked him more than in this moment.

★ ★ ★

Kitty's birthday party with all her friends won't be for a few weeks. She insisted on a sleepover, and Daddy's on call for weekends in February. Tonight, we'll celebrate with a family dinner.

One of Daddy's most go-to dinners is roast chicken. He calls it the house specialty. He'll slather it in butter, pop an onion and an apple inside, sprinkle some poultry seasoning, and stick it in the oven. Usually a potato in some form as the side. Tonight I've mashed sweet potatoes and sprinkled brown sugar and cinnamon on top, then put them under the broiler so the sugar burns like crème brûlée.

Kitty is in charge of setting the table and putting out the condiments: Texas Pete's hot sauce for Daddy, mustard for Kitty, strawberry jam for me. Chutney for Margot if she were here. "What kind of sauce did Mommy like with her chicken?" Kitty asks me suddenly.

"I . . . can't remember," I say. We both look at Daddy, who is checking on the chicken.

"Did she like mustard like me?" she asks.

Closing the oven door, Daddy says, "Hmm. Well, I know she liked balsamic vinegar. A lot. A lot a lot."

"Just on chicken?" Kitty asks.

"On everything, actually. Avocados, with butter on toast, tomatoes, steak."

I file this away under Misc. Facts about M.

"Are you guys ready to eat?" Daddy asks. "I want to get this bird out while it's still nice and juicy."

"In a minute," Kitty says, and literally a minute later the doorbell rings. Kitty springs into action. She comes back with Ms. Rothschild from across the street. She's in skinny jeans and a black turtleneck sweater and high-heeled boots, a chunky black-and-gold necklace around her neck. Her mahogany brown hair is half up, half down. She's carrying a wrapped present in her hands. Jamie Fox-Pickle's puppy legs can't get to her fast enough; he is sliding all over the place, wagging his little tail.

Laughing, she says, "Well, hello, Jamie." She sets her gift on the counter and kneels down and pets him. "What's up, everybody?"

"Hi, Ms. Rothschild," I say.

"Trina!" Daddy says, surprised.

Ms. Rothschild lets out an awkward laugh. "Oh, did you not know I was coming? Kitty invited me when she was over with Jamie today. . . ." She reddens. "Kitty," she chides.

"I did tell him—it's just that Daddy's absentminded," Kitty says.

"Hm," Ms. Rothschild says, giving her a look, which Kitty pretends not to see. "Well, thank you anyway!" Jamie starts jumping all over her, another of his bad habits. Ms. Rothschild sticks her knee out and Jamie settles down immediately. "Sit, Jamie."

And then he actually sits! Daddy and I exchange an impressed look. Clearly Jamie needs to continue under Ms. Rothschild's tutelage.

"Trina, what can I get you to drink?" Daddy asks her.

"I'll have whatever's open," she says.

"I don't have anything open, but I'm happy to open whatever you like—"

"Ms. Rothschild likes pinot grigio," Kitty says. "With an ice cube."

She turns even redder. "God, Kitty, I'm not a lush!" She turns to us and says, "I'll have a small glass after work, but not every night."

Daddy laughs. "I'll put some white wine in the freezer. It'll get cold soon."

Kitty looks pleased as punch, and when Daddy and Ms. Rothschild go into the living room, I grab her by the collar and whisper, "What are you up to?"

"Nothing," she says, trying to squirm away.

"Is this a setup?" I hiss.

"So what if it is? They'd be a good match."

Huh! "What makes you say that?"

Kitty ticks off her fingers. "She loves animals, she's hot, she makes her own money, and I like her."

Hmm. All of that does sound good. Plus she lives across the street, which is convenient.

"Do you think Ms. Rothschild watches documentaries?"

"Who cares about dusty old documentaries? He can watch them with you or Margot. The important thing is chemistry." Kitty tries to jerk loose from my grip. "Let go of me so I can see if they have any!"

I release her collar. "No, don't go in yet." Kitty huffs and flounces away and I say meaningfully, "Let's let it *simmer* for a minute."

She stops short and then gives me an appreciative nod. "Let's let it simmer," she repeats, savoring the words.

Kitty is sawing her way through a piece of white meat, the only kind she'll eat—she likes it sliced thin like deli meat, and Daddy tries but it always ends up kind of shredded and sad-looking. I think maybe I'll get him an electric carving knife for this birthday. Personally, I like the thigh. I honestly don't know why anyone would bother eating anything but thigh if they had the choice.

When Ms. Rothschild shakes some hot sauce on her chicken, Kitty's eyes glow like a lightning bug. I make note of the way Ms. Rothschild laughs at Daddy's corny jokes with sincerity. I also appreciate the way she goes wild for my snickerdoodles. I threw some frozen ones in the oven when Daddy put the coffee on.

"I love how this cookie is crunchy but also soft. You're telling me you made this from scratch?"

"Always," I tell her.

"Well, give me the recipe, girl." Then she laughs. "Wait, don't bother. I know my strengths, and baking is not one of them."

"We'll share with you anytime—we always have lots of cakes and cookies," Kitty says, which is rich coming from her, because it's not like Kitty ever helps. She only shows up for the fun parts, the decorating and eating.

I sneak a look at Daddy, who is placidly sipping his coffee. I sigh. He's completely oblivious.

We all do the washing up and wrapping up of leftovers together, and it feels very natural. Without anyone telling her, Ms. Rothschild knows to hand-wash the wineglasses and not put them in the dishwasher, and on the first try she finds the aluminum foil and plastic wrap drawer. Which might say more about Margot's organizational skills than Ms. Rothschild's intuition, but still. I think I could see her fitting in with us pretty seamlessly. And, as I said, she does live across the street, which is convenient. People say absence makes the heart grow fonder, but I think they're wrong: *Proximity* makes the heart grow fonder.

As soon as Ms. Rothschild's gone home and Daddy's in his study, Kitty pounces on me in my room, where I'm setting out school clothes. Navy sweater with a fox on it that I've been saving for a rainy day, mustard-yellow skirt, knee socks.

"Well?" she demands. She has Jamie Fox-Pickle in her arms.

"I like the way she started Saran-wrapping things; that was some good initiative," I say, pinning a tortoiseshell bow in my hair and checking it out in the mirror. "She also complimented my snickerdoodles a lot, which I appreciated. But I don't know if I necessarily saw any sparks with Daddy. I mean, did you think he seemed interested?"

"I think he could be if she gave him a chance. She was dating a guy from her office, but it didn't work out because he reminded her of her ex-husband."

I raise my eyebrows. "It sounds like you guys have had some serious talks."

Proudly Kitty says, "She doesn't treat me like a little kid."

If Kitty's that crazy about her, that says a lot. "Well, she might not be Daddy's type, but if we keep throwing them together, who knows?"

"What do you mean she might not be Daddy's type?"

"Her style seems really different than Mommy's. Doesn't she smoke? Daddy hates that."

"She's trying to quit. She's got an electronic cigarette now."

"Let's keep inviting her to things and see what happens," I say, picking up my hairbrush. "Hey, do you think if you watched a video, you could give me a little side cornrow?"

"I could give it a shot," Kitty says. "Curl the ends first and then check with me after I watch my shows."

"Got it."

# 19

I break the news to her. She's sitting at her desk, wearing a Fair Isle sweater, light blue and hunter green, and her hair is wet. She has a Saint Andrews mug she's drinking tea out of. "That's a cute sweater," I say, nestling my laptop on my thighs and getting cozy against my pillows. "So guess who Kitty's been trying to set Daddy up with."

*"Who?"*

"Ms. Rothschild."

Margot practically chokes on her tea. "From across the street? You've got to be kidding me. That's literally the craziest thing I ever heard."

"Really? You think so?"

"Yes! Don't you?"

"I don't know. Kitty's been spending a lot of time with her because she's teaching her how to train Jamie. She seems pretty nice."

"I mean, sure, she's nice, but she wears so much makeup and she's always spilling hot coffee all over her cleavage and shrieking like a banshee. Remember how she and her ex-husband used to get into those screaming matches in their yard?" Margot shudders. "What would she and Daddy even have to talk about? She's like a Real Housewife of Charlottesville. Except she's divorced."

"She did mention that *Real Housewives* is her favorite show," I admit, feeling like a tattletale. "But she said it's a guilty pleasure!"

"Which city?"

"I think all of them?"

"Lara Jean, promise me you won't let her get her hooks in Daddy. He doesn't know the first thing about dating in the twenty-first century, and she'll just eat him alive. He needs to be with someone mature, someone with wisdom in her eyes."

I snort. "Like who? A grandma? If so, I know a few from Belleview I could set him up with."

"No, but someone who's at least the same age as him! She should be sophisticated, but also enjoy nature and hiking and that kind of thing."

"When's the last time Daddy hiked?"

"Not for years, but that's the point—he needs a woman who will encourage those kinds of interests. Keep him active, physically *and* mentally."

Giggling, I say, "And . . . sexually?" I simply cannot resist the joke, or the opportunity to gross Margot out.

"Ew!" she screams. "You're depraved!"

"I'm just joking!"

"I'm hanging up on you right now."

"No, don't. If Ms. Rothschild isn't the one, I was think-ing he should try online dating. I've found a dating site for him and everything. He's a handsome guy, you know. And at Thanksgiving, Grandma was bugging him about dating more. She says it's not good for a man to be alone."

"He's perfectly happy." She pauses. "Isn't he?"

"I think he's perfectly . . . content? But that's not the same thing as happy, is it? Gogo, I hate to think of him being lonely . . . and the way Kitty's so bent on setting him up with Ms. Rothschild, it makes me think she's longing for a mother figure."

Margot sighs and takes a sip of tea. "Okay, work on his profile and send me the login info so I can weigh in on everything. We'll handpick a few and present him with a really curated selection so he doesn't get overwhelmed."

Impulsively I say, "Why don't we hold off until we see how this thing with Ms. Rothschild plays out? We should at least give her a chance, don't you think? For Kitty's sake."

Margot sighs again. "How old do you think she is?"

"Like, thirty-nine? Forty?"

"Well, she dresses much younger."

"You shouldn't hold that against her," I say, though I will admit to feeling slight discomfort when she said we shop at the same places. Does that mean she dresses too young or I dress too old? Chris has called my style "granny meets little-girl chic" and "Lolita went to library school." Which reminds me. "Hey, if you see any cute kilts, will you bring one back for me? Red tartan, maybe with a big safety pin button?"

"I'll keep my eyes open for you," she promises. "Maybe I

can find matching for the three of us. Actually, the four of us. It can be next year's Christmas card."

I snort. "Daddy in a kilt!"

"You never know, he might be into it. He's always talking up his one-quarter Scottish heritage. He can put his money where his mouth is." She wraps both hands around her mug and takes a sip of tea. "Guess what. I met a cute boy. His name is Samuel, and he's in my British pop culture class."

"Ooh. Does he have a posh accent?"

"Indubitably," she says in a posh English accent. We both giggle. "We're meeting up at a pub tonight. Wish me luck."

"Luck!" I shout.

I like seeing Margot like this, so light and happy and unserious. I think it must mean she's really and truly over Josh.

# 20

*"DON'T STAND IN FRONT OF THE TV," KITTY* snaps.

I'm dusting the bookshelves with a new feather duster that I ordered online. I don't know the last time anybody dusted in here. I whirl around and say, "Why are you being such a mean little crab apple today?"

"I'm just in a mood," she mutters, stretching her string-bean legs out in front of her. "Shanae was supposed to come over today and now she isn't."

"Well, don't take it out on me."

Kitty scratches her knee. "Hey, what would you think about me sending Ms. Rothschild a valentine on Daddy's behalf?"

"Don't you dare!" I shake my feather duster at her. "You've got to stop with this meddling habit of yours, Katherine. It's not cute."

Kitty gives me a deep eye roll. "Ugh, I never should have told you."

"Too late now. Look, if two people are meant to be, they'll find their way to each other."

"Would you and Peter have 'found your way to each other' if I hadn't sent those letters?" she challenges.

Point one for Kitty. "Probably not," I admit.

"No, definitely not. You needed my little push."

"Don't act like sending my letters was some altruistic act on your part. You know you did it out of spite."

Kitty sails right past that and asks, "What does 'altruistic' mean?"

"Selfless, charitable, generous of spirit . . . a.k.a. the opposite of you." Kitty shrieks and lunges at me, and we struggle briefly, both of us breathless and giggling and bumping into the shelves. I used to be able to disarm her with not much effort, but she's gaining on me. Her legs are strong, and she's good at wriggling out of my grasp like a worm. I finally get both her arms behind her back, and she yells, "I give, I give!" As soon as I release her, she jumps up and attacks me again, tickling under my arms and going for my neck.

"Not the neck, not the neck!" I shriek. The neck is my weak spot, which everyone in my family knows. I fall to my knees, laughing so hard it hurts. "Stop, stop! Please!"

Kitty stops tickling. "And that's me being altru . . . altruistic," she says. "That's my altruicity."

"Altruism," I pant.

"I think 'altruicity' works too."

If Kitty hadn't sent those letters, would Peter and I still have found our way to each other? My first impulse is to say no, but maybe we would have kept going down different paths and converged at some other fork in the road. Or maybe not, but either way, we're here now.

# 21

"TELL ME MORE ABOUT YOUR YOUNG MAN," Stormy says. We're sitting cross-legged on her floor, setting aside pictures and mementos for her scrapbook. She was the only one to show up for Scrapbooking to the Oldies today, so we moved it over to her apartment. I'd worried Janette would notice the low attendance, but since I started volunteering, she hasn't so much as popped her head in. All the better.

"What do you want to know about him?

"Does he play any sports?"

"He plays lacrosse."

"Lacrosse?" she repeats. "Not football or baseball or basketball?"

"Well, he's very good. He's being recruited by colleges."

"Can I see a picture of him?"

I get my phone out and pull up a picture of the two of us in his car. He's wearing a hunter green sweater that I think he looks particularly handsome in. I like him in sweaters. I get the urge to cuddle and pet him like a stuffed animal.

Stormy looks at it closely. "Huh," she says. "Yes, he is very handsome. I don't know if he's as handsome as my grandson, though. My grandson looks like a young Robert Redford."

Whoa.

"I'll show you if you don't believe me," she says, getting up and rooting around for a picture. She's opening drawers, moving papers around. Any other grandmother at Belleview would already have a picture of her beloved grandson on display. Framed, above the TV or on the mantel. Not Stormy. The only pictures she has framed are pictures of herself. There's a huge black-and-white bridal portrait in the entry-way that takes up nearly the whole wall. Though I suppose if I was once that beautiful, I would want to show it off too. "Huh. I can't find a picture."

"You can show me next time," I say, and Stormy lowers herself back down on the couch.

She puts her legs up on the ottoman. "Where do young people go these days for a little alone time? Is there no 'Lookout Point' type of place?" She's digging, she's definitely digging for information. Stormy's a bloodhound when it comes to sniffing out juicy goods, but I'm not giving up a thing. Not that I even have much juice to offer her.

"Um, I don't know . . . I don't think so." I busy myself with cleaning up a pile of scraps.

She starts to cut up some trimmings. "I remember the first boy I ever went parking with. Ken Newbery. He drove a Chevy Impala. God, the thrill of a boy putting his hands on you for the first time. There's nothing quite like it, is there, dear?"

"Mm-hmm. Where's that stack of old Broadway playbills you had? We should do something with those, too."

"They might be in my hope chest."

*The thrill of a boy putting his hands on you for the first time.*

I get a shivery feeling in my stomach. I do know that thrill. I remember it perfectly, and I would even if it hadn't been caught on camera. It's nice to think of it again as its own memory, separate from the video and everything that followed.

Stormy leans in close and says, "Lara Jean, just remember, the girl must always be the one to control how far things go. Boys think with their you-know-whats. It's up to you to keep your head and protect what's yours."

"I don't know, Stormy. Isn't that kind of sexist?"

"Life is sexist. If you were to get pregnant, you're the one whose life changes. Nothing of significance changes for the boy. You're the one people whisper about. I've seen that show, *Teen Moms*. All those boys are worthless. Garbage!"

"Are you saying I shouldn't have sex?" This whole time, Stormy has been telling me to stop being such a stick-in-the-mud, to live life, to love boys. And now this?

"I'm saying you should be careful. As careful as life and death, because that's what it is." She gives me a meaningful look. "And never trust the boy to bring the condom. A lady always brings her own."

I cough.

"Your body is yours to protect *and* to enjoy." She raises both eyebrows at me meaningfully. "Whoever you should choose to partake in that enjoyment, that is your choice, and choose wisely. Every man that ever got to touch me was afforded an *honor*. A privilege." Stormy waves her hand over me. "All this? It's a privilege to worship at this temple, do you understand my meaning? Not just any young fool can approach the throne. Remember my words, Lara Jean. You decide who, how far, and how often, if ever."

"I had no idea you were such a feminist," I say.

"Feminist?" Stormy makes a disgusted sound in her throat. "I'm no *feminist*. Really, Lara Jean!"

"Stormy, don't get worked up about it. All it means is that you believe men and women are equal, and should have equal rights."

"I don't think any man is my equal. Women are far superior, and don't you forget it. Don't forget any of the things I just told you. In fact you should probably be writing it down for my memoirs." She starts to hum "Stormy Weather."

There was never a threat of things going too far when we were fake. But I see now how fast things can change without you even realizing it. It can go from a kiss to hands under my shirt in two seconds, and it's so feverish, so frenzied. It's like we're on a high-speed train that's going somewhere fast, and I like it, I do, but I also like a slow train where I can look out the window and appreciate the countryside, the buildings, the mountains. It's like I don't want to miss the little steps; I want it to last. And then the next second I want to grow up faster, more, now. To be as ready as everyone else is. How is everyone else so ready?

I still find it very surprising, having a boy in my personal space. I still get nervous when he puts his arm around my waist or reaches for my hand. I don't think I know how to date in the 2010s. I'm confused by it. I don't want what Margot and Josh had, or Peter and Genevieve. I want something different.

I guess you could call me a late bloomer, but that implies that we're all on some predetermined blooming schedule, that there's a right or a wrong way to be sixteen and in love with a boy.

*My body is a temple not just any boy gets to worship at.*

*I won't do any more than I want to do.*

# 22

*PETER AND I ARE AT STARBUCKS, SITTING* side by side, studying for our chemistry exam. Idly, he puts his arm around my chair and starts twisting my hair around his pencil and letting it unfurl like a slice of ribbon. I ignore him. He pulls my chair closer to his and plants a warm kiss on my neck, which makes me giggle. I scoot away from him. "I can't concentrate when you do that."

"You said you like when I play with your hair."

"I do, but I'm trying to study." I look around and then whisper, "Besides, we're in public."

"There's hardly anybody in here!"

"There's the barista, and that guy over there by the door." I try to discreetly point with my pencil. Things have been quiet at school; the last thing we need is another meme flare-up.

"Lara Jean, nobody's going to film us if that's what you're worried about. We're not doing anything."

"I told you from the start I'm not into PDAs," I remind him.

Peter smirks. "Really? Let's not forget who kissed who in the hallway. You literally jumped on top of me, Covey."

I blush. "There was a purpose for that and you know it."

"There's a purpose now," he pouts. "The purpose is I'm

bored and I feel like kissing you. Is that a crime?"

"You're such a baby," I say, pinching his nose hard. "If you stay quiet and study for forty-five more minutes, I'll let you kiss me in the privacy of your car."

Peter's face lights up. "Deal." His phone buzzes, and he reaches down to check it. He frowns and texts something, his fingers lightning quick.

"Is everything okay?" I ask.

He nods, but he looks distracted, and he keeps texting, even as we're supposed to be studying. And now I'm distracted too, wondering what it could be. Or who.

# 23

*I'M PUSHING MY GROCERY CART AROUND,* looking for condensed milk for key lime pie, when I spot Josh in the cereal aisle. I roll right up to him and bump him with my cart.

"Hey, neighbor," I say.

"Hey, so guess what." Josh grins a pleased, proud sort of grin. "I got into UVA early."

I let out a high-pitched shriek and let go of my cart. "Josh! That's amazing!" I throw my arms around him and jump up and down. I shake his shoulders. "Be more excited, you loon!"

He laughs and jumps up and down a few times too before releasing me. "I am excited. My parents are out of their heads excited because now they don't have to pay out-of-state tuition. They haven't fought in days." Shyly he asks, "Will you tell Margot? I feel like I can't call her myself, but she deserves to know. She's the one who helped me study all that time. It's partly because of her that this is even happening."

"I'll tell her. I know she'll be really happy for you, Josh. My dad and Kitty, too." I lift my hand for a high five, and he smacks it. I can't believe it—Josh is going to college, and soon he won't be my neighbor anymore. Not like before.

Now that he'll be graduating and leaving town, maybe his parents will finally get their divorce, and then they'll sell the house and he won't even be my sort-of neighbor. Things have been off with us for months, even before the Margot breakup, and we haven't hung out in ages . . . but I liked knowing that he was there, right next door if I needed him. "Once a little more time has passed . . . ," I begin. "Once we have the all clear from Margot, will you come over for dinner again like before? Everyone misses you. I know Kitty's dying to show you Jamie's new tricks. I'll tell you right now, it's nothing fancy, so don't get excited. But still."

A smile spreads across his face, that slow smile I know so well. "All right," he says.

# 24

*THE SONG GIRLS TAKE VALENTINE MAKING* very seriously. A valentine is humble and sweet and sincere in its old-fashionedness, and as such, homemade is best. I have plenty of raw materials from my scrapbooking, but in addition I've saved snippets of lace and ribbon and doilies. I have a tin with little beads and pearls and rhinestones in it; I have antiquey rubber stamps, too—a Cupid, hearts of all kinds, flowers.

Historically, Daddy gets one valentine from the three of us. This year is the first that Margot will be sending one of her own. Josh will get one too, though I let Kitty take the lead on it and merely sign my name under hers.

I've spent the better part of the afternoon on Peter's. It's a white heart, edged in white lace. In the center I've stitched *YOU'RE MINE, PETER K* in pink string. I know it will make him smile. It's lighthearted, teasing; it doesn't take itself too seriously, much like Peter himself. Still, it acknowledges the day and the fact that we, Peter Kavinsky and Lara Jean Song Covey, are in a relationship. I was going to make a much more extravagant card, big and beaded and lacy, but Kitty said it would be a bit much.

"Don't use all my pearls," I tell Kitty. "It's taken me years to build up my collection. Literally, years."

Pragmatic as ever, Kitty says, "What's the point of collecting them if you don't use them? All that work so they can just live in a little tin box where no one can even see them?"

"I guess," I say, because she does have a point. "I'm just saying, only put pearls on the valentines of the people you really like."

"What about the purple rhinestones?"

"Use as many of those as you want," I say in a benevolent tone, much like a wealthy landowner to a less-fortunate neighbor. The purple rhinestones don't go with my motif. I'm shooting for a Victorian look, and purple rhinestones are more Mardi Gras, but you won't see me saying that to Kitty. Kitty's temperament is such that when she knows you don't much value something, she grows suspicious of it too and the appeal is lost to her. For a long time I had her convinced that raisins were my absolute favorite, and she must never ever eat more than her share, when in actuality I hate raisins and was grateful someone else was eating them. Kitty used to hoard raisins; she was probably the most regular kid in kindergarten.

I'm hot-gluing white bric-a-brac around a heart as I wonder aloud, "Should we do a special breakfast for Daddy? We could buy one of those juicers at the mall and make fresh-squeezed pink grapefruit juice. And I think I saw heart waffle makers online for not very expensive."

"Daddy doesn't like grapefruit," Kitty says. "And we barely use our regular waffle maker as it is. How about we just cut the waffle into the shape of a heart instead?"

"That would look so cheap," I scoff. But she's right. There's no sense in buying something we'd only ever use once a year, even if it only costs $19.99. As Kitty gets older, I see that she is far more like Margot than me.

But then she says, "What if we use our cookie cutter to make heart-shaped pancakes instead? And put in red food coloring?"

I beam at her. "Attagirl!" So maybe she's got a little bit of me in her after all.

Kitty continues. "We could put red food coloring in the syrup, too, to make it look like blood. A bloody heart!"

No, never mind. Kitty is all her own.

# 25

*THE NIGHT BEFORE VALENTINE'S DAY, I GET* it in my head that my card for Peter isn't enough and cherry turnovers would be a fantastic idea, so I wake up before the sun rises to bake them fresh, and now the kitchen looks like a crime scene. Cherry juice splattered all over the countertops and tiles. It's a bloodbath, a cherry-juice bloodbath. Worse than the time I made red velvet cake and got red food coloring in the backsplash tiles. I had to take a toothbrush to the grout.

But my turnovers turn out so perfect, right out of a cartoon, each one so golden and homey, with their fork-tined edges and the little holes to let out steam. My plan is to bring these to the lunch table; I know that Peter and Gabe and Darrell will appreciate them. I'll give one to Lucas, too. And Chris, if she shows up for school.

I text Peter that I don't need a ride, because I want to get there early and put the valentine in his locker. There's something sweet about a valentine in a locker—when you think about it, a locker is much like a mailbox, and everyone knows that letters sent in the mail are far more romantic than when they're unceremoniously handed over in person.

Kitty comes downstairs around seven, and the two of us

set a beautiful Valentine's table setting for Daddy, with his valentines from me, Kitty, and Margot arranged around his plate. I leave him two turnovers. I miss the big reaction because I don't want to get to school after Peter. He always cuts it close, so I figure I'm fine being just five minutes early.

When I get to school, I slip the valentine into Peter's locker, then head to the cafeteria to wait for him.

But when I walk in, he's already there, standing by the vending machines with . . . Genevieve. He has his hands on her shoulders, and he is talking to her intently. She's nodding, her eyes downcast. What could it be, this thing that has her so sad? Or is it just an act, a way to keep Peter close?

Here it is Valentine's Day and I feel like I'm interrupting my boyfriend and his ex-girlfriend. Is he really just being a good friend to her, or is it something more? With her I feel like it's always something more, whether he knows it or not. Have they exchanged Valentine's gifts, for old times' sake? Is that me being paranoid or is that a thing that exes who are still friends do?

She spots me then, says something to Peter, and walks past me and out of the cafeteria. He strides over to me. "Happy Valentine's Day, Covey." He puts his hands on my waist and picks me up for a hug like I weigh nothing. Setting me down, he says, "Can we kiss in public since it's a holiday?"

"Where's my valentine first?" I say, holding my hand out.

Peter laughs. "Damn, it's in my backpack. Geez. So greedy."

Whatever it is, I can tell he is excited to give it to me, which in turn excites me. He takes my hand and leads me over to the table where his backpack is. "First sit down," he says, and I obey. He sits down next to me. "Close your eyes and hold out your hand."

I do, and I hear him unzip his bag, and then he puts something in my hand, a piece of paper. I open my eyes.

"It's a poem," he says. "For you."

*The moon never beams without bringing me dreams*
*Of beautiful Lara Jean.*
*And stars never rise but I feel the bright eyes*
*Of beautiful Lara Jean.*

I touch my hand to my lips. *Beautiful Lara Jean!* I can't even believe it. "This is my favorite thing anyone has ever done for me. I could squeeze you to death right now I'm so happy." To picture him, sitting at his desk at home, scribbling away with a pen and paper, endears him to me so completely. It gives me shivers. Currents of electricity from my scalp down to my toes.

"Really? You like it?"

"I *love* it!" I throw my arms around him and squeeze with all my might. I will put this valentine in my hatbox, and when I'm old like Stormy, I will take it out and look at it and remember this exact moment. Forget Genevieve; forget everything. Peter Kavinsky wrote me a poem.

"That's not the only present I brought you. It's not even

the best one." He peels away from me and pulls a little vel-vet jewelry box out of his backpack. I gasp. Pleased, he says, "Hurry up and open it already."

"Is it a pin?"

"It's better."

My hands fly to my mouth. It's my necklace, the heart locket from his mom's antique store, the very same necklace I admired for so many months. At Christmas when Daddy said the necklace had been sold, I thought it was gone from my life forever. "I can't believe it," I whisper, touching the diamond chip in the middle.

"Here, let me put it on for you."

I lift my hair up, and Peter comes around and fastens the necklace around my neck. "Can I even accept this?" I won-der aloud. "It was really expensive, Peter! Like, really really expensive."

He laughs. "I know how much it cost. Don't worry, my mom cut me a deal. I had to sign over a bunch of week-ends to driving the van around picking up furniture for the store, but you know, no biggie. It's whatever, as long as you're into it."

I touch the necklace. "I am! I'm so, so into it." Surreptitiously I look around the cafeteria. It's a petty thought, a small thought, but I wish Genevieve were here to see this.

"Wait, where's my valentine?" Peter asks me.

"It's in your locker," I say. Now I'm sort of wishing I didn't listen to Kitty and let myself go a little overboard this first Valentine's Day with a boyfriend. With Peter. Oh, well. At least there are the cherry turnovers still warm in my backpack. I'll give them all to him. Sorry, Chris and Lucas and Gabe.

I can't stop looking at myself in this necklace. At school, I wear it over my sweater, so all can see and admire. That night I show it to Daddy, to Kitty, to Margot over video chat. As a joke I show it off to Jamie Fox-Pickle. Everyone's impressed. I don't take it off, ever: I wear it in the shower; I wear it to sleep.

It's like in *Little House in the Big Woods*, when Laura got a rag doll for Christmas. It had black button eyes, and berry-stained lips and cheeks. Red flannel stockings and a pink-and-blue calico dress. Laura couldn't take her eyes off of it. She held that doll tight and forgot the rest of the world. Her mother had to remind her to let the other girls hold it.

That's how I feel. When Kitty asks to try it on, I hesitate for a tiny second and then feel guilty for being so stingy. "Just be careful with it," I tell her as I unclasp the necklace.

Kitty pretends to drop the locket off the chain and I shriek. "Just kidding," she giggles. She goes over to my mirror and looks at herself, her head tilted, neck arched. "Not bad. Aren't you so glad I set this whole you-and-Peter thing in motion?"

I throw a pillow at her.

"Can I borrow it for a special occasion?"

"No!" Then I think of Laura and the doll again. "Yes. If it's a very special occasion."

"Thank you," Kitty says. Then she cocks her head and looks at me with serious eyes. "Lara Jean, can I ask you a question?"

"You can ask me anything," I say.

"It's about boys."

I try not to look too eager as I nod. Boys! So we're here already. All right. "I'm listening."

"And you promise you'll answer honestly? Sister swear?"

"Of course. Come sit by me, Kitty." She sits down next to me on the floor and I put my arm around her, feeling generous and warm and maternal. Kitty really is growing up.

She looks up at me, doe-eyed. "Are you and Peter doing it?"

"What?" I shove her away. "Kitty!"

Gleefully she says, "You promised you'd answer!"

"Well, the answer is no, you sneaky little fink. God! Get out of my room." Kitty skips off, laughing like a mad hyena. I can hear her all the way down the hallway.

# 26

JUST WHEN I THOUGHT THE HOT-TUB-VIDEO ordeal was well and truly over with, another version pops up and reminds me that this particular nightmare will never be over. Nothing on the Internet ever dies; isn't that what people say? This time I'm in the library, and out of the corner of my eye I see two sophomore girls sharing a pair of earbuds, watching the video, giggling. There I am, in my nightgown, draped all over Peter's lap like a blanket. For a few seconds I just sit there, trapped in my indecision. To confront or not to confront. I remember Margot's words about rising above it and acting like I couldn't care less. And then I think, *Screw it.*

I stand up, stalk over to them, and snatch the earbuds out of the laptop. "Part of Your World" comes blasting out the speakers.

"Hey!" the girl says, whirling in her seat.

Then she sees it's me, and she and her friend exchange a panicky look. She slams the laptop shut. "Go ahead, play it," I say, crossing my arms.

"No thanks," she says.

I reach over her and open it and push play. Whoever's made this video has spliced it with scenes from *The Little Mermaid.* "When's it my turn? Wouldn't I love, love to explore that shore up above . . ." I snap the computer shut. "Just so you know, watching this video is the equivalent of child pornography, and you guys could be charged for it. Your IP address is already in the system. Think about that before you forward it on. That's distribution."

The red-haired girl gapes. "How is this child porn?"

"I'm underage and so is Peter."

The other girl smirks and says, "I thought you guys claimed you weren't having sex."

I'm stumped. "Well, we'll let the Justice Department sort that out. But first I'm notifying Principal Lochlan."

"It's not like we're the only ones looking at it!" the red-haired girl says.

"Think about how you'd feel if it were you in that video," I say.

"I'd feel great," the girl mutters. "You're lucky. Kavinsky's hot."

Lucky. Right.


It catches me off guard how upset Peter is when I show him the *Little Mermaid* video. Because nothing bad ever sticks to Peter; it just rolls off his back. That's why people like him so much, I think. He's sure of himself; he's self-possessed. It sets people at ease.

But it's the *Little Mermaid* video that breaks him. We watch it in his car, on his phone, and he's so mad I'm afraid he's going to throw the phone out the window. "Those fuckers! How dare they!" Peter punches the steering wheel, and the horn beeps. I jump. I've never seen him upset like this. I'm not sure what to say, how to calm him down. I grew up in a house full of women and one gentle dad. I don't know anything about teenage boys' tempers.

"Shit!" he yells. "I hate that I can't protect you from this."

"I don't need you to," I say, and I realize as I say it that it's true. I'm coping on my own just fine.

He stares straight ahead. "But I want to. I thought I fixed it before, but here it is again. It's like fucking herpes."

I want to comfort him, to make him laugh and forget. Teasingly I ask him, "Peter, do you have herpes?"

"Lara Jean, it's not funny."

"Sorry." I put my hand on his arm. "Let's get out of here."

Peter starts the car. "Where do you want to go?"

"Anywhere. Nowhere. Let's just drive." I don't want to run into anybody, I don't want any knowing looks or whispers. I want to hide. Peter's Audi, our little haven. To cover up my bleak thoughts, I give Peter a bright smile, bright enough to make him smile back, just.

The drive calms Peter down, and by the time we get to my house, Peter seems to be in good spirits again. I ask him if he wants to come inside and have pizza, it being pizza night and all. I tell him he can order whichever toppings he wants. But he shakes his head, says he should get home. For the first time he doesn't kiss me good-bye, and it makes me feel guilty, how bad he feels. It's partly my fault, I know it is. He feels like he has to make things right for me, and now he knows he can't, and it's killing him.

★ ★ ★

When I walk into the house, Daddy is waiting for me at the kitchen table, just sitting and waiting, eyebrows knit together. "Why haven't you been answering your phone?"

"Sorry . . . my battery died. Is everything okay?" Judging by the serious look on his face, everything is definitely not okay.

"We need to talk, Lara Jean. Come sit down."

Dread hits me like a tidal wave. "Why, Daddy? What's wrong? Where's Kitty?"

"She's in her room." I put down my bag and make my way over to the kitchen table, feet moving as slow as I can make them. I sit down next to him and he sighs heavily, hands folded.

Just as I say, "Is this about the dating profile I set up for you? Because I haven't even activated it yet," he says, "Why didn't you tell me what was going on at school?"

My heart drops all the way to the floor. "What do you mean?" I'm still hoping, praying this is about something else. Tell me I failed my chemistry test; say anything but the hot tub.

"The video of you and Peter."

"How did you find out?" I whisper.

"Your guidance counselor called me. She was worried about you. Why didn't you tell me what was going on, Lara Jean?"

He looks so stern, and so very disappointed, which I hate most of all. I feel pressure building behind my eyes. "Because . . . I was ashamed. I didn't want you to think of me that way. Daddy, I swear, all we were doing was kissing. That's it."

"I haven't seen the video, and I won't. That's private, between you and Peter. But I wish you had used better judgment that day, Lara Jean. There are long-lasting consequences to our actions."

"I know." Tears roll down my cheeks.

Daddy takes my hand out of my lap and holds it in his. "It pains me that you didn't come to me when things were so hard for you at school. I knew you were going through something, but I didn't want to push too hard. I always try to think about what your mom would do if she were here. I know it's not easy, only having a dad to talk to—" His voice breaks, and I cry harder. "But I'm trying. I really am trying."

I jump out of my seat and throw my arms around him. "I know you're trying," I cry.

He hugs me back. "You have to know you can come to me, Lara Jean. No matter what it is. I've spoken to Principal Lochlan, and he's going to make an announcement tomorrow saying that anyone who watches or distributes the video will be suspended."

Relief floods over me. I should've come to my dad in the first place. I stand up straight, and he reaches up and wipes my cheeks. "Now, what's this about a dating profile?"

"Oh . . ." I sit back down again. "Well . . . I started one for you on Singleparentloveconnection.com." He's frowning, so I quickly say, "Grandma doesn't think it's good for a man to be alone for so long, and I agree with her. I thought online dating could help you get back out there."

"Lara Jean, I can handle my own dating life! I don't need my daughter managing my dates."

"But . . . you never go on any."

"That's my concern, not yours. I want you to take down that profile tonight."

"It was never even active; I just set it up in case. It's a whole new world out there, Daddy."

"Right now we're talking about your love life, not mine, Lara Jean. Mine we'll save for another time. I want to hear about yours."

"Okay." Primly, I fold my hands in front of me on the table. "What do you want to know?"

He scratches his neck. "Well . . . are you and Peter pretty serious?"

"I don't know. I mean, I think I might love him. But maybe it's too early to say. How serious can you be in high school, anyway? Look at Margot and Josh and how that turned out."

Wistfully, Daddy says, "He never comes around here anymore."

"Exactly. I don't want to be the girl crying in her dorm room over a boy." I stop suddenly. "That's something Mommy said to Margot. She said don't be the girl who goes to college with a boyfriend and then misses out on everything."

He smiles a knowing kind of smile. "That sounds like her."

"Who was her high school boyfriend? Did she love him a lot? Did you ever meet him?"

"Your mom didn't have a high school boyfriend. That was her roommate she was talking about. Robyn." Daddy chuckles. "She drove your mom crazy."

I rest back in my seat. All this time I thought Mommy was talking about herself.

"I remember the first time I saw your mom. She was throwing a dinner in her dorm called Fakesgiving, and a buddy of mine and I went. It was a big Thanksgiving meal in May. She had on a red dress, and her hair was long back then. You know, you've seen the pictures." He pauses, a smile flickering on his face. "She gave me a hard time because I brought canned green beans and not fresh ones. That's how you knew if she liked someone, if she teased them. Of course, I didn't know it at the time. I was pretty clueless about girls back then."

Ha! *Back then.* "I thought you guys met in a psychology class," I say.

"According to your mom, we took the same class one semester, but I don't remember seeing her. It was in one of those lecture halls with hundreds of people."

"But she noticed you," I say. That, I've heard before. She said she liked the way he paid attention in class, and how his hair was a little too long in the back, like an absent-minded professor.

"Thank God she did. Where would I be without her?"

This gives me pause. Where *would* he be? Without us,

certainly, but probably he wouldn't be a widower either. Would his life have been happier if he'd married some other girl, made some other choice?

Daddy tips my chin. Firmly he says, "I would be nowhere without her, because I wouldn't have my girls."

I call Peter and tell him Mrs. Duvall called my dad and he knows all about the video, but he's talked to Principal Lochlan and everything will be fine now. I expect him to be relieved, but he still sounds down. "Now your dad probably hates me," he says.

"He doesn't," I assure him.

"Do you think I should say something to him? I don't know, like, apologize, man to man?"

I shudder. "Definitely not. My dad is super awkward."

"Yeah, but—"

"Please stop worrying, Peter. It's like I told you, my dad's sorted it all out. Principal Lochlan will make the announcement and people will leave us alone. Besides, there's nothing for you to apologize for. I was in it just as much as you were. You didn't make me do anything I didn't want to do."

We hang up soon after, and even though I feel better about the video, I still feel unsettled about Peter. I know he's upset about not being able to protect me, but I also know that part of why he's upset is because his pride was injured, and that has nothing to do with me. Is a boy's ego really such a fragile, breakable thing? It must be so.

*JENNY HAN*

## 27

*THE LETTER COMES ON A TUESDAY, BUT I* don't see it until Wednesday morning before school. I'm at the kitchen window seat, eating an apple, going through the stack of mail while I wait for Peter to pick me up. Electric bill, cable bill, a Victoria's Secret catalog, Kitty's issue of this month's *Dog Fancy (For Kids!)*. And then a letter, in a white envelope, addressed to me. A boy's handwriting. A return address I don't recognize.

Dear Lara Jean,

A tree fell in our driveway last week and Mr. Barber of Barber Landscaping came by to haul it away. The Barbers are the family who moved into our old house in Meadowridge, and not to overstate, but they own a landscaping company. Mr. Barber brought your letter. I saw on the postmark you sent it way back in September, but I only just got it this week, because it was sent to my old house. That's why it took me so long to write back.

Your letter made me remember all kinds of stuff I thought I'd forgotten. Like that time your older sister

made peanut brittle in the microwave and you guys
decided we should have a break dancing contest for who
got the biggest piece. Or the time I got locked out of
my house one afternoon and I went to the tree house
and you and I just read until it got really dark and we
had to use a flashlight. I remember your neighbor was
grilling hamburgers and you dared me to go ask for one
for us to share, but I was too chicken. When I went
home I was in so much trouble because no one knew
where I was, but it was worth it.

I stop reading. I remember that day we both got locked
out! It was Chris and John and me, and then Chris had to
leave and it was just John and me. My dad had been at a
seminar; I don't remember where Margot and Kitty were.
We got so hungry, we tore into the bag of Skittles that
Trevor had stashed under a loose floorboard. I suppose I
could have gone to Josh's for food and shelter, but there
was something fun in being vagabonds with John Ambrose
McClaren. It was like we were runaways.

I have to tell you, your letter blew me away, because
when I was thirteen, I was still such a little kid, and
here you were this actual person with complex thoughts
and emotions. My mom still cut my apple up for me for
afternoon snack. If I had written a letter to you
in eighth grade it would have said, your hair is pretty.

*JENNY HAN*

That's it. Just, your hair is pretty. I was so clueless.
I had no idea you liked me back then.

A few months ago I saw you at a Model UN scrimmage
at Thomas Jefferson. I doubt you recognized me, but
I was there representing the Republic of China. You
dropped off a note for me and I called your name but
you kept walking. I tried to find you later, but you
were gone. Did you see me?

I guess what I'm most curious about is why you decided
to send me the letter after all this time. So if you
want to call me, or email me, or write me, please do.

Yours truly, John

PS. Since you asked—the only people that call me Johnny
are my mom and my grandma, but feel free.

I let out a long sigh.

In middle school John Ambrose McClaren and I had
all of two "romantic" encounters—the spin-the-bottle kiss,
which honestly wasn't the least bit romantic, and that day
in the rain during gym, which up until this year was the
most romantic moment of my life. I'm sure John doesn't
remember it that way. I doubt he remembers it at all. To get
this letter from him, after all this time, it's like he's come

back from the dead. It feels different from seeing him for those few seconds at Model UN in December. That was like seeing a ghost. This is a real, living person I used to know, who used to know me.

John was smart; he made the best grades of the boys, and I made the best grades of the girls. We were in honors classes together. He liked history best—he always did his readings—but he was good at math and science, too. I'm sure that hasn't changed.

If Peter was the last boy in our grade to get tall, John was the first. I liked his yellow hair, sunny and fair like white summer corn. He was innocent and sweet-cheeked, he had the face of a boy who'd never been in trouble, and the neighborhood mothers loved him best. He just had this look about him. That's what made him such a good partner in crime. He and Peter used to get into all kinds of mischief together. John was the clever one, he had the great ideas, but he was a little bit shy to talk because he used to have a stutter.

He liked to play a supporting role, whereas Peter loved to be the star. So everyone always gave the credit, and the blame, to Peter, because he was the scamp and how could an angel like John Ambrose McClaren really be to blame for anything? Not that there was even much blame. People are so charmed by beautiful boys. Beautiful boys get an indulgent shake of the head and an "Oh, Peter," not even a slap on the wrist. Our English teacher Ms. Holt used to call them Butch Cassidy and the Sundance Kid, which none of us had ever heard of. Peter convinced her to show the movie to us in class one day, and then they argued all year over who got to be Butch and who had to be the Sundance Kid, even though it was very clear to everyone who was who.

I bet all the girls at his school like him. When I saw him at the Model UN scrimmage, he looked so assured, the way he sat tall in his seat, shoulders squared, utterly focused. If I went to John's school, I bet I would be right there at the front of the pack, with binoculars and a granola bar, camping out at his locker. I'd have his schedule memorized; I'd know his lunch by heart. Does he still eat double-decker peanut butter and jelly sandwiches on whole wheat bread? I wonder. There are so many things I don't know.

Peter's car honking out front is what shakes me out of my reverie. I jump guiltily at the sound. I have this crazy impulse to hide the letter, to tuck it away in my hatbox for safekeeping and never think about it again. But then I think, no, that would be crazy. Of course I'll write John Ambrose McClaren back. It would be rude not to.

So I tuck the letter in my bag, throw on my white puffer coat, and run outside to Peter's car. There's still a bit of snow on the ground from the last storm, but it looks shabby, like a threadbare rug. I'm an all-or-nothing kind of girl when it comes to weather, I'd much rather it all melt away or have feet and feet of snow, so deep your knees sink in.

When I get in Peter's car, he's texting on his phone. "What's up?" I ask him.

"Nothing," he says. "It's just Gen. She wanted me to give her a ride, but I told her we can't."

My skin prickles. It rankles that they still text so much, that they're in such easy contact, enough to ask for rides. But they're friends, just friends. That's what I keep telling myself. And he's telling me the truth, just like we promised we would. "Guess who I got a letter from."

He backs out of the driveway. "Who?"

"Guess."

"Um . . . Margot?"

"Why would that be surprising? No, not Margot. John Ambrose McClaren!"

Peter just looks confused. "McClaren? Why would he write you a letter?"

"Because I wrote him one, remember? Same as I did to you. There were five love letters, and his was the only letter that never came back. I thought it was lost forever, but then a tree fell in John's driveway after this last ice storm, and Mr. Barber came to haul it away and he brought the letter."

"Who's Mr. Barber?"

"He's the man who bought John's old house. He owns a landscaping company—that's all beside the point, anyway. The point is, John only just got my letter last week; that's why it took him so long to write back."

"Hm," Peter says, messing with the heating vents. "So he wrote you an actual letter? Not an email?"

"No, it was a real letter that came in the mail." I watch to see if he is jealous, to see if this new development gets under his skin even a little.

"Hm," Peter says again. The second *hm* is bored-sounding, noncommittal. Not the slightest bit jealous. "How is the Sundance Kid anyway?" He snickers. "McClaren used to hate when I called him that."

"I remember," I say. We're at the stoplight; there's a line to get into school.

"What'd the letter say?"

"Oh, you know, just 'how are you,' the usual sort of things." I look out the window. I'm feeling a bit stingy about sharing extra information because his ho-hum reaction hasn't merited any. Doesn't he have the decency to at least *act* like he cares?

Peter drums his fingers on the steering wheel. "We should hang out with him sometime."

The thought of Peter and John Ambrose McClaren in the same space together again is discomfiting. Where would I even look? Vaguely I say, "Hmm, maybe." Perhaps bringing up the letter wasn't such a great idea.

"I think he still has my old baseball glove," he muses. "Hey, did he say anything about me?"

"Like what?"

"I don't know. Like did he ask what I was up to?"

"Not really."

"Hmm." Peter's mouth turns down into a miffed sort of expression. "What'd you write him back?"

"I just got it! I haven't had time to write anything back."

"Tell him I say hey when you do," he says.

"Sure," I say. I feel around in my bag to make sure the letter is still in there.

"So, wait, if you sent a love letter to five of us, does that mean you liked us all equally?"

He's looking at me with expectant eyes, and I know he thinks I'm going to say I liked him best, but that wouldn't be true. "Yes, I liked you all exactly the same," I tell him.

"Bullshit! Who'd you like best? Me, right?"

"That's a really impossible question to answer, Peter. I mean, it's all relative. I could say I liked Josh best, because I liked him longest, but you can't judge who you love the most by how long you love them."

"Love?"

"Like," I say.

"You definitely said 'love.'"

"Well, I meant 'like.'"

"What about McClaren?" he asks. "How much did you like him in comparison to the rest of us?"

Finally! A little jealousy at last. "I liked him . . ." I'm about to say "the same," but I hesitate. According to Stormy, no one can ever like anyone exactly the same. But how can you possibly quantify how much you like a person, much less two? Peter always has to be liked the best. He expects it. So

I just say, "It's unknowable. But I like you best now."

Peter shakes his head. "For someone who's never had a boyfriend before, you really know how to work a guy."

I raise my eyebrows. *I* know how to work a guy? That's the first time I've ever heard that in my life. Genevieve, Chris, *they* know how to work guys. Not me. Never me.

# 28

Dear John(ny),

First of all, thanks for writing me back. That was a really nice surprise. Second of all . . . the story behind the letter. I wrote you that letter in eighth grade, but I never meant for you to see it. It sounds crazy, I know, it was just a thing I used to do—when I liked a boy, I'd write the letter and then I'd hide it away in my hatbox. The letters were just for me. But then my little sister Kitty—remember her? Scrawny and willful?— sent them all out back in September, including yours.

I do remember that break-dancing contest. I think Peter won. He would've taken the biggest piece of peanut brittle either way, though! This is random but do you remember how he used to always take the last piece of pizza? So annoying. Do you remember how he and Trevor got into a fight over it and they ended up dropping the pizza and nobody got to have it? Do you remember how all of us went to

your house to say good-bye when you moved?
I made a chocolate cake with chocolate peanut
butter frosting, and I brought a knife but your
forks and plates were all packed up, so we ate
it on the front porch with our hands. When
I got home, I realized that the corners of my
mouth were stained brown from the chocolate.
I was so embarrassed. It feels like such a long
time ago.

I'm not in Model UN but I was there that
day and I did see you. Actually, I had a feeling
you might be there because I remembered how
into Model UN you were in middle school. I'm
sorry I didn't stick around so we could catch up.
I think I was just startled because it had been
so long. You looked the same to me too. Much
taller, though.

I have a favor to ask—would you mind
sending me back my letter? The other ones have
found their way back to me, and though I'm
sure it will be excruciating, I'd really like to
know what I said.

Your friend, Lara Jean

# 29

*IT'S LATE, AND ALL THE LIGHTS ARE OFF AT* my house. Daddy's at the hospital; Kitty's at a sleepover. I can tell Peter wants to come inside, but my dad will be home soon and he might be freaked out if he gets home and it's just the two of us alone in the house so late. Daddy hasn't said anything in so many words, but since the video, something shifted just the tiniest fraction. Now when I go out with Peter, Daddy oh-so-casually asks what time I'll be home, where we'll be. He never used to ask those kinds of questions, though I suppose he never had much reason to before.

I look over at Peter, who has turned off the ignition. Suddenly I say, "Why don't we go up to Carolyn Pearce's old tree house?"

Readily, he agrees. "Let's do it."

It's dark outside; I've never been up here in such darkness. There was always a light on from the Pearces' kitchen or garage or from our house. Peter climbs up first and then shines his phone flashlight down on me as I make my way up.

He marvels at how, inside, nothing's changed. It's just like we left it. Kitty never had much interest in coming up here. It's just been sort of abandoned since we stopped using it in eighth grade. "We" was the neighborhood kids my age: Genevieve, Allie Feldman, sometimes Chris, sometimes the boys—Peter, John Ambrose McClaren, Trevor. It was just a private place; we weren't doing anything bad like smoke or drink. We'd sit up there and talk.

Genevieve was always thinking up games of Who Would You Choose. If we were on a deserted island, which of us here would you choose? Peter picked Genevieve without hesitation, because she was his girlfriend. Chris said she'd pick Trevor because he was the meatiest and also the most obnoxious, and who knew if at some point she'd have to resort to cannibalism. I said I'd pick Chris because I'd never get bored. Chris liked that; Genevieve frowned at me, but she'd already been picked once. And besides, it was true: Chris would be the funner island companion, and probably more helpful around the island. I doubted Genevieve would help gather firewood or spear a fish. John took a long time to decide. He went around the circle, weighing all of our merits. Peter was a fast runner, Trevor was strong, Genevieve was crafty, Chris could handle herself in a fight, and for me he said I would never give up hope of being rescued. So he picked me.

It was the last summer we spent outside. Just, every day was outside. As you grow up, you spend less and less time outside. Nobody can say "Go play outside" anymore to you. But that summer we did. It was the hottest summer in a hundred years, they said. We spent most of it on bikes, at the pool. We played games.

Peter sits down on the floor and takes off his coat and spreads it out like a blanket. "You can sit here."

I sit down, and he pulls me toward him by my ankles, reeling me in carefully like a big fish that might jump off the line. When we're knees to knees, he kisses me: soft-lipped, *we have all the time in the world* kisses. I'm shaking, but not from the cold. I feel jittery heart-palpitations kind of nerves. Peter bends his head and starts kissing my neck, making his way down to my collarbone. I'm so keyed up, it doesn't even tickle the way it normally does when someone touches my neck. His mouth is warm, and it feels nice. I fall back against my hands, and he moves over me. Is this it? Is this when it's supposed to happen? On the floor of Carolyn Pearce's tree house?

When his hand moves under my blouse, but still over my bra, a panicky thought leaps into my head, one I haven't thought before—Genevieve's boobs are definitely bigger than mine. Will he be disappointed?

Suddenly I blurt out, "I'm not ready to have sex with you."

His head jerks up in alarm. "God, Lara Jean! You scared me."

"Sorry. I just wanted to make that clear, in case it wasn't."

"It was clear." Peter flashes a hurt look at me and sits up, his back ramrod straight. "I'm not some caveman. Damn!"

"I know," I say. I sit up and fix my necklace so the heart is in front. "Just . . . I hope you weren't thinking that because you gave me this beautiful necklace, that . . ." I stop talking because he's glaring at me. "Sorry, sorry. But . . . do you miss sex? Since you and Genevieve used to do it all the time, I mean?" We've all heard the stories about Kavinsky and Gen's sex life, how they did it in Steve Bledell's parents' bedroom at his last-day-of-school party, how she went on the pill in ninth grade. How can someone who's used to having sex 24/7 be content with someone like me, a virgin who's so far barely been to second base with him? Not content. "Content" is the wrong word. Happy.

"We didn't do it all the time! I don't want to talk about this with you. It's too weird."

"I'm just saying, since I've never done it, but you've done it a lot, is that, like, a void in your life? Do you maybe feel like . . . like you're missing out? Is it, like, if I never had an ice cream sundae, so I don't know how good it is, but then I finally try one and I'm craving it all the time?" I chew on my bottom lip. "Are you . . . craving it all the time?"

"No!"

"Be honest!"

"Do I wish we were having sex? I mean, okay, yes. But it's not like I'm trying to pressure you. I've never even brought it up! And it's not like guys don't have other ways of . . ." He goes red. "Of release."

"So . . . do you look at porn, then?"

"Lara Jean!"

"I have a naturally inquisitive personality! You know that about me. You used to answer all my questions."

"That was before. Now it's different."

Sometimes Peter can say the most insightful thing and

not even realize he's said it. Things *are* different. They were easier before. Before sex was ever up for discussion.

Haltingly I say, "In the contract we said we'd always tell the truth."

"Fine, but I'm not talking to you about porn." I start to ask another question and Peter adds, "All I'll say about it is, any guy that says he never looks at porn is a liar."

"So you do." I nod to myself. Okay. Good to know. "You know those statistics people are always spouting off, about teenage boys thinking about sex every seven seconds? Is that really true?"

"Nope. And I just want to point out that you're the one who keeps bringing up sex. I think teenage girls might be more obsessed than boys."

"Maybe," I say, and his eyes widen, all excited. Hastily I add, "I mean, I'm definitely curious about it. It's definitely a *thought*. But I don't see myself doing it anytime soon. With anybody. Including you."

I can tell Peter is embarrassed, the way he rushes to say, "Okay, okay, I got it. Let's just change the subject." Under his breath he mutters, "I didn't even want to talk about it in the first place."

It's sweet that he's embarrassed. I didn't think he would be, with all his experience. I tug on his sweater sleeve. "At some point, when I'm ready, if I'm ready, I'll let you know." And then I pull him toward me and press my lips against his softly. His mouth opens, and so does mine, and I think, *I could kiss this boy for hours.*

Mid-kiss, he says, "Wait, so we're never having sex? Like ever?"

"I didn't say never. But not now. I mean, not until I'm really, really sure. Okay?"

He lets out a laugh. "Sure. You're the one driving this bus. You have been from the start. I'm still catching up." He snuggles closer and sniffs my hair. "What's this new shampoo you're wearing?"

"I stole it from Margot. It's juicy pear. Nice, right?"

"It's all right, I guess. But can you go back to the one you used to wear? The coconut one? I love the smell of that one." A dreamy look crosses his face, like evening fog settling over a city.

"If I feel like it," I say, which makes him pout. I'm already thinking I should buy a bottle of the coconut hair mask, too, but I like to keep him on his toes. Like he said, I'm the one driving this bus. Peter pulls me against him so he's curved around my back like shelter. I let my head rest on his shoulder, rest my arms on his kneecaps. This is nice. This is cozy. Just me and him, just for a while, apart from the rest of the world.

We're sitting there like that when suddenly I remember something, an important something. The time capsule. John Ambrose McClaren's grandmother gave it to him for his birthday in seventh grade. He'd asked for a video game, but the time capsule was what he got. He said he was going to throw it away, but then he thought one of us girls might want it. I said I wanted it, and then Genevieve said she wanted it, so of course Chris chimed in too. And then I had the idea to bury it right there in the Pearces' backyard under the tree house. I got really excited and said everybody needed to put in something that they had on them at that very moment. I said we should come back the day we graduate from high school and open it up and reminisce.

"Do you remember that time capsule we buried?" I ask him.

"Oh, yeah! McClaren's. Let's dig it up!"

"We can't open it without everybody else," I say. "Remember, we were going to do it after high school graduation?" This was when I still thought we'd all be friends. "You, me, John, Trevor, Chris, Allie." I don't say Genevieve's name.

Peter doesn't appear to notice. "All right, then we'll wait. Whatever my girl wants."

# 30

Dear Lara Jean,

I will give you your letter back on one condition. You have to make a ~~solemn~~ unbreakable vow that you will return it to me after you're done reading it. I need physical proof that a girl liked me in middle school, otherwise who would ever believe it?

And for what it's worth, that peanut butter chocolate cake you baked was the best I ever ate. I never had another cake quite like that one, with my name written in Reese's Pieces. I still think about it sometimes. A guy doesn't forget a cake like that.

I have one question for you. How many letters did you write? Just wondering how special I should feel.

John


Dear John,

I, Lara Jean, hereby make a solemn vow—nay, an <u>unbreakable</u> vow—to return my letter to you, intact and unchanged. Now give me my letter back!

Also you're such a liar. You know very well that plenty of girls liked you in middle school. At sleepovers, girls would be like, are you Team Peter or Team John? Don't pretend like you didn't know that, Johnny!

And to answer your question—there were five letters. Five meaningful boys in my whole life history. Though, now that I'm writing it down, five sounds like a lot, considering the fact that I'm only sixteen. I wonder how many there'll have been by the time I'm twenty! There's this lady at the nursing home I volunteer at, and she's had so many husbands and lived so many lives. I look at her and I think, she must not have even one regret, because she's done and seen it all.

Did I tell you my older sister Margot's all the way in Scotland, at St. Andrews? It's where Prince William and Kate Middleton met. Maybe she'll meet a prince, too, haha! Where do you want to go to college? Do you know what you want to study? I think I want to stay in state. Virginia has great public schools *and it'll be much cheaper, but I guess the main reason is I'm very close to my family and I don't want to be too-too far away. I used to think I might want to go to UVA and live at home, but now I'm thinking dorms are the way to go for a true college experience.*

*Don't forget to send back my letter, Lara Jean*

Daddy's at the hospital, but he's made a big pot of oatmeal, a vat of it like you see in a soup kitchen. By this time it's gummy and I have to put half a bottle of maple syrup and dried cherries on mine to make it palatable, and even then I'm not sure if I like oatmeal. I make a bowl for me with some chopped-up pecans on top, and a bowl with just honey on top for Kitty. "Have some gruel," I call out. She's in front of the TV, of course.

We sit on stools at the breakfast bar and eat our gruel. I will say there is something satisfying about it, the way it sticks to your insides like paste. As I eat, I keep my eyes toward the window.

Kitty snaps her fingers in my face. "Hello! I asked you a question."

"Has the mail come yet?" I ask.

"The mailman doesn't come until after twelve on Saturdays," Kitty says, licking honey off her spoon. Eyeing me she says, "Why have you been so excited about the mail all week?"

"I'm waiting for a letter," I say.

"From who?"

"Just . . . no one important." A rookie mistake. I should've made up a name, because Kitty's eyes narrow, and now she's really interested.

"If it wasn't someone important, you wouldn't be so gaga looking out the window for it. Who's it from?"

"If you must know, it's actually a letter from me. One of those love letters of mine *you* sent out." I reach across the table and pinch her arm. "It's coming back my way."

"From the boy with the funny name. Ambrose. What kind of name is Ambrose?"

"Do you remember him at all? He used to live on our street."

"He had yellow hair," Kitty says. "He had a skateboard. He let me play with it once."

"That sounds like him," I say, remembering. Of all the boys, he had the most patience with Kitty, even though she was a pain.

"Stop smiling," Kitty commands. "You already have a boyfriend. You don't need two."

My smile slips. "We're just writing letters, Kitty. Also don't snap at me." I lean in to give her another pinch, and she jumps up before I can. "What are you going to do today?"

"Ms. Rothschild said she'd take me and Jamie to the dog park," Kitty says, putting her dirty bowl in the sink. "I'm gonna go over and remind her."

"You've been hanging out with her a lot lately." Kitty

shrugs and gently I say, "Just don't become a nuisance, all right? I mean, she's like, forty; she might have other things she wants to be doing with her Saturday. Like go to a winery or a spa. She doesn't need you harassing her about dating our dad."

"Ms. Rothschild loves hanging out with me, so keep your little opinions to yourself."

I frown at her. "Seriously, you have such bad manners, Kitty."

"Blame my manners on you and Margot and Daddy, then. You're the ones who raised me this way."

"Then I guess nothing will ever be your fault in life because of the shoddy way you were raised."

"I guess not."

I let out a scream of frustration, and Kitty skips off, humming to herself, pleased as punch to have annoyed me.

Dear Lara Jean,

For the record, the only reason girls ever paid me any attention was because I was Peter's best friend. It's why Sabrina Fox asked me to be her date to the eighth grade formal! She even tried to sit next to Peter at Red Lobster before the dance.

As for college, my dad went to UNC, so he's really pushing for that. He says I have tar in my blood. My mom wants me to stay in state. I haven't told anyone *this, but I really want to go to Georgetown. Knock on wood. Studying for the SATs as we speak.*

*Anyway . . . here's your letter back. Don't forget your promise. I'm really enjoying writing letters back and forth, but can I also have your phone number? You're pretty hard to find online.*

My very first thought is: He hasn't seen the video. He can't possibly have! Not if he's saying I'm so hard to find online. I suppose deep down I must have been worrying about it, because I feel so relieved to know for certain. What a comfort, to know that he can still have a certain idea of me in his head, the same as I have of him. And truly, John Ambrose McClaren isn't the type of boy to look at Anonybitch. Not the John Ambrose McClaren I remember.

I look back down at the letter, and there, at the bottom, is his phone number.

I blink. Letters were harmless enough, but if John and I started talking on the phone, would that be a betrayal of sorts? Is there even a difference between texting and letter writing? One is more immediate. But the act of writing a letter, of selecting paper and pen, addressing the envelope, finding a stamp, let alone putting pen to paper . . . it's far more deliberate. My cheeks heat up. It's more . . . romantic. A letter is something to keep.

Speaking of which . . . I unfold the second piece of paper in the envelope. It's creased, a stationery I recognize well.

Thick creamy paper with *LJSC* engraved in navy at the top. A birthday gift from my dad because of my delight in anything monogrammed.

Dear John Ambrose McClaren,

I know the exact day it all started. Fall, eighth grade. We got caught in the rain when we had to put all the softball bats away after gym. We started to run back to the building, and I couldn't run as fast as you, so you stopped and grabbed my bag too. It was even better than if you'd grabbed my hand. I still remember the way you looked—your T-shirt was stuck to your back, your hair wet like you just came out of the shower. When it started to pour, you whooped and hollered like a little kid. There was this moment—you looked back at me, and your grin was as wide as your face. You said, "Come on, LJ!"

It was right then. That's when I knew, all the way down to my soaking-wet Keds. I love you, John Ambrose McClaren. I really love you. I might have loved you for all of high school. I think you might have loved me back. If only you weren't moving away, John! It's so unfair when people move away. It's like their parents *just decide something and no one else gets a say in it. Not that I even deserve a say—I'm not your girlfriend or anything. But you at least deserve a say.*

*I was really hoping that one day I would get to call you Johnny. Your mom came to get you after school once, and a bunch of us were hanging out on the front steps. And you didn't see her car, so she honked and called out, "Johnny!" I loved the sound of that. Johnny. One day, I bet your girlfriend will call you Johnny. She's really lucky. Maybe you already have a girlfriend right now. If you do, know this—once upon a time in Virginia, a girl loved you.*

*I'm going to say it just this once, since you'll never hear it anyway. Good-bye, Johnny.*

*Love,*

*Lara Jean*

I let out a scream, so loud and so piercing that Jamie barks in alarm. "Sorry," I whisper, falling back against my pillows.

I cannot believe that John Ambrose McClaren read that letter. I didn't remember it to be so . . . naked. With so much . . . yearning. God, why do I have to be a person who yearns so much? How horrible. How perfectly horrible. I've never been naked in front of a boy before, but now I feel like I have. I can't bear to look at it again, to even think about it. I scramble up and stuff it back inside the envelope and push it under my bed so it no longer exists. Out of sight, out of mind.

Obviously John won't be getting this letter back. In fact I don't know if I should write him back at all. Things feel . . . altered, somehow.

I'd forgotten that letter, how ardently I longed for him. How certain I was, how absolutely certain I believed we were meant to be, if only. The memory of that belief shakes me up; it leaves me feeling unsettled and even uncertain. Unmoored. What was it about him, I wonder, that made me so sure?

Strangely, there's no mention of Peter in my letter. In the letter I say I started liking him in the fall of eighth grade. I liked Peter in eighth grade too, so there was a definite cross-over. When did one begin and the other end?

The one person who would know is the one person I could never ask.

She is the one who foretold that I would like John.

Genevieve slept over at my house most nights that summer. Allie was only allowed to sleep over on special occasions, so it was usually just the two of us. We'd go over what happened that day with the boys, every detail. "This is going to be our crew," she said to me one night, her lips barely moving. We were doing Korean face masks my grandma had sent, the kind that look like ski masks, and drip with "essence" and vitamins and spa-like things. "This is what high school is going to be like. It'll be me and Peter and you and McClaren, and Chrissy and Allie can share Trevor. We'll all be power couples."

"But John and I don't like each other like that," I said, teeth clenched to keep my face mask from shifting.

"You will," she said. She said it like it was a preordained fact, and I believed her. I always believed her.

But none of it came to be, except for the Gen and Peter part.

# 31

*LUCAS AND I ARE SITTING CROSS-LEGGED IN*
the hallway, sharing a strawberry-shortcake ice cream bar.
"Stick to your side," he reminds me as I lower my head for
another bite.

"I'm the one who bought it!" I remind him. "Lucas . . . do
you think it's cheating to write letters to someone? Not me,
I'm asking for a friend."

"No," Lucas says. He raises both eyebrows. "Wait, are they
sexy letters?"

"No!"

"Are they the kind of letter you wrote me?"

A meek little "no" from me. He gives me a look like
he isn't buying whatever I'm selling. "Then you're fine.
Technically you're in the clear. So who are you writing
to?"

I hesitate. "Do you remember John Ambrose McClaren?"

He rolls his eyes. "Of course I remember John Ambrose
McClaren. I had a crush on him in seventh grade."

"I had a crush on him in eighth!"

"Of course you did. We all did. In middle school you
either liked John or you liked Peter. Those were the two
main choices. Like Betty and Veronica. Obviously John is
Betty and Peter's Veronica." He pauses. "Remember how

John used to have that really endearing stutter?"

"Yes! I mourned it a little when it went away. It was so sweet. So boyish. And do you remember how his hair was the color of pale butter? Like, the way I bet freshly churned butter looks."

"I thought it was more like moonlit corn silk, but yeah. So how did he turn out?"

"I don't know. . . . It's strange because there's the him I remember from middle school, and that's just my memory of him, but then there's the him now."

"Did you guys ever go out back then?"

"Oh no! Never."

"So that's probably why you're curious about him now."

"I didn't say I was *curious*."

Lucas gives me a look. "You basically did. I don't blame you. I'd be curious too."

"It's just fun to think about."

"You're lucky," he says.

"Lucky how?"

"Lucky that you have . . . *options*. I mean, I'm not officially 'out,' but even if I was, there are, like, two gay guys at our school. Mark Weinberger, who's a pizza face, and *Leon Butler*." Lucas shudders.

"What's wrong with Leon?"

"Don't patronize me by asking. I just wish our school was bigger. There's nobody for me here." He stares off into space moodily. Sometimes I look at Lucas and for a second I forget he's gay and I want to like him all over again.

I touch his hand. "One day soon you'll be in the world, and you'll have so many options you won't know what to do with them. Everyone will fall in love with you, because you're so beautiful and so charming, and you'll look back on high school as such a tiny blip."

Lucas smiles, and his moodiness lifts away. "I won't forget you, though."

# 32

"*THE PEARCES FINALLY SOLD THEIR HOUSE,*"
Daddy says, heaping more spinach salad on Kitty's plate.
"We'll have new backyard neighbors in a month."

Kitty perks up. "Do they have kids?"

"Donnie says they're retired."

Kitty makes a gagging noise. "Old people. Boring! Do
they have grandkids, at least?"

"He didn't say, but I don't think so. They're probably going
to take down that old tree house."

I stop mid-chew. "They're demolishing our tree house?"

Daddy nods. "I think they're putting in a gazebo."

"A gazebo!" I repeat. "We used to have so much fun up
there. Genevieve and I would play Rapunzel for hours. She
always got to be Rapunzel, though. I just got to stand underneath it and call up"—I pause to put on my best English
accent—"Rapunzel, Rapunzel, let down your hair, miss."

"What kind of accent is that supposed to be?" Kitty asks me.

"Cockney, I think. Why? Was it not good?"

"Not really."

"Oh." I turn to Daddy. "When are they tearing the tree
house down?"

"I'm not sure. I'd imagine before they move in, but you
never know."

There was this one time I looked out the window and saw that John McClaren was up in the tree house alone. He was just sitting by himself, reading. So I went out there with a couple of Cokes and a book and we read up there all afternoon. Later in the day Peter and Trevor Pike showed up, and we put the books away and played cards. At the time I was deep in the throes of liking Peter, so it wasn't romantic in the slightest, of that I'm sure. But I do remember feeling that our quiet afternoon had been disrupted, that I'd rather have just kept reading in companionable silence.

"We buried a time capsule under that tree house," I tell Kitty as I squeeze toothpaste onto my toothbrush. "Genevieve, Peter, Chris, Allie, Trevor, me, and John Ambrose McClaren. We were going to dig it up after we graduated high school."

"You should have a time capsule party before they demolish the tree house," Kitty says from the toilet. She's peeing and I'm brushing my teeth. "You can send invitations and it can be a fun little thing. An unveiling."

I spit out toothpaste. "I mean, in theory. But Allie moved, and Genevieve is a—"

"Witch with a *b*," she supplies.

I giggle. "Definitely a witch with a *b*."

"She's scary. One time when I was little, she locked me in the towel closet!" Kitty flushes the toilet and gets up. "You can still have a party, just don't invite Genevieve. It doesn't make sense for you to invite your boyfriend's ex-girlfriend to a time capsule party anyway."

As if there were some set etiquette for who to invite to a time capsule party! As if there were really such a thing as a time capsule party! "I got you out of the closet right away," I remind her. I set my toothbrush back down. "Wash your hands."

"I was going to."

"And brush your teeth." Before Kitty can open her mouth, I say, "Don't say you were going to, because I know you weren't."

Kitty will do anything to get out of brushing her teeth.

We can't just let this tree house go without a proper send-off. It wouldn't be right. We always said we'd come back. I will have a party, and it will be themed. Genevieve would sneer at that, how babyish—but it's not like I'm inviting her, so who cares what she thinks. It will just be Peter, Chris, Trevor, and . . . John. I'll have to invite John. As friends, just friends.

What did we eat that summer? Cheez Doodles. Melty ice cream sandwiches—the chocolate wafer would stick to our fingers. Lukewarm Hawaiian Punch flowed freely. Capri Suns when we could get them. John always had a double-decker peanut butter and jelly sandwich with him in a ziplock bag that his mother packed. I'll be sure to have all of those snacks for the party.

What else? Trevor had portable speakers he used to carry around. His dad was big into Southern rock, and that summer Trevor played "Sweet Home Alabama" so much that Peter threw his speakers out of the tree house and Trevor wouldn't speak to him for days. Trevor Pike had brown hair that curled when it was wet, and he was chubby in the way that middle school boys are (in the cheeks, around the middle) right before they have a big growth spurt and everything sort of evens out. He was always hungry and hanging around other people's cupboards. He'd have to go pee, and he'd come back with a Popsicle or a banana, or cheese crackers, whatever he could scam. Trevor was Peter's number three. It went John and Peter and then Trevor. They don't hang out so much anymore. Trevor's more friends with the track guys. We don't have any classes together; I'm in all honors and APs and Trevor was never that into school or grades. He was fun, though.

I remember the day Genevieve showed up at my house crying, saying she was moving. Not far, she'd still go to school with us, but she wouldn't be able to ride her bike or walk over anymore. Peter was sad; he comforted her, put his arms around her. I remember thinking how grown-up they seemed in that moment, like real teenagers in love. And then Chris and Gen had a fight about something, a bigger fight than usual; I don't even remember what it was about. I think something with their parents. Whenever their parents weren't getting along, things trickled down to them like trash floating down a river.

Gen moved away, and we were still friends, and then, around the time of the eighth grade dance, she dropped me. I guess there was no place for me in her life anymore. I thought Genevieve was someone I would know forever. Those people in your life that you just always know, no matter what. But it's not that way. Here we are, three years later, and we're worse than strangers. I know she took that video; I know she sent it to Anonybitch. How could I forgive that?

# 33

*JOSH HAS A NEW GIRLFRIEND: LIZA BOOKER,*
a girl from his comic-book club. She has frizzy brown hair,
nice eyes, big boobs, braces. She's a senior like Josh, smart like
Josh. I just can't believe he's with a girl who's not Margot.
Next to my sister, Liza Booker's nice eyes and big boobs are
nothing.

I kept seeing a car I didn't recognize in Josh's driveway,
and then today, when I was getting the mail, she and Josh
came out of the house and he walked her to her car and
then he kissed her. Just like how he used to kiss Margot.

I wait until she's driven away and he's about to walk back
inside his house before I call out to him. "So you and Liza
are a thing now, huh?"

He turns around and at least looks sheepish. "We've been
hanging out, yes. It's not serious or anything. But I like her."
Josh comes a few feet closer, so we're not so far apart.

I can't resist saying, "There's no accounting for taste. I
mean, that you'd pick her over Margot?" I let out a huffy
little laugh that surprises even me, because Josh and I are
fine now—not like before, but fine. It was a mean thing to
say. But I'm not saying it to be mean to Liza Booker, who
I don't even know; I'm saying it for my sister. For what she
and Josh used to be to each other.

Quietly he says, "I didn't pick Liza over Margot and you know it. Liza and I barely knew each other in January."

"Okay, well, why not Margot then?"

"It just wasn't going to work out. I still care about her. I'll always love her. But she was right to break things off when she left. It would only have been harder if we'd kept it going."

"Wouldn't it have been worth it just to see? To know?"

"It would've ended the same way even if she hadn't gone to Scotland."

His face has that stubborn look to it; that weak chin of his is firmly set. I know he isn't going to say anything more: It isn't really my business, not truly. It's his and Margot's, and maybe he doesn't even fully know, himself.

# 34

CHRIS SHOWS UP AT MY HOUSE WITH OMBRÉ
lavender hair. Pulling her jacket hood all the way off, she
asks me, "What do you think?"

"I think it's pretty," I say.

Kitty mouths, *Like an Easter egg.*

"I mostly did it to piss off my mom." There's the tiniest
bit of uncertainty in her voice that she's trying to conceal.

"It makes you look sophisticated," I tell her. I reach out
and touch the ends, and her hair feels synthetic, like Barbie
doll hair after it's been washed.

Kitty mouths, *Like a grandma,* and I cut my eyes at her.

"Does it look like shit?" Chris asks her, chewing on her
bottom lip nervously.

"Don't cuss in front of my sister! She's ten!"

"Sorry. Does it look like crap?"

"Yeah," Kitty admits. Thank God for Kitty—you can
always count on her to tell the hard truths. "Why didn't you
just go to a salon and have them do it for you?"

Chris starts running her fingers through her hair. "I did."
She exhales. "Shi—I mean, crap. Maybe I should just cut off
the bottom."

"I've always thought you would look great with short
hair," I say. "But honestly, I don't think the lavender looks

bad. It's kind of beautiful, actually. Like the inside of a seashell." If I was as gutsy as Chris, I'd chop my hair off short like Audrey Hepburn in *Sabrina*. But I'm not that brave, and also, I'm sure I'd feel immediate remorse for my ponytails and braids and curls.

"All right. Maybe I'll keep it for a bit."

"You should try deep-conditioning it and see if that helps," Kitty suggests, and Chris glares at her.

"I have a Korean hair mask my grandma bought me," I say, putting my arm around her.

We go upstairs, and Chris goes to my room while I root around in the bathroom for the hair mask. When I get back to my room with the jar, Chris is sitting cross-legged on the floor, sifting through my hatbox.

"Chris! That's private."

"It was out in the open!" She holds up Peter's valentine, the poem he wrote me. "What's this?"

Proudly I say, "That's a poem Peter wrote for me for Valentine's Day."

Chris looks down at the paper again. "He said he wrote it? He's so full of shit. This is from an Edgar Allan Poe poem."

"No, Peter definitely wrote it."

"It's from that poem called 'Annabel Lee'! We studied it in my remedial English class in middle school. I remember because we went to the Edgar Allan Poe museum, and then we went on a riverboat called the *Annabel Lee*. The poem was framed on the wall!"

I can't believe this. "But . . . he told me he wrote it for me."

She cackles. "Classic Kavinsky." When Chris sees that I'm not cackling with her, she says, "Eh, whatever. It's the thought that counts, right?"

"Except it isn't his thought." I was so happy to receive that poem. No one had ever written me a love poem before, and now it turns out it was plagiarized. A knockoff.

"Don't be pissed. I think it's funny! Clearly he was trying to impress you."

I should've known Peter didn't write it. He hardly ever reads in his spare time, much less writes poetry. "Well, the necklace is real, at least," I say.

"Are you sure?"

I shoot her a dirty look.

When Peter and I talk on the phone that night, I'm all set to confront him about the poem, to at least tease him about it. But then we get to talking about his upcoming away game on Friday. "You're coming, right?" he says.

"I want to, but I promised Stormy I'd dye her hair on Friday night."

"Can't you just do it on Saturday?"

"I can't, the time capsule party is on Saturday, and she has a date that night. That's why her hair needs to be done on Friday. . . ." It sounds like a weak excuse, I know. But I promised. And also . . . I wouldn't be able to ride on the bus with Peter, and I don't feel comfortable driving forty-five minutes away to a school I've never been to. He doesn't need me there anyway. Not like Stormy needs me.

He's silent.

"I'll come to the next one, I promise," I say.

Peter bursts out, "Gabe's girlfriend comes to every single game and she paints his jersey number on her face every game day. She doesn't even go to our school!"

"There have only been four games and I've gone to two!" Now I'm annoyed. I know lacrosse is important to him, but it's no less important than my commitments at Belleview. "And you know what? I know you didn't write that poem for me on Valentine's Day. You copied it off of Edgar Allan Poe!"

"I never said I *wrote* it," he hedges.

"Yes you did. You acted like you wrote it."

"I wasn't going to, but then you were so happy about it! Sorry for trying to make you happy."

"You know what? I was going to bake you lemon cookies on game day, and now I don't know."

"Fine, then I don't know if I'm going to make it to your tree-house party on Saturday. I might be too tired from the game."

I gasp. "You'd better be there!" This party is small as it is, and Chris isn't the most reliable person. It can't just be me and Trevor and John. Three people does not a party make.

Peter makes a harrumph sound. "Well, then I'd better see some lemon cookies in my locker come game day."

"Fine."

"Fine."

★ ★ ★

*JENNY HAN*

On Friday I bring his lemon cookies *and* wear his jersey number on my cheek, which delights Peter. He grabs me and throws me in the air, and his smile is so big. It makes me feel guilty for not doing it sooner, because it took so very little on my part to make him happy. I can see now that it's the little things, the small efforts, that keep a relationship going. And I know now too that in some small measure I have the power to hurt him and also the power to make it better. This discovery leaves me with an unsettling, queer sort of feeling in my chest for reasons I can't explain.

# 35

*I'D WORRIED IT WOULD BE TOO COLD FOR US* to stay in the tree house for long, but it's unseasonably warm, so much so that Daddy starts on one of his rants about climate change, to the point where Kitty and I have to tune him out.

After his rant I get a shovel from the garage and set about digging under the tree. The ground is hard, and it takes me a while to get into a good groove digging, but I finally hit metal a couple of feet in. The time capsule's the size of a small cooler; it looks like a futuristic coffee thermos. The metal has eroded from the rain and snow and dirt, but not as much as you'd think, considering it's been nearly four years. I take it back to the house and wash it in the sink so it gleams again.

Close to noon, I load up a shopping bag with ice cream sandwiches, Hawaiian Punch, and Cheez Doodles and take it all out to the tree house. I'm crossing our backyard to the Pearces', trying to juggle the bag and the portable speakers and my phone, when I see John Ambrose McClaren standing in front of the tree house, staring up at it with his arms crossed. I'd know the back of his blond head anywhere.

I freeze, suddenly nervous and unsure. I'd thought Peter

or Chris would be here with me when he arrived, and that would smooth out any awkwardness. But no such luck.

I put down all my stuff and move forward to tap him on the shoulder, but he turns around before I can. I take a step back. "Hi! Hey!" I say.

"Hey!" He takes a long look at me. "Is it really you?"

"It's me."

"My pen pal the elusive Lara Jean Covey who shows up at Model UN and runs off without so much as a hello?"

I bite the inside of my cheek. "I'm pretty sure I at least said hello."

Teasingly he says, "No, I'm pretty sure you didn't."

He's right: I didn't. I was too flustered. Kind of like right now. It must be that distance between knowing someone when you were a kid and seeing them now that you're both more grown-up, but still not all the way grown-up, and there are all these years and letters in between you, and you don't know how to act.

"Well—anyway. You look . . . taller." He looks more than just taller. Now that I can take the time to really look at him, I notice more. With his fair hair and milky skin and rosy cheeks, he looks like he could be an English farmer's son. But he's slim, so maybe the sensitive farmer's son who steals away to the barn to read. The thought makes me smile, and John gives me a curious look but doesn't ask why.

With a nod, he says, "You look . . . exactly the same."

Gulp. Is that a good thing or a bad thing? "I do?" I get

up on my tiptoes. "I think I've grown at least an inch since eighth grade." And my boobs are at least a little bigger. Not much. Not that I want John to notice—I'm just saying.

"No, you look . . . just like how I remembered you." John Ambrose reaches out, and I think he's trying to hug me but he's only trying to take my bag from me, and there's a brief but strange dance that mortifies me but he doesn't seem to notice. "So thanks for inviting me."

"Thanks for coming."

"Do you want me to take this stuff up for you?"

"Sure," I say.

John takes the bag from me and looks inside. "Oh, wow. All of our old snacks! Why don't you climb up first and I'll pass it to you." So that's what I do: I scramble up the ladder and he climbs up behind me. I'm crouched, arms outstretched, waiting for him to pass me the bag.

But when he gets halfway up the ladder, he stops and looks up at me and says, "You still wear your hair in fancy braids."

I touch my side braid. Of all the things to remember about me. Back then, Margot was the one who braided my hair. "You think it looks fancy?"

"Yeah. Like . . . expensive bread."

I burst out laughing. "Bread!"

"Yeah. Or . . . Rapunzel."

I get down on my stomach, wriggle over to the edge, and pretend like I'm letting down my hair for him to climb. He climbs up to the top of the ladder and passes me the bag, which I take, and then he grins at me and gives my braid a tug. I'm still lying down but feel an electric charge like he's zapped me. I'm suddenly feeling very anxious about the worlds that will be colliding, the past and the present, a pen pal and a boyfriend, all in this little tree house. Probably I should have thought this through a bit better. But I was so focused on the time capsule, and the snacks, and the *idea* of it—old friends coming back together to do what we said we'd do. And now here we are, in it.

"Everything okay?" John asks, offering me his hand as I rise to my feet.

I don't take his hand; I don't want another zap. "Everything's great," I say cheerily.

"Hey, you never sent back my letter," he says. "You broke an unbreakable vow."

I laugh awkwardly. I'd kind of been hoping he wouldn't bring that up. "It was too embarrassing. The things I wrote. I couldn't bear the thought of another person seeing it."

"But I already saw it," he reminds me.

Luckily, Chris and Trevor Pike show up and break up the conversation about the letter. They immediately tear into the snacks. Meanwhile Peter's late. I text him a stern You better be on your way. And then: Don't text back if you're driving. That's dangerous.

Just as I'm texting again, Peter's head pops up in the door and he climbs inside. I'm about to give him a hug, but then right behind him is Genevieve. My whole body goes cold.

I look from him to her. She sails right past me and sweeps

John into a hug. "Johnny!" she squeals, and he laughs. I feel the sharp twist of envy in my stomach. Must every boy be charmed by her?

While she's hugging John, Peter's looking at me with pleading eyes. He mouths, *Don't be mad*, and he clasps his hands in prayer. I mouth back, *What the hell*, and he grimaces. I never explicitly said I wasn't inviting her, but I would have thought it was pretty clear. And then I think, *Wait a minute.* They came here together. He was with her and he never said a word to me about it, and then he brought her here, here, to my house. Specifically to my neighbors' tree house. This girl who has hurt me, hurt us both.

Then Peter and John are hugging and high-fiving and slapping each other on the back, like old war buddies, long-lost brothers in arms. "It's been too fucking long, man," Peter says.

Genevieve is already unzipping her puffy white bomber jacket and making herself comfortable. Whatever fleeting moment there was for me to kick her and Peter both out of my neighbors' tree house is gone. "Hi, Chrissy," she says, smiling as she settles on the ground. "Nice hair."

Chris glares at her. "What are you even doing here?" I love that she says this—I love *her*.

"Peter and I were hanging out and he told me about what you guys were doing today." Shrugging out of her jacket, Genevieve says to me, "I guess my invitation got lost in the mail."

I don't reply, because what can I say in front of all these

people? I just hug my knees to my chest. Now that I'm sitting next to her, I realize how small this tree house has become. There's hardly enough room for all the arms and legs, and the boys are so big now. Before, we were more or less the same size, boys and girls.

"God, was this place always so tiny?" Genevieve says to no one in particular. "Or did we all just get really big?" She laughs. "Except you, Lara Jean. You're still itty-bitty pocket-sized." She says it sweetly. Like sweetened condensed milk. Sweet and condescending. Poured on super thick.

I play along: I smile. I won't let her get a rise out of me.

John rolls his eyes. "Same old Gen." He says it dryly, with weary affection, and she smiles her cute wrinkly-nose smile at him like he's paid her a compliment. But then he looks at me and raises one sardonic eyebrow, and I feel better about everything, just like that. In a strange way, maybe her presence here completes the circle. She can take whatever's hers in that time capsule, and this history of ours can be done.

"Trev, throw me an ice cream sandwich," Peter says, squeezing in between Genevieve and me. He stretches his legs out into the center of the circle, and everyone else adjusts to make room for his long legs.

I push his legs over so I can set the time capsule down in the center. "Here it is, everybody. All your greatest treasures from seventh grade." I try to whip off the aluminum top with a flourish, but it's really stuck. I'm struggling with it, using my nails. I look over at Peter and he's digging into the ice cream bars, oblivious, so John gets up and helps me unscrew it. He smells like pine soap. I add this to the list of new things I've learned about him.

"So how are we gonna do this?" Peter asks me, his mouth full of ice cream. "Do we dump it all out?"

I've given this some thought. "I think we should take turns pulling something out. Let's make it last, like opening presents on Christmas morning."

Genevieve leans forward in anticipation. Without looking, I reach into the cylinder and pull out the first thing my fingers touch. It's funny, I'd forgotten what I put inside, but I know what it is instantly; I don't have to look down. It's a friendship bracelet that Genevieve made for me when we were in our weaving phase in fifth grade. Pink, white, and light blue chevron. I made one for her too. Purple and yellow chevron. She probably doesn't even remember it. I look over at her, and her face is blank. No recognition.

"What is it?" Trevor asks.

"It's mine," I say. "It's . . . it's a bracelet I used to wear."

Peter touches his shoe to mine. "That piece of string was your most treasured thing?" he teases.

John is watching me. "You used to wear it all the time," he says, and it's sweet that he even remembers.

Once it goes on, it's never supposed to come off, but I sacrificed it to the time capsule because I loved it so much. Maybe this is where Gen's and my friendship went sour. The curse of the friendship bracelet. "You go next," I say to him.

He reaches inside the box and pulls out a baseball.

"That's mine," Peter crows. "That's from when I hit a home run at Claremont Park." John throws the ball to him, and Peter catches it. Examining it, he says, "See, I signed and dated it!"

"I remember that day," Genevieve says, tilting her head. "You came running off the field, and you kissed me in front of your mom. Remember?"

"Uh . . . not really," Peter mumbles. He's staring down at the baseball, turning it in his hand like he's fascinated by it. I can't believe him. I really can't.

"Awk-ward," Trevor says with a chortle.

In a soft voice, like no one else is here, she says to him, "Can I keep it?"

Peter's ears are turning red. He looks at me, panicky. "Covey, do you want it?"

"Nope," I say, keeping my head turned away from them. I grab the bag of Cheez Doodles and stuff a handful in my mouth. I'm so mad all I can do is eat Cheez Doodles or else I'll scream at him.

"Okay, then I'm gonna keep it," Peter says, putting the baseball in his coat pocket. "Owen might want it. Sorry, Gen." He grabs the time capsule and starts rifling through it. He holds up a worn-out baseball cap. Orioles. Too loudly he says, "McClaren, look what I got here."

A smile spreads across John's face like a slow sunrise. He takes it from Peter and puts it on his head, adjusting the bill.

"That really was your most prized possession," I say. He wore it deep into the fall, too. I asked my dad to buy me an

Orioles T-shirt because I thought John McClaren would be impressed. I wore it twice but I don't think he ever noticed. My smile fades when I notice Genevieve watching me. Our eyes meet; there is some knowing light in her gaze that makes me feel twitchy. She looks away; now she is the one smiling to herself.

"The Orioles suck," Peter says, leaning against the wall. He reaches for the box of ice cream sandwiches and pulls one out.

"Pass me one of those," Trevor says.

"Sorry, last one," Peter says, biting into it.

John catches my eye and winks. "Same old Kavinsky," he says, and I laugh. I know he's thinking of our letters.

Peter grins at him. "Hey, no more stutter."

I freeze. How could Peter bring that up so cavalierly? None of us ever talked about John's stutter back in middle school. He was so shy about it. But now John just flashes a smile and shrugs and says, "I'll pass that along to my eighth grade speech therapist, Elaine." He's so confident!

Peter blinks, and I can see that he is caught off guard. He does not know this John McClaren. It used to be that Peter was the shot caller, not John. He followed Peter's lead. Peter might still be the same, but John has changed. Now Peter's the one who is less sure-footed.

Chris goes next. She pulls out a ring with a tiny pearl in the center. Allie's, a confirmation gift from her aunt. She loved that ring. I'll have to send it to her. Trevor pulls out his own treasure—an autographed baseball card.

Genevieve is the one to pull out Chris's—an envelope with a twenty-dollar bill inside.

"Yes!" Chris screams. "I was such a little genius." We high-five.

"What about yours, Gen?" Trevor asks.

She shrugs. "I guess I didn't put anything in the capsule."

"Yes you did," I say, brushing orange Cheez dust off my fingers. "You were there that day." I remember she went back and forth between putting in a picture of her and Peter or the rose he gave her for her birthday. I can't remember what she decided on.

"Well, there's nothing inside, so I guess I didn't. Whatever."

I look inside the time capsule just to be sure. It's empty.


"Remember how we used to play Assassins?" Trevor says, squeezing the last bit of juice out of his Capri Sun.

Oh, how I loved that game! It was like tag: Everybody picked a name out of a hat, and you had to tag the person out. Once you got your person, you had to take out whoever *they* had. It involved a lot of sneaking around and hiding. A game could last for days.

"I was the Black Widow," Genevieve says. She does a little shoulder shimmy at Peter. "I won more than anybody."

"Please," Peter scoffs. "I won plenty."

"So did I," Chris says.

Trevor points at me. "L'il J, you were the worst at it. I don't think you won once."

I make a face. *L'il J.* I'd forgotten he used to call me that.

And he's right: I never did win. Not even once. The one time I came close, Chris tagged me out at Kitty's swim meet. I'd thought I was safe because it was late at night. I was so close to that win, I could almost taste it.

Chris's eyes meet mine, and I know she's remembering too. She winks at me, and I give her a sour look.

"Lara Jean just doesn't have the killer instinct," Genevieve says, looking at her nails.

I say, "We can't all be black widows."

"True," she says, and my teeth clench.

John says to Peter, "Remember that one time I had you, and I was hiding behind your dad's car before school, but it was your dad that came out, not you? And I scared him, and he and I both screamed?"

"Then we had to quit altogether when Trevor came to my mom's store in his ski mask," Peter guffaws.

Everyone laughs, except for me. I'm still smarting from Genevieve's "killer instinct" dig.

Trevor's laughing so hard he can barely speak. "She almost called the cops!" he manages to sputter.

Peter nudges my sneaker toe with his. "We should play again."

He's trying to get back in my good graces, but I'm not ready to let him, so I just shrug a chilly little shrug. I wish I weren't mad at him, because I really do want to play again. I want to prove I've got the killer instinct too, that I'm not some Assassins loser.

"We should do it," John says. "For old times' sake." He catches my eye. "One last shot, Lara Jean."

I smile.

Chris raises an eyebrow. "What does the winner get?"

"Well . . . nothing," I say. "It would just be for fun." Trevor makes a face at this.

"There should be a prize," Genevieve says. "Otherwise what's the point?"

I think fast. What would be a good prize? "Movie tickets? A baked good of the winner's choice?" I blurt out. No one says a word.

"We could all put in a twenty," John offers. I throw him a grateful look and he smiles.

"Money's boring," Genevieve says, stretching like a cat.

I roll my eyes. Who asked for her two cents? I didn't even ask for her to be here.

Trevor says, "Um, how about the winner gets breakfast in bed every day for a week? It could be pancakes on Monday, omelet on Tuesday, waffle on Wednesday, and so forth. There are six of us, so—"

Shuddering, Genevieve says, "I don't eat breakfast." Everyone groans.

"Why don't you suggest something instead of shooting everybody down," Peter says, and I hide my face behind my braid so no one sees me smile.

"Okay." Genevieve thinks for a minute, and then a smile spreads across her face. It's her Big Idea look, and it makes me nervous. Slowly, deliberately, she says, "The winner gets a wish."

"From who?" Trevor asks. "Everybody?"

"From any one of us who are playing."

"Wait a minute," Peter interjects. "What are we signing on for here?"

Genevieve looks very pleased with herself. "One wish, and you have to grant it." She looks like an evil queen.

Chris's eyes gleam as she says, "Anything?"

"Within reason," I quickly say. This isn't at all what I had in mind, but at least people are willing to play.

"Reason is subjective," John points out.

"Basically, Gen can't force Peter to have sex with her one last time," Chris says. "That's what everyone's thinking, right?"

I stiffen. That wasn't what I was thinking, like at all. But now I am.

Trevor busts up laughing and Peter shoves him. Genevieve shakes her head. "You're *disgusting*, Chrissy."

"I only said what everyone was thinking!"

I'm barely even listening at this point. All I can think is, I want to play this game and I want to win. Just once I want to beat Genevieve at something.

I only have one pen and no paper, so John tears up the ice cream sandwich box and we take turns writing our names down on our cardboard scraps. Then everybody puts their names in the empty time capsule, and I shake it up. We pass it around and I go last. I pull out the piece of cardboard, hold it close to my chest, and open it.

*JOHN.*

Well, that complicates things. I sneak a peek at him. He's carefully tucking his piece of cardboard in his jeans pocket. Sorry, (pen) pal, but you're going down. I take a quick look around the room for clues to who might have my name, but everyone's got their poker faces on.

# 36

*THE RULES ARE: YOUR HOUSE IS A SAFE ZONE.*
School is a safe zone, but not the parking lot. Once you step
out the door, it's all fair game. You're out if you get hit with
a two-hand touch.

And if you renege on your wish, your life is forfeit.
Genevieve comes up with that last part and it gives me shivers. Trevor Pike shudders and says, "Girls are scary."

"No, girls in *their* family are scary," Peter says, gesturing at
Chris and Genevieve. They both smile, and in those smiles I
see the family resemblance. Casting a sidelong glance at me,
Peter says hopefully, "You're not scary, though. You're sweet,
right?" Suddenly I remember something Stormy said to me.
*Don't ever let him get too sure of you.* Peter is very sure of me.
As sure as a person could be.

"I can be scary too," I quietly say back, and he blanches.
Then, to everyone else, I say, "Let's just have fun with it."

"Oh, it'll be fun," John assures me. He puts his Orioles cap
on his head and pulls the brim down. "Game on." He catches
my eye. "If you thought I was good at Model UN, wait till
you see my *Zero Dark Thirty* skills."

I walk with everyone out front to their cars, and I hear
Peter tell Genevieve to get a ride with Chris, which they
both balk at. "Figure it out amongst yourselves," Peter

says. "I'm hanging out with my girlfriend."

Genevieve rolls her eyes and Chris groans. "Ugh. Fine." To Genevieve she says, "Get in."

Chris's car is backing out of the driveway when John says to Peter, "Who's your girlfriend?" My stomach does a dip.

"Covey." Peter gives him a funny look. "You didn't know? That's weird."

Now they're both looking at me. Peter's confused, but John gets it, whatever "it" is.

I should have told him. Why didn't I tell him?

Everyone leaves soon after, except for Peter.

"So are we going to talk about this?" he asks, trailing after me into the kitchen. I've got the trash bag with all the ice cream wrappers and Capri Suns, and I refused his help carrying it down. Almost tripped going down the ladder with it, but I don't care.

"Sure, let's talk." I spin around and advance toward him, trash bag swinging in my hand. He lifts his hands up in alarm. "Why did you bring Genevieve here?"

Peter grimaces. "Ugh, Covey, I'm sorry."

"Were you hanging out with her? Is that why you didn't come early to help me set up?"

He hesitates. "Yeah, I was with her. She called me crying, so I went over there, and then I couldn't just leave her by herself . . . so I brought her."

Crying? I've never known her to cry. Even when her cat Queen Elizabeth died, she didn't cry. She must have been faking to get Peter to stay. "You couldn't just leave her?"

"No," he says. "She's going through some shit right now. I'm just trying to be there for her. As a friend. That's it!"

"Gosh, she really knows how to work you, Peter!"

"It's not like that."

"It's always like that. She pulls the strings and you just . . ." I dangle my arms and head like a marionette doll.

Peter frowns. "That was mean."

"Well, I feel mean right now. So watch out."

"You're not mean, though. Not usually."

"Why can't you just tell me? You know I won't tell anyone. I really want to understand it, Peter."

"Because it's not for me to say. Don't try to make me tell you, because I can't."

"She's just doing this to manipulate you. It's what she does." I hear the jealousy in my voice, and I hate it, I hate it. This isn't me.

He sighs. "Nothing's happening with us. She just needs a friend."

"She has a lot of friends."

"She needs an old friend."

I shake my head. He doesn't get it. Girls understand each other in a way boys never will. It's how I know this is all just another one of her games. Showing up at my house today was just another way for her to exert dominance over me.

Then Peter says, "Speaking of old friends, I didn't realize you and McClaren were so buddy-buddy."

I flush. "I told you we were pen pals."

Raising his eyebrows, he says, "You're pen pals but he doesn't know we're together?"

"It never came up!" Wait a minute—I'm the one who's supposed to be mad at him right now, not the other way around. Somehow this whole conversation has flipped around, and now I'm the one flailing.

"So that day you went to the Model UN thing a few months ago, I asked you if you saw McClaren and you said no. But then today he brought up Model UN, and you clearly did see him there. Did you not?"

I swallow. "When did you turn into a prosecutor? Sheesh. I saw him there but we didn't even talk; I just handed him a note—"

"A note? You gave him a note?"

"It wasn't from me—it was from a different country, for Model UN." Peter opens his mouth to ask another question, and I quickly add, "I just didn't mention it because nothing came of it."

Incredulous, he says, "So you want me to be honest with you, but you don't want to be honest with me?"

"It wasn't like that!" I cry out. What is even happening here? How did our fight get so big so fast?

Neither of us says anything for a moment. Then, quietly, he asks, "Do you want to break up?"

*Break up?* "No." All of a sudden I feel shaky, like I could cry. "Do you?"

"No!"

"You asked me first!"

"So that's it. Neither of us wants to break up, so we just move on." Peter sinks down on a chair at the kitchen table and rests his head on it.

I sit across from him. He feels so far away from me. My hand is itching to reach out and touch his hair, smooth it out, to make this fight be over and in our rearview.

He lifts his head; his eyes are sad and enormous. "Can we hug now?"

Shakily I nod, and we both get up and I wrap my arms around his middle. He holds me tight against him. His voice is muffled against my shoulder as he says, "Can we never fight again?"

I laugh a shaky kind of laugh, shaky and relieved. "Yes, please."

And then he's kissing me; his mouth is urgent against mine, like he's searching for some sort of reassurance, some kind of promise only I can give. In answer I kiss him back— *yes, I promise, promise, promise, let's never fight again.* I start to lose my balance, and his arm locks around me tight, and he kisses me until I am breathless.

# 37

ON THE PHONE THAT NIGHT, CHRIS SAYS,
"Spill it. Who do you have?"

"I'm not telling." I've made this mistake in the past,
telling Chris too much, only to have her tag her way to
victory.

"Come on! I'll help you if you help me. I want my wish!"
Chris's strength in this game is how bad she wants it, but
it's also her weakness. You have to play Assassins in a cool,
measured way, not go too hot too fast. I say this as someone who's observed all the nuances but has never personally
won, of course.

"You might have my name. Besides, I want to win too."

"Let's just help each other out on this first round of hits,"
Chris wheedles. "I don't have your name, I swear."

"Swear on your blankie that you won't let your mom
throw away."

"I swear on my blankie Fredrick and I double swear on
my new leather jacket that cost more money than my damn
car. Do you have *my* name?"

"No."

"Swear on your ugly beret collection."

I make an indignant sound. "I swear on my *charming* and

*jaunty* beret collection! So who do you have then?"

"Trevor."

"I've got John McClaren."

"Let's team up to take them out," Chris suggests. "Our alliance can last as long as this first round, and then it's every girl for herself."

Hmm. Is she for real or is this all strategy? "What if you're lying just to smoke me out?"

"I swore on Fredrick!"

I hesitate and then say, "Text me a picture of the name slip and then I'll believe you."

"Fine! Then text me yours."

"Fine. Bye."

"Wait. Tell me the truth. Does my hair look like shit? It doesn't, right? Gen's just a heinous troll. Right?"

I hesitate the tiniest of beats. "Right."

Chris and I are slumped down in her car. We are one neighborhood over from mine; it's the neighborhood Trevor will drive through to shortcut to school for track practice. We're parked in some random person's driveway. She says, "Tell me what you're going to wish for if you win." The way she says it, I know she doesn't think I'm going to win.

I thought about the wish all last night when I was trying to fall asleep. "There's a craft expo in North Carolina in June. I could get Peter to drive me. There's no way he'd take me otherwise. We could take his mom's van, so there's plenty of room for all the supplies and things that I'll buy."

"A craft expo?" Chris is giving me a look like I'm a cockroach that flew into her car. "You would waste a wish on a craft expo?"

"I was just getting warmed up with that idea," I lie. "Anyway, if you're so smart, what would you wish for if you were me?"

"I would make it so that Peter never talks to Gen again. I mean, right? I'm an evil genius, am I not?"

"Evil, yes; genius, hardly." Chris gives me a shove, and I giggle. We're both shoving each other when Chris stops short and says, "Two fifty-five. It's go time." Chris unlocks the doors and gets out and hides behind an oak tree in the yard.

My adrenaline is pumping as I hop out of Chris's car, grab Kitty's bike out of her trunk, and push it a few houses. Then I set it on the ground and drape myself over it in a dramatic heap. Then I pull out the bottle of fake blood I bought for this very purpose and squirt some on my jeans—old jeans I've been planning on giving to Goodwill. As soon as I see Trevor's car approaching, I start to pretend sob. From behind the tree Chris whispers, "Tone it down a little!" I immediately stop sobbing and start moaning.

Trevor's car pulls up beside me. He rolls down the window. "Lara Jean? Are you okay?"

I whimper. "No . . . I think I might have sprained my ankle. It really hurts. Can you give me a ride home?" I'm willing myself to tear up, but it's harder to cry on cue than I would have thought. I try to think about sad things—the *Titanic*, old people with Alzheimer's, Jamie Fox-Pickle dying—but I can't focus.

Trevor regards me suspiciously. "Why are you riding your bike in this neighborhood?"

Oh no, I'm losing him! I start talking fast but not too fast. "It's not my bike; it's my little sister's. She's friends with Sara Healey. You know, Dan Healey's little sister? They live over there." I point to their house. "I was bringing it to her—oh my God, Trevor. Do you not believe me? Are you seriously not going to give me a ride?"

Trevor looks around. "Do you swear this isn't a trick?"

Gotcha! "Yes! I swear I don't have your name, okay? Please just help me up. It really hurts."

"First show me your ankle."

"Trevor! You can't *see* a sprained ankle!" I whimper and make a show of trying to stand up, and Trevor finally turns the car off and gets out. He stoops down and pulls me to my feet and I try to make my body heavy. "Be gentle," I tell him. "See? I told you I didn't have your name."

Trevor pulls me up by my armpits, and over his shoulder Chris creeps up behind him like a ninja. She dives forward, both hands out, and claps them on his back hard. "I got you!" she screams.

Trevor shrieks and drops me, and I narrowly escape falling for real. "Damn it!" he yells.

Gleefully Chris says, "You're done, sucker!" She and I high-five and hug.

"Can you guys not celebrate in front of me?" he mutters.

Chris holds her hand out. "Now gimme gimme gimme."

Sighing, Trevor shakes his head and says, "I can't believe I fell for that, Lara Jean."

I pat him on the back. "Sorry, Trevor."

"What if I had had your name?" he asks me. "What would you have done then?"

Huh. I never thought of that. I shoot Chris an accusing glare. "Wait a minute! What if he had had my name?"

"That was a chance we were willing to take," she says smoothly. "So Trev, what was your wish going to be?"

"You don't have to say if you don't want," I tell him.

"I was gonna wish for tickets to a UVA football game. McClaren's dad has season tickets! Damn you, Chris."

I feel bad. "Maybe he'll take you anyway. You should ask. . . ."

He reaches into his pocket and pulls out his wallet and hands her a small piece of folded cardboard. Before Chris opens it, I quickly say, "Don't forget, if it's my name, you can't tag me. This is a demilitarized zone right here."

Chris nods, opens the cardboard, and then grins.

I can't resist. "Is it me?"

Chris stuffs it in her pocket.

"If it's me, you can't take me out!" I start to back away from her. "We agreed to be allies this first round, and you haven't helped me with mine yet."

"I know, I know. But I don't have your name."

I'm not entirely convinced. This is how she beat me another time we played. She can't be trusted, not in this game. I should have remembered that. It's why I always lose; I don't look down the line far enough.

"Lara Jean! I just told you, I don't have your name!"

I shake my head. "Just get in the car, Chris. I'll ride Kitty's bike home."

"Are you serious?"

"Yes. I'm playing to win this time."

Chris shrugs. "Have it your way. I'm not helping you with your kill, then, if you don't trust me."

"Fine by me," I say, and swing my leg over Kitty's bike.

# 38

PETER AND I ARE ONLY TALKING ON THE
phone and at school until one of us gets tagged out. It won't
be me. I've been super careful. I drive myself to and from
school. I look around before I jump out of my car and run
like the wind to our front door. I've enlisted Kitty as my
scout—she always gets out of the car or the house first and
makes sure the coast is clear for me. I've already promised
her that whatever I wish for if I win, she'll get a piece of.

But so far I've only been playing defense. I haven't tried to
tag out John McClaren yet. It's not because I'm afraid—not
of the game, anyway. I just don't know what I'm going to say
to him. I'm embarrassed. Maybe I wouldn't even need to say
anything; maybe I'm being presumptuous even thinking he
might be interested in me.

After lunch, Chris comes flying down the hall and skids to
a stop when she sees me and Lucas on the floor at our lock-
ers. Today we're sharing a grape Popsicle. Chris sinks down
to the floor. "I'm out," she says.

I gasp. "Who got you?"

"John freaking McClaren!" She snatches the Popsicle out
of Lucas's hands and finishes it in a gulp.

"Rude," Lucas says.

"Tell us everything," I urge.

"John tailed me on the way to school this morning. I stopped to get gas and he jumped out of the car as soon as my back was turned. I didn't even know he was following me!"

"Wait, how did he know you were going to stop for gas?" Lucas asks. He knows all about the game, which will hopefully come in handy if it comes down to Genevieve and me, seeing as how he lives in her neighborhood.

"He siphoned gas out of my tank!"

"Whoa," I breathe. It warms my heart that John is taking it so seriously. I'd worried people wouldn't, but it seems like they are. I wonder what John's wish is? It must be something good to go to all this trouble.

"That's legit," Lucas says with a nod.

"I almost can't be mad because it's so hard-core." She blows her hair out of her face. "I'm just so pissed I can't make Gen give me our grandma's car."

Lucas's eyes bulge. "That's what you were going to wish for? A *car*?"

"That car holds a lot of sentimental value for me," Chris says. "Our grandma used to take me to the beauty parlor with her in it on Sunday afternoons. By all rights it should be mine. Gen's poisoned Granny's mind against me!"

"What kind of car is it?" Lucas asks.

"It's an old Jaguar."

"What color?" he wants to know.

"Black."

If I didn't know Chris better, I would think that was a tear forming in her eye. I put my arm around her. "Want me to buy you another Popsicle?"

Chris shakes her head. "I've got to wear a crop top tonight. I can't have a gut."

"So if you're out, who does John have now?" Lucas asks.

"Kavinsky," Chris says. "I haven't been able to get him because he's always with fucking Gen, and I thought for sure Gen had me." She glances at me. "Sorry, LJ."

Lucas and Chris are looking at me with pity eyes.

If Chris had Peter, and John took her out, that means John has Peter now. Which means either Peter or Genevieve has me. And since I have John, that means one of them has the other—which means they must be in an alliance. That means they've confided in each other, told each other who they have.

Swallowing, I say, "I knew from the start they were still friends. And, she's going through a hard time, you know?"

"What's she going through?" Chris asks, one eyebrow way high up.

"Peter said family stuff." She looks blank. "So you haven't heard anything?"

"I mean, she was acting kind of weird at Aunt Wendy's birthday dinner last week. Like, more of a bitch than usual. She barely said a word all night to anybody." She shrugs. "So something probably is up, but I don't know what." Chris blows her hair out of her face. "Damn it. I can't believe I'm not getting that car."

"I'll take John McClaren out for you," I vow. "Your death will not be in vain."

She gives me side-eye. "If you'd have gotten him out sooner, this wouldn't have happened."

"He lives half an hour away! I don't even know how to get to his house."

"Whatever, I still partially blame you." The bell rings and Chris stands up. "Later, *chicas*." She heads off down the hall, in the opposite direction of her next class.

"She just called me *chica*," Lucas says, frowning at me. "Did you tell her I'm gay?"

"No!"

"Okay, because I told you that in confidence. Remember?"

"Lucas, of course I remember!" Now I'm nervous—*did* I ever say anything to Chris? I'm almost one hundred percent sure not, but he has me doubting myself all of a sudden.

"Fine," he says with a sigh. "It's whatever." He rises to his feet and offers his hand to help me up. He is ever the gentleman.

# 39

*IT'S MY FIRST OFFICIAL FRIDAY NIGHT* cocktail hour at Belleview and the night isn't going . . . as well as I'd hoped. We're already half an hour in and it's just Stormy, Mr. Morales, Alicia, and Nelson, who has Alzheimer's and whose nurse brought him in for a change of scenery. He is, however, wearing a dapper navy sport coat with copper buttons. Not that many people came when Margot was in charge, either—Mrs. Maguire was a regular, but she was moved to a different nursing home last month, and Mrs. Montero died over the holidays. But I made such a fuss to Janette about how I would breathe new life into cocktail hour, and now look at me. I feel a little olive pit of dread in the bottom of my stomach, because if Janette catches wind of how low the attendance is, she might cancel Friday night social after all, and I had the funnest idea for the next one—a USO party. If tonight's a flop, there's no way she'll let me run it. Also, throwing a party and having four people show up, one of whom is dozing off, feels like a huge failure. Stormy either doesn't notice or doesn't mind; she just keeps singing and playing the piano. The show must go on, as they say.

I'm trying to keep busy, keep a smile on my face: *Tra-la-la, everything is loverly.* I've lined up the glassware in neat rows so it looks like a real bar and brought a bunch of things from home—our one good tablecloth (no gravy stains, freshly ironed), a little bud vase I put next to the plate of peanut butter cookies (at first I hesitated at peanut butter, what with allergies and all, but then I remembered that old people don't have as many food allergies), Mommy and Daddy's silver ice bucket with their monogram, a matching silver bowl with cut-up lemons and limes.

I've already gone around knocking on doors of some of the more active residents, but most weren't home. I guess if you're active, you're not staying in your apartment on a Friday night.

I'm pouring salted peanuts into a heart-shaped crystal bowl (a contribution from Alicia, who brought it out of storage, along with her ice tongs) when John Ambrose McClaren walks into the room in a light blue Oxford shirt and navy sport coat, not dissimilar to Nelson's! I nearly scream out loud. Clapping my hands to my mouth, I drop to the floor, behind the table. If he sees me, he might run off. I don't know what he's doing here, but this is my perfect chance to take him out. I crouch behind the table, running through options in my head.

And then the piano music stops and I hear Stormy call out, "Lara Jean? Lara Jean, where are you? Come out from behind the table. I want to introduce you to someone."

Slowly, I rise to my feet. John McClaren is staring at me. "What are you doing here?" he asks me, tugging on his shirt collar like it's choking him.

"I volunteer here," I say, still keeping a safe distance. Don't want to spook him.

Stormy claps her hands. "You two know each other?"

John says, "We're friends, Grandma. We used to live in the same neighborhood."

"Stormy's your *grandma*?" My mind is blown. So John is her grandson she wanted to set me up with! Of all the nursing homes in all the towns in all the world! *My grandson looks like a young Robert Redford.* He does; he really does.

"She's my great-grandmother by marriage," John says.

Stormy's eyes dart around the room. "Hush up! I don't want people knowing you're my great-anything."

John lowers his voice. "She was my great-grandpa's second wife."

"My favorite of all my husbands," Stormy says. "May he rest in peace, that old buzzard." She looks from John to me. "Johnny, be a dear and bring me a vodka soda with lots of lemons." She sits back at the piano bench and starts to play "When I Fall in Love."

John starts toward me and I point at him. "Stop right there, John Ambrose McClaren. Do you have my name?"

"No! I swear I don't. I have—I'm not saying who I have." He pauses. "Wait a minute. Do you have mine?"

I shake my head, innocent as a little lost lamb. He still looks suspicious, so I busy myself with making Stormy's drink. I know just how she likes it. I drop in three ice cubes, an eight-second pour of vodka, and a splash of soda water. Then I squeeze three lemon slices and drop them in the glass. "Here," I say, holding out the glass.

"You can put it on the table," he says.

"John! I'm telling you, I don't have your name!"

He shakes his head. "Table."

I set the glass back down. "I can't believe you don't believe me. I feel like I remember you being a trusting kind of person who sees the good in people."

Sober as a judge, John says, "Just . . . stay on your side of the table."

Shoot. How am I supposed to take him out if he makes me stay ten feet away all night?

Airily I say, "Fine by me. I don't know if I believe you, either, so! I mean, this is a pretty big coincidence, you showing up here."

"Stormy guilted me into coming!"

I snap my head in Stormy's direction. She's still playing the piano, looking over at us with a big smile.

Mr. Morales sidles up to the bar and says, "May I have this dance, Lara Jean?"

"You may," I say. To John I warn, "Don't you dare come close to me."

He throws his hands out like he's warding me off. "Don't you come close to me!"

As Mr. Morales leads me in a slow dance, I press my face against his shoulder to hide my smile. I'm really quite good at this espionage thing. John McClaren is sitting on a love seat now, watching Stormy play and chatting with Alicia. I've got him right where I want him. I can't even believe how lucky I am. I'd been planning on showing up at his next Model UN meeting, but this is so much better.

I'm thinking I'll come up from behind him, take him by surprise, when Stormy stands up and declares she needs a piano break, she wants to dance with her grandson. I go turn on the stereo and cue up the CD we decided on for her break.

John is protesting: "Stormy, I told you I don't dance." He used to try and fake sick during the square-dancing unit in gym—that's how much he hates dancing.

Stormy doesn't listen, of course. She pulls him off the love seat and starts trying to teach him how to fox-trot. "Put your hand on my waist," she orders. "I didn't wear heels to sit behind a piano all night." Stormy's trying to teach him the steps, and he keeps stepping on her feet. "Ouch!" she snaps.

I can't stop giggling. Mr. Morales is too. He dances us over closer. "May I cut in?" he asks.

"Please!" John practically pushes Stormy into Mr. Morales's arms.

"Johnny, be a gentleman and ask Lara Jean to dance," Stormy says as Mr. Morales twirls her.

John gives me a searching look, and I have a feeling he's still suspicious of me and whether or not I have his name.

"Ask her to dance," Mr. Morales urges, grinning at me. "She wants to dance, don't you, Lara Jean?"

I shrug a sad kind of shrug. Wistful. The very picture of a girl who is waiting to be asked to dance.

"I want to see the young people dance!" Norman yells.

John McClaren looks at me, one eyebrow raised. "If

we're just swaying back and forth, I probably won't step on your feet."

I feign hesitation and then nod. My pulse is racing. Target acquired.

We step toward each other, and I thread my arms around his neck, and he puts his around my waist, and we sway, off beat. I'm short, not even five-two, and he looks just under six feet tall, but in my heels we're a good height for dance partners. From across the room Stormy smiles knowingly at me, which I pretend not to see. I should probably go ahead and take him out before he's onto me, but the residents are so enjoying watching us dance. It couldn't hurt to hold off just a few minutes.

As we sway, I'm remembering the eighth grade formal, how everyone paired up and no one asked me to go. I'd thought Genevieve and I were riding over together, but then she said Peter's mom was taking them, and they were going to a restaurant first, like a real date, and it would be awkward if I tagged along. So it ended up being her and Peter and Sabrina Fox and John. I'd hoped John McClaren would ask me for a slow dance, but he didn't; he didn't dance with anyone. The only guy who really danced was Peter. He was always in the center of the cool-people dance circle.

John's hand is pressed against my back, leading me, and I think he's forgotten all about the game. I've got him in my crosshairs now.

"You're not so bad," I tell him. Song's halfway over. I'd

better hop to the beat. *I've got you in five, four, three, two*—

"So . . . you and Kavinsky, huh?"

He's distracted me completely, and I've forgotten all about the game for a moment. "Yeah . . ."

Clearing his throat, he says, "I was pretty surprised that you guys were together."

"Why? Because I'm not his type?" I say it casually, like it's nothing, a fact, but it stings like a little pebble thrown directly at my heart.

"No, you are."

"Then why?" I'm pretty sure John's going to say "because I didn't think he was *your* type," just like Josh did.

He doesn't answer right away. "That day you came to Model UN, I tried to follow you out to the parking lot, but you were already gone. Then I got your letter, and I wrote you back, and you wrote me back, and then you invited me to the tree-house thing. I guess I didn't know what to think. You know what I mean?" He looks at me expectantly, and I feel like it's important that I say yes.

All the blood rushes to my face, and I hear a pounding in my ears, which I belatedly realize is the sound of my heart beating really fast. My body is still dancing, though.

He keeps talking. "Maybe it was dumb to think that, because all that stuff was such a long time ago."

*All what stuff?* I want to know, but it wouldn't be right to ask. "Do you know what I remember?" I ask suddenly.

"What?"

"The time Trevor's shorts split open when you guys were

playing basketball. And everybody was laughing so hard that Trevor started getting mad. But not you. You got on your bike and you rode all the way home and brought Trevor a pair of shorts. I was really impressed by that."

He has a faint half smile on his face. "Thanks."

Then we're both quiet and still dancing. He's an easy person to be quiet with. "John?"

"Hmm?"

I look up at him. "I have to tell you something."

"What?"

"I've got you. I mean, I have your name. In the game."

"Seriously?" John looks genuinely disappointed, which makes me feel guilty.

"Seriously. Sorry." I press my hands against his shoulders. "Tag."

"Well, now you have Kavinsky. I was really looking forward to taking him out, too. I had a whole plan and everything."

All eagerness I ask, "What was your plan?"

"Why should I tell the girl who just tagged me out?" he challenges, but it's a weak challenge, just for show, and we both know he's going to tell me.

I play along. "Come on, Johnny. I'm not just the girl who tagged you out. I'm your *pen pal.*"

John laughs a little. "All right, all right. I'll help you."

The song ends and we step apart. "Thanks for the dance," I say. After all this time, I finally know what it's like to dance with John Ambrose McClaren. "So what would you have asked for if you won?"

*JENNY HAN*

He doesn't hesitate even one beat. "Your peanut butter chocolate cake with my name written in Reese's Pieces."

I stare at him in surprise. *That's* what he would have wished for? He could have anything and he wants my cake? I give him a curtsy. "I'm so honored."

"Well, it was a really good cake," he says.

# 40

ON THE PHONE A FEW NIGHTS LATER, PETER
suddenly says, "You have me, don't you?"

"No!" I haven't told him I took out John over the weekend. I don't want him—or Genevieve, for that matter—to
have any extra info. It's down to the three of us now.

"So you do have me!" He lets out a groan. "I don't
want to play this game anymore. It's making me lonely and
really . . . frustrated. I haven't seen you outside of school
for a week! When is this going to be over?"

"Peter, I don't have you. I have John." I feel a little guilty
for lying, but this is how winners play this game. You can't
second-guess yourself.

There's a silence on the other end. Then he says, "So are
you going to drive over to his house to tag him out? He lives
in the middle of nowhere. I could take you if you want."

"I haven't figured out my game plan yet," I say. "Who do
you have?" I know it has to be me or Genevieve.

He gets quiet. "I'm not saying."

"Well, have you told anyone else?" Like, say, Genevieve?
"No."

Hmm. "Okay, well, I just told you, so you obviously owe
me that same courtesy."

Peter bursts out, "I didn't make you, you offered up that

information yourself, and look, if it was a lie and you have me, please just freaking take me out already! I'm begging you. Come to my house right now, and I'll let you sneak up to my room. I'll be a sitting duck for you if it means I can see you again."

"No."

"No?"

"No, I don't want to win like that. When I get your name, I want to have the satisfaction of knowing I beat you fair and square. My first ever Assassins win can't be tainted." I pause. "And besides, your house is a safe zone."

Peter lets out an aggravated sigh. "Are you at least coming to my lacrosse game on Friday?"

His lacrosse game! That's the perfect place to take him out. I try to keep my voice calm and even as I say, "I can't come. My dad has a date, and he needs me to watch Kitty." A lie, but Peter doesn't know that.

"Well, can't you bring her? She's been asking to go to one of my games."

I think fast. "No, because she has a piano lesson after school."

"Since when does Kitty play the piano?"

"Recently, in fact. She heard from our neighbor that it helps with training puppies; it calms them down." I bite my lip. Will he buy it? I hurry to add, "I promise I'll be at the next game no matter what."

Peter groans, this time even louder. "You're killing me, Covey."

Soon, my dear Peter.

I will surprise him at the game; I'll get all decked out in our school colors; I'll even paint his jersey number on my face. He'll be so happy to see me, he won't suspect a thing!

I can't fully explain why this game of Assassins is so important to me. I only know that with each passing day I want it more and more—the win. I want to beat Genevieve, yes, but it's more than that. Maybe it's to prove that I've changed too: I'm not a soft little marshmallow; I've got some fight in me.

After Peter and I hang up, I text John my idea, and he offers to drive me to the game. It's at his school. I ask if he's sure he doesn't mind coming all the way to get me, and he says it'll be worth it to see Kavinsky get taken down. I'm relieved, because the last thing I need is to get lost on the way there.

After school on Friday, I rush home to get ready. I change into school colors—light blue T-shirt, white shorts, white and light blue striped knee socks, a blue ribbon in my hair. I paint a big 15 on my cheek and outline it with white eyeliner.

I run outside as soon as John pulls into our driveway. He's wearing his faded old Orioles baseball cap, pulled down low. He eyes me as I climb inside.

Smiling, John says, "You look like a rally girl."

I tap him on the bill of his hat. "You used to wear this, like, every day that one summer."

As he backs out of our driveway, John grins like he has a secret. It's contagious. Now I'm smiling too, and I don't even know why. "What? Why are you smiling?" I ask, pulling up my knee socks.

"Nothing," he says.

I jab him in the side. "Come on!"

"My mom gave me a really bad haircut at the beginning of summer, and I was embarrassed. I never let my mom cut my hair again after that." He checks the time on the dashboard. "What time did you say the game started? Five?"

"Yup!" I'm practically bouncing up and down in my seat I'm so excited. Peter will be proud of me for pulling this off, I know he will.

We get to John's school in under half an hour, and there's still time before the school bus arrives, so John jogs inside to get us snacks out of the vending machine. He comes back with two cans of soda and a bag of salt-and-vinegar chips to share.

He hasn't been back long before a tall black guy in a lacrosse uniform comes jogging over to the car. He calls out, "McClaren!" He bends down and puts his face up close to the window, and he and John bump fists. "Are you coming to Danica's after this?" he asks.

John glances over at me and then says, "Nah, I can't."

His friend notices me then; his eyes widen. "Who's this?"

"I'm Lara Jean, I don't go here," I say, which is dumb, because he probably knows that already.

"You're Lara Jean!" He nods enthusiastically. "I've heard about you. You're why McClaren's hanging around a nursing home, am I right?"

I blush and John laughs an easy sort of laugh. "Get outta here, Avery."

Avery reaches over John and shakes my hand. "Nice to meet you, Lara Jean. See you around." Then he runs off toward the field. As we sit and wait, a few more people come up to John's car to say hi, and I see it's just like I thought: He has lots of friends, lots of girls who admire him. A group of girls walks by the car, toward the field, and one in particular stares into the car and right at me, questions in her eyes. John doesn't seem to notice. He is asking me what TV shows I watch, what I'm going to do for spring break in April, summer vacation. I tell him about Daddy's idea to go to Korea.

"I have a funny story about your dad," John says, looking at me sideways.

I groan. "Oh no. What did he do?"

"It wasn't him; it was me." He clears his throat. "This is embarrassing."

I rub my hands together in anticipation.

"So, I went over to your house to ask you to eighth grade formal. I had this whole extravagant plan."

"You never asked me to formal!"

"I know, I'm getting to that part. Are you going to let me tell the story or not?"

"You had a whole extravagant plan," I prompt.

John nods. "So I gathered a bunch of sticks and some flowers and I arranged them into the letters FORMAL? in front of your window. But your dad came home while I was in the middle of it, and he thought I was going around cleaning people's yards. He gave me ten bucks, and I lost my nerve and I just went home."

I laugh. "I . . . can't believe you did that." I can't believe that this almost happened to me. What would that have felt like, to have a boy do something like that for me? In the whole history of my letters, of my liking boys, not once has a boy liked me back at the same time as I liked him. It was always me alone, longing after a boy, and that was fine, that was safe. But this is new. Or old. Old and new, because it's the first time I'm hearing it.

"The biggest regret of eighth grade," John says, and that's when I remember—how Peter once told me that John's biggest regret was not asking me to formal, how elated I was when he said it, and then how he quickly backtracked and said he was only joking.

The school bus pulls up then. "Showtime," I say. I'm giddy as we watch the players get off the bus—I see Gabe, Darrell, no Peter yet. But then the last person gets off the bus and still no Peter. "That's weird . . ."

"Could he have driven his own car?" John asks.

I shake my head. "He never does." I grab my phone out of my bag and text him.

Where are you?

No reply. Something's wrong, I know it. Peter never misses a game. He even played when he had the flu.

"I'll be right back," I tell John, and I jump out of the car and run for the field. The guys are warming up. I find Gabe on the sideline lacing his cleats. I call out, "Gabe!"

He looks up, surprised. "Large! What's up?"

Breathlessly I ask him, "Where's Peter?"

"I don't know," he says, scratching the back of his neck. "He told Coach he had a family emergency. It sounded pretty legit. Kavinsky wouldn't miss a game if it wasn't important."

I'm already running back to the car. As soon as I'm in, I pant, "Can you drive me to Peter's?"

I see her car first. Parked on the street in front of his house. The next thing I see is the two of them, standing together on the street for all to see. He has his arms wrapped around her; she is leaning in to him like she can't stand on her own two feet. Her face is buried in his chest. He is saying something in her ear, petting her hair tenderly.

It all happens in the span of seconds, but it feels like time goes in slow-motion, like I'm moving through water. I think I stop breathing; my head goes fuzzy; everything around me blurs. How many times have I seen them stand just like that? Too many to count.

"Keep driving," I manage to say to John, and he obeys. He drives right past Peter's house; they don't even look up. Thank God they don't look up. Quietly I say, "Can you take me home?" I can't even look at John. I hate that he saw too.

John begins, "It might not be . . ." Then he stops. "It was just a hug, Lara Jean."

"I know." Whatever it was, he missed his game for her.

We're almost at my house when he finally asks, "What are you going to do?"

I've been thinking it over this whole ride. "I'm going to tell Peter to come over tonight, and then I'm going to tag him out."

"You're still playing?" He sounds surprised.

I stare out the window, at all the familiar places. "Sure. I'm going to take him out and then I'm going to take Genevieve out and I'm going to win."

"Why do you want to win so badly?" he asks me. "Is it the prize?"

I don't answer him. If I open my mouth, I will cry.

We're at my house now. I mumble, "Thanks for the ride," and I get out of the car before John can reply. I run into the house, kick off my shoes, and run up the stairs to my room, where I lie down and stare at the ceiling. I put glow-in-the-dark stars up there years ago, and I scraped most of them off except for one, which hung on tight as a stalactite.

Star light, star bright, the first star I see tonight. I wish I may, I wish I might, have the wish I wish tonight. I wish not to cry.

I text Peter: Come over after you're finished hanging out with Genevieve.

He writes back one word: Okay.

Just "okay." No denials, no explanations or clarifications. All this time I've been making excuses for him. I've been trusting Peter and not trusting my own gut. Why am I the one making all these concessions, pretending to be okay with something I'm not actually okay with? Just to keep him?

In the contract we said we'd always tell each other the truth. We said we'd never break each other's hearts. So I guess two times now he's broken his word.

# 41

PETER AND I ARE SITTING ON MY FRONT PORCH;
I can hear the TV on in the living room. Kitty's watching
a movie. There is an interminably long silence between us,
only the sound of crickets chirping.

He speaks first. "It isn't what you think, Lara Jean; it really
isn't."

I take a moment to gather my thoughts together, to string
them into something that makes any kind of sense. "When
we first started all this, I was really happy just being at home
with my sisters and my dad. It was cozy. And then we started
hanging out, and it was like . . . it was like you brought me
out into the world." At this his eyes go soft. "At first it was
scary, but then I liked it too. Part of me wants to just stay
next to you forever. I could easily do that. I could love you
forever."

He tries to make his voice light. "Then just do that."

"I can't." I take a shaky breath. "I saw you two. You were
holding her; she was in your arms. I saw everything."

"If you'd seen everything, you'd know that it wasn't
anything like what you're saying," he begins. I just stare at
him, and his face falls. "Come on. Don't look at me like
that."

"I can't help it. It's the only way I can look at you right now."

"Gen needed me today, so I was there for her, but just as a friend."

"It's no use, Peter. She laid claim to you a long time ago, and there's just no room for me here." My eyesight is going fuzzy with tears. I wipe my eyes with my jacket sleeve. I can't be here anymore, around him. It's hurting me too much to look at his face. "I deserve better than that, you know? I deserve . . . I deserve to be someone's number one girl."

"You *are*."

"No, I'm not. She is. You're still protecting her, her secret, whatever that is. From what, though? From me? What have I ever done to her?"

He spreads his hands helplessly. "You took me away from her. You became my most important person."

"But I'm not, though. That's the thing. She is." He sputters and tries to deny it, but there's no use. How could I believe him when the truth is right in front of me? "You know how I know she's your most important person? You pick her every time."

"That's bullshit!" he explodes. "When I found out she took that video, I told her that if she ever hurt you again, we were done." Peter's still talking, but I don't hear anything more that comes out of his mouth.

*He knew.*

He knew it was Genevieve who posted that video; he knew and he never told me.

Peter isn't talking anymore; he's peering at me. "Lara Jean? What's the matter?"

"You knew?"

His face goes gray. "No! It's not like how you think. I haven't known this whole time."

I wet my lips and press them together. "So at some point you found out the truth, and you didn't tell me." It's hard to breathe. "You knew how upset I was, and you kept defending her, and then you found out the truth, and you never told me."

Peter starts talking very fast. "Let me explain it. It's only recently I found out Gen was behind the video. I asked her about it, and she broke down and admitted everything to me. That night at the ski trip, she saw us in the hot tub; she took the video. She's the one who sent it to Anonybitch and played it at the assembly."

I knew it, and I let myself go along with Peter and pretend not to know what I knew. And for what? For him?

"She's been really fucked up over stuff she's going through with her family, and she was jealous, and she took it out on you and me—"

"Like what? What is she going through?" I don't ask expecting an answer; I know he won't tell me. I'm asking to prove a point.

He looks pained. "You know I can't tell you. Why do you keep putting me in a position where I have to say no to you?"

"You put yourself in that position. You have her name, don't you? In the game, you have her name and she has mine."

"Who cares about the stupid game? Covey, we're talking about us."

"I care about the stupid game." Peter is loyal to her first, me second. It's first Genevieve, then me. That is the deal. That's always been the deal. And I'm sick of it. Something clicks in my head. Suddenly I ask him, "Why was Genevieve outside that night at the ski trip? All of her friends were in the lodge."

Peter closes his eyes briefly. "Why does it matter?"

I think back to that night in the woods. How he looked surprised to see me. Startled, even. He wasn't waiting for me. He was waiting for *her*. He still is. "If I hadn't gone out to apologize that night, would you have kissed her?"

He doesn't answer right away. "I don't know."

Those three words confirm everything for me. They take my breath away. "If I win . . . do you know what I would wish for?" Don't say it, don't say it. Don't say the thing you can't take back. "I'd wish we never started any of this." The words echo in my head, in the air.

He sucks in his breath. His eyes get small; so does his mouth. I've hurt him. Is that what I wanted? I thought so, but now, looking at his face, I'm not sure. "You don't have to win the game to have that, Covey. You can have that right now if you want it."

I reach out, put both hands on his chest. My eyes fill. "You're out. Who do you have?" I already know the answer.

"Genevieve."

I stand up. "Bye, Peter." And then I walk into my house and shut the door. I don't look back, not once.

We broke so easily. Like it was nothing. Like we were nothing. Does that mean it was never meant to be in the first place? That we were an accident of fate? If we were meant to be, how could we both walk away just like that?

I guess the answer is, we weren't.

# 42

*PETER AND ME, OUR BREAKUP, IT'S ALL SO* very high school. By that I mean it's ephemeral. Even this pain will be fleeting, finite. Even the sharp sting of this betrayal I should hold on to and remember and cherish, because it is my first true breakup. It's all just part of it, the process of falling in love. And it's not like I thought we'd stay together forever; we're only sixteen and seventeen. One day I will look back on all of this fondly.

This is what I keep telling myself, even as tears are filling my eyes, even as I'm lying in bed that night, crying myself to sleep. I cry until my cheeks sting from wiping away my tears. This well of sadness, it starts with Peter but it doesn't end there.

Because over and over one thought runs in my head on a loop: *I miss my mother. I miss my mother. I miss her so much.* If she were here, she would bring me a cup of Night-Night tea, she would sit at the foot of my bed. She would put my head in her lap, and run her fingers through my hair, and whisper in my ear, *It will all be fine, Lara Jean. It will all be fine.* And I would believe her, because her words were always true.

*Oh, Mommy. How I miss you. Why aren't you here, when I need you most?*

So far I've saved a napkin Peter drew a little sketch of my face on, a ticket stub from the first time we went to the movies, the poem he gave me on Valentine's Day. The necklace. Of course the necklace. I haven't been able to bring myself to take it off. Not yet.

I lie in bed all day Saturday, only getting up for snacks and to let Jamie out to pee in the backyard. I fast-forward to the sad parts of romantic comedies. What I should be doing is coming up with a plan to take Genevieve out, but I can't. It hurts every time I think of her, of the game, of Peter most of all. I resolve to put it out of my mind until I can really concentrate.

John texts me once to see if I'm all right, but I can't bring myself to reply. I put that off for later too.

The only time I leave the house is on Sunday afternoon to go to Belleview for a party planning committee meeting. With a little cajoling on Stormy's part, Janette has okayed my USO party idea, and the show must go on, breakups be damned.

Stormy says the whole retirement community is abuzz about it. She's particularly excited because there's been talk that Ferncliff, the other big nursing home in town, might bus over some of their residents. Stormy says they have at least one eligible widower that she knows from the seniors book club at the local library. This gets the other female residents stirred up. "He's a very distinguished silver," she keeps telling everyone. "He still drives, too!" I make sure to spread that info around myself. Anything to build excitement.

At the party everyone will get five "war bonds," which you can use for a cup of whiskey punch, a little flag pin, or a dance. That was Mr. Morales's idea. Actually, his exact idea was one war bond for a dance with a lady, but we all slapped him down for being sexist and said that it should be a dance with a man *or* a lady. Alicia, pragmatic as ever, said, "There will be many more women than men, so it's the women who will be in charge anyway."

I've been going from apartment to apartment asking people to lend pictures from the forties if they have them, especially in uniform or at a USO party. One resident sniffed at me and said, "Excuse me, but I was six in 1945!" Hastily I told her that pictures of her parents would be welcome too, of course—but she was already closing the door in my face.

Scrapbooking to the Oldies has turned into a de facto dance-planning committee. I printed out war bonds, and Mr. Morales is using my paper cutter to cut them. Maude, who is new to the group and is Internet savvy, is clipping news articles from the war to decorate the refreshments table. Her friend Claudia is working on the playlist.

Alicia will have a little table of her own. She's making a paper-crane garland, all different-colored papers, lilac and peach and turquoise and floral. Stormy balked at the deviation from the red, white, and blue theme, but Alicia held firm and I backed her up. Classy as always, her pictures of Japanese Americans in internment camps are in fancy silver frames.

"Those pictures are really going to bring the mood down," Stormy stage-whispers to me.

Alicia whirls around. "These pictures are meant to educate the ignorant."

Stormy gathers herself up to her full five feet three inches, five-six in heels. "Alicia, did you just call me *ignorant?*" I wince. Stormy's been putting a lot of work into this party, and she's been a little extra Stormy lately.

I just can't take another fight between them right now. I'm about to plead for peace when Alicia fixes Stormy with a steely look and says, "If the muumuu fits."

Stormy and I both gasp. Then Stormy stalks over to Alicia's table and sweeps Alicia's paper cranes to the floor with a flourish. Alicia screams, and I gasp again. Everyone else in the room looks up. "Stormy!"

"You're taking *her* side? She just called me ignorant! Stormy Sinclair might be a lot of things, but I am not ignorant."

"I'm not taking anybody's side," I say, bending down to pick up the paper cranes.

"If you're taking a side, it should be mine," Alicia says. She thrusts her chin in Stormy's direction. "She thinks she's some grand dame, but she is a child, throwing a tantrum over a party."

"A child!" Stormy shrieks.

"Will you two please stop fighting?" To my mortification, tears spurt out the corners of my eyes. "I can't take it today." My voice trembles. "I really just can't."

They exchange a look, and then they both rush to my side. "Darling, what's wrong?" Stormy croons. "It must be a boy."

"Sit, sit," Alicia says. They lead me over to the couch and sit on either side of me.

"Everybody, get out!" Stormy yells, and the others scatter. "Now you tell us what's wrong."

I wipe my eyes with the corner of my shirtsleeve. "Peter and I broke up." It's the first time I've said the words out loud.

Stormy gasps. "You and Mr. Handsome broke up! Was it over another boy?" She looks hopeful, and I know she is thinking of John.

"It wasn't over another boy. It's complicated."

"Darling, it's never that complicated," Stormy says. "In my day—"

Alicia glares at her. "Will you just let her talk?"

"Peter never got over his ex-girlfriend, Genevieve," I say, sniffling. "She was the one who posted that video of us in the hot tub, and Peter found out and he didn't tell me."

"Perhaps he wanted to spare your feelings," Alicia says.

Vehemently Stormy shakes her head, so hard her earrings whoosh. "The boy is a dog, pure and simple. He ought to treat you like a queen, not this other girl Genevieve."

Alicia accuses, "You just want Lara Jean to date your great-grandson."

"So what if I do!" With a gleam in her eye she says, "Say, Lara Jean. Have you got any plans tonight?"

At that we all laugh. "I can't think about any boy but Peter right now," I say. "Do you still remember your first love?"

Stormy's had so many—could she possibly? But she nods. "Garrett O'Leary. I was fifteen and he was eighteen and we only ever had a dance, but the way I felt when he looked at me . . ." She shivers.

I look to my left at Alicia. "And yours was your husband, Phillip, right?"

To my surprise she shakes her head. "My first love was named Albert. He was my older brother's best friend. I thought I would marry him. But it was not to be. I met my Phillip." She smiles. "Phillip was the love of my life. And yet I never forgot Albert. How young I was once! Stormy, can you believe we were ever so young?"

Stormy does not give her usual blithe reply. Her eyes go moist, and as softly as I've ever heard her speak she says, "It's all a million lifetimes ago. And yet."

"And yet," Alicia echoes.

They both smile at me fondly, with such true and genuine affection that new tears come to my eyes. "What will I do now that Peter's not my boyfriend anymore?" I wonder out loud.

"You'll just do what you did before he was your

boyfriend," Alicia says. "You'll go about your day, and you will miss him at first, but over time it will ease. It will lessen." She reaches out, touches her papery hand to my cheek. A smile plays at her lips. "All you need is time, and you, little one, have all the time in the world."

It's a comforting thought, but I don't know if I believe it is true, not completely. I think that time might be different for young people. The minutes longer, stronger, more vibrant. All I know is that every minute without him feels interminably long, like I'm waiting, just waiting for him to come back to me. I, Lara Jean, know he isn't, but my heart doesn't seem to understand it's over.

After, energies renewed, tears dried, I am with Janette in her office, going over party details. When she offhandedly mentions the sitting room, I freeze. "Janette, the sitting room isn't going to be big enough."

"I don't know what to tell you. The main activities room is booked for bingo. They have a standing Friday night reservation."

"But this party is a huge event! Can't the bingo people be in the sitting room just for one night?"

"Lara Jean, I can't move bingo. People from all over the community come here for that, including the leasing agent's own mother. There are a lot of politics at play here. My hands are tied."

"Well, what about the dining room?" We could move

all the tables and set up the dance floor at the center of the room and then put the refreshments on a long table against the wall. It could work.

Janette gives me a look like *Girl, please.* "And who's going to put away all the tables and chairs? You?"

"Well, me, and I'm sure I could round up some volunteers—"

"And have one of the residents put out their back and sue the home? No, *gracias*."

"We wouldn't need to put away all of the tables, just half. Couldn't you get the staff to help?" Janette's already shaking her head when inspiration hits me. "Janette, I heard that Ferncliff might bus over some of their residents. *Ferncliff*. They already call themselves the premier retirement community of the Blue Ridge Mountains."

"Oh my God, Ferncliff is a dump. The people who work at that place are garbage. I have a *master's*. 'Premier retirement community of the Blue Ridge Mountains'? Ha! My ass."

Now I just need to bring it home. "I'm telling you, Janette, if this dance isn't up to par, it's going to make us look like fools. We can't let that happen. I want those Ferncliff residents to walk or wheel out of here wishing they were Belleview!"

"All right, all right. I'll get the janitors to help set up the dining room." Janette shakes her finger at me. "You're like a dog with a bone, girl."

"You won't regret it," I promise her. "For the pictures alone. We'll put them all over the website. Everyone will want to be us!"

At this Janette's eyes narrow with satisfaction, and I let out the breath I've been holding. This party has to go right. It just has to. It is my one bright spot.

# 43

SUNDAY NIGHT I CURL MY HAIR. CURLING
your hair is an intrinsically hopeful act. I like to curl mine
at night and think about all the things that could happen
tomorrow. Also, it generally looks much better slept on and
not so poofy.

I've got half of it clipped and I'm almost done with one
side when Chris comes climbing through my window.
"I'm supposed to be grounded right now, so I have to wait
until my mom falls asleep before I go home," she says, taking off her motorcycle jacket. "Are you still depressed over
Kavinsky?"

I wind another section of hair around the curling iron barrel. "Yes. I mean, it hasn't even been forty-eight hours yet."

Chris puts her arm around me. "I hate to say it, but this
has been a train wreck from the start."

I give her a wounded look. "Thanks a lot."

"Well, it's true. The way you guys got together was weird,
and then the whole hot tub video thing." She takes the curling iron from me and starts curling her own hair. "Although,
I will say that it was probably good for you to go through all
that. You were really sheltered, hon. You can be very judg-
mental."

I snatch the curling iron back from her and make like I'm

going to bonk her over the head with it. "Are you here to cheer me up or to tell me all of my flaws?"

"Sorry! I'm just saying." She offers me a cheery smile. "Don't be sad for too long. It's not your style. There are other guys besides Kavinsky. Guys who aren't my cousin's sloppy seconds. Guys like John McClaren. He's hot. I'd go for him myself if he wasn't into you."

Softly, I say, "I can't think about anyone else right now. Peter and I just broke up."

"There's heat between you and Johnny boy. I saw it with my own two eyes at the time capsule thing. He wants you." She bumps her shoulder against mine. "You liked him before. Maybe there's still something there."

I ignore her and keep curling my hair, one lock at a time.

Peter still sits in front of me in chemistry. I didn't know you could miss someone even more acutely when they're only a few feet away. Maybe it's because he doesn't look at me, not even once. I didn't fully comprehend what a big part of my life he'd become. He'd become so . . . familiar to me. And now he's just gone. Not gone, still here, just not available to me, which might be even worse. For a minute there it was really good. It was really, really good. Wasn't it good? Maybe really, really good things aren't meant to last for too long; maybe that's what makes them all the more sweet, the temporariness of them. Maybe I'm just trying to make myself feel better. It's working, barely. Barely is enough for now.

*JENNY HAN*

After class is over, Peter lingers at his desk, and then he turns around and says, "Hey."

My heart leaps. "Hey." I have this sudden, wild thought that if he wants me back, I'll say yes. Forget my pride, forget Genevieve, forget it all.

"So I want my necklace back," he says. "Obviously."

My fingers fly to the heart locket hanging from around my neck. I wanted to take it off this morning, but I couldn't bear to.

Now I have to give it back? Stormy has a whole box of trinkets and tokens from old boyfriends. I didn't think I'd have to return my one token from a boy. But it *was* expensive, and Peter is practical. He could get his money back, and his mom could resell it. "Of course," I say, fumbling with the clasp.

"I didn't mean you had to give it back right this second," he says, and my hand stills. Maybe he'll let me keep it awhile longer, or even forever. "But I'll take it."

I can't get the clasp undone, and it's taking forever, and it's excruciating because he's just standing there. Finally he comes up behind me and pulls my hair away from my neck so it rests on one shoulder. It might be my imagination, but I think I hear his heart beating. His is beating and mine feels like it's breaking.

# 44

KITTY FLIES INTO MY BEDROOM. I'M AT MY
desk, doing homework. It's been so long since I sat here
and did homework; Peter and I usually go to Starbucks
after school. Life is lonely already.

"Did you and Peter break up?" Kitty demands.

I flinch. "Who told you?"

"Don't worry about it. Just answer the question."

"Well . . . yes."

"You don't deserve him," she spits out.

I reel backward in my seat. "What? You're *my* sister—it's
not fair for you to take Peter's side. You haven't even heard
my side. Not that you should have to. Don't you know that
you never take a side against your sister?"

She purses her lips. "What's your side?"

"My side is, it's complicated. Peter still has feelings for
Genevieve—"

"He doesn't think of her that way anymore. Don't make
an excuse."

"You didn't see what I saw, Kitty!" I burst out.

"What did you see?" she challenges, chin thrust out like a
weapon. "Tell me."

"It isn't just what I saw. It's what I knew all along. Just—
never mind. You wouldn't understand it, Kitty."

"Did you see him kiss her? Did you?"

"No, but—"

"But nothing." She squints at me. "Does this have anything to do with that guy with the weird name? John Amberton McClaren or whatever?"

"No! Why would you say that?" I let out a gasp. "Wait a minute! Have you been reading my letters again?"

She screws up her face, and I know she has, the fiend. "Don't change the subject! Do you like him or not?"

"This doesn't have anything to do with John McClaren. It's just about me and Peter."

I want to tell her that he knew it was Genevieve who made that video, spread it around. He knew and he still protected her. But I can't mar her little-girl notion of who Peter is. It would be too cruel a thing to do to her. "Kitty, it doesn't matter. Peter still has feelings for Genevieve, and I've always known it. And besides, what's even the point of a serious thing with Peter when we're only going to break up like Margot and Josh did? High school romances hardly ever last, you know. And for a good reason. We're too young to be so serious." Even as I'm saying the words, tears are leaking out the corners of my eyes.

Kitty softens. She puts her arm around me. "Don't cry."

"I'm not crying. I'm tearing up a little."

Sighing heavily, she says, "If this is love, no thanks. I don't want any part of it. When I'm older, I'm just going to do my own thing."

"What does that mean?" I ask her.

Kitty shrugs. "If I like a boy, fine, I'll date him, but I'm not going to sit at home and cry over him."

"Kitty, don't act like you never cry."

"I cry over important things."

"You cried the other night because Daddy wouldn't let you stay up to watch TV!"

"Yes, well, that was important to *me*."

I sniffle. "I don't know why I'm arguing over this stuff with you." She's too little to understand. Part of me hopes she never does. It was better when I didn't.

That night, Daddy and I are doing the dishes when he clears his throat and says, "So Kitty told me about the big breakup. How are you holding up?"

I rinse off a glass and set it in the dishwasher. "Kitty has such a big mouth. I was going to tell you about it later." Maybe deep down I was hoping I wouldn't have to.

"Do you want to talk about it? I can make some Night-Night tea. Not as good as Mommy's, but still."

"Maybe later," I say, just to be kind. His version of Night-Night tea isn't the best.

He puts his arm around my shoulders. "It'll get easier, I promise. Peter Kavinsky isn't the only boy in the world."

Sighing, I say, "I just don't want to hurt like this ever again."

"There's no way to protect yourself against heartbreak, Lara Jean. That's just a part of life." He kisses me on the top of my head. "Go upstairs and rest. I'll finish up here."

"Thanks, Daddy." I leave him alone in the kitchen, humming to himself as he dries a pan with a dishcloth.

My dad said Peter isn't the only boy in the world. I know this is true, of course it's true. But look at Daddy. My mom was the only girl in the world for him. If she wasn't, he'd have found somebody new by now. Maybe he's been trying to protect himself from heartbreak too. Maybe we're more alike than I ever realized.

# 45

*IT'S RAINING AGAIN. I'D HAD THE THOUGHT* that I might take Kitty and Jamie to the park after school, but that's out now. Instead I sit in bed and curl my hair and watch the rain shoot down like silver pellets. Weather to match my mood, I suppose.

In the midst of our breakup, I forgot about the game. Well, now I'm remembering all too well. I will win. I will take her out. She can't have Peter *and* win the game. It's too unfair. And I will think of some perfect wish, some perfect something to take from her. If only I knew what to wish for!

I need help. I call Chris, and she doesn't pick up. I'm about to call again, but at the last second I text John:

Will you help me take out Genevieve?

It takes a few minutes for him to write back.

It would be my honor.

John settles into the couch and leans forward, looking at me intently. "All right, so how do you want to do this? Do you want to flush her out? Go black ops on her?"

I set down a glass of sweet tea in front of him. Sitting next to him, I say, "I think we have to run surveillance on her first. I don't even know what her schedule is like." And . . . if in winning this game, I find out her big secret, well, that would be a nice bonus.

"I like where your head is at," John says, tipping his head back and drinking his tea.

"I know where they keep the emergency key. Chris and I had to pick up a vacuum cleaner from her house once. What if . . . what if I try to get under her skin? Like I could leave a note on her pillow that says *I'm watching you*. That would really creep her out."

John nearly chokes on his iced tea. "Wait, what would that even get you?"

"I don't know. You're the expert at this!"

"Expert? How am I an expert? If I was really any good, I'd still be in the game."

"There's no way you could have known I'd be at Belleview," I point out. "That was just your bad luck."

"We have a lot of coincidences. Belleview. You being at Model UN that day."

I look down at my hands. "That . . . wasn't a total coincidence. It actually wasn't a coincidence at all. I went there looking for you. I wanted to see how you turned out. I knew you'd be in Model UN. I remembered how much you liked it in middle school."

"The only reason I joined was so I could work on my public speaking. For my stutter." He stops. "Wait. Did you say you went there for me? To see how I turned out?"

"Yeah. I . . . I always wondered."

John's not saying anything; he's just staring at me. He sets down his glass abruptly. Then he picks it back up and puts a coaster under it. "You haven't said what happened with you and Kavinsky that night after I left."

"Oh. We broke up."

"You broke up," he repeats, his face blank.

That's when I notice Kitty lurking in the doorway like a little spy. "What do you want, Kitty?"

"Um . . . is there any red pepper hummus left?" she asks.

"I don't know—go check."

John is wide-eyed. "This is your little sister?" To Kitty he says, "The last time I saw you, you were still a little kid."

"Yeah, I grew up," she says, not even a little bit nicely.

I throw her a look. "Be polite to our guest." Kitty turns on her heels and runs upstairs. "Sorry about my sister. She's really close with Peter and she gets crazy ideas. . . ."

"Crazy ideas?" John repeats.

I could slap myself. "Yeah, I mean, she thinks that something's going on with us. But obviously there isn't, and you don't, like, like me like that, so, yeah, it's crazy." Like, why do I speak? Why did God give me a mouth if I'm just going to say dumb stuff with it?

It's so quiet I open my mouth to say more dumb stuff, but then he says, "Well . . . it's not *that* crazy."

"Right! I mean, I didn't mean *crazy*—" My mouth snaps shut, and I stare straight ahead.

"Do you remember that time we played spin the bottle in my basement?"

I nod.

"I was nervous to kiss you, because I'd never kissed a girl before," he says, and picks up the glass of sweet tea again. He takes a swig, but there's no tea left, just ice. His eyes meet mine, and he grins. "All the guys gave me such a hard time afterward for whiffing it."

"You didn't whiff it," I say.

"I think that was around when Trevor's old brother told us he made a girl . . ." John hesitates, and I nod eagerly so he'll go on. "He claimed he gave a girl an orgasm just by kissing her."

I let out a shrieky laugh and clap my hands to my mouth. "That's the biggest lie I ever heard! I never saw him talk to even one girl. Besides, I don't think that's even possible. And if it was possible, I highly doubt Sean Pike was capable of it."

John laughs too. "Well, I know it's a lie now, but at the time we all believed him."

"I mean, was it a great kiss? No, it wasn't." John winces and I quickly continue. "But it wasn't an altogether *terrible* one. I swear. And listen, it's not like I'm an expert on kissing anyway. Who am I to say?"

"Okay okay, you can stop trying to make me feel better." He sets down his glass. "I've gotten much better at it. That's what the girls tell me."

This conversation has taken a strange and confessional turn, and I'm nervous but not in a bad way. I like sharing secrets, being coconspirators. "Oh, so you've kissed that many, huh?"

He laughs again. "A respectable number." He pauses. "I'm surprised you even remember that day. You were so into Kavinsky, I don't think you even noticed who else was there."

I push him in the shoulder. "I was not 'so into Kavinsky'!"

"Yes you were. You kept your eyes on that bottle the whole game, like this." John picks up the bottle and lasers his eyes at it. "Waiting for your moment."

I'm bright red, I know I am. "Oh, be quiet."

Laughing, he says, "Like a hawk on its prey."

"Shut up!" Now I'm laughing too. "How do you even remember that?"

"Because I was doing the same thing," he says.

"You were staring at Peter too?" I say it like a joke, to tease, because this is fun. For the first time in days I'm having fun.

He looks right at me, navy-blue eyes sure and steady, and my breath catches in my chest. "No. I was looking at you."

There's a humming in my ears, and it's the sound of my heart beating in triple measure. *In memory, everything seems to happen to music.* One of my favorite lines from *The Glass Menagerie.* If I close my eyes I can almost hear it, that day in John Ambrose McClaren's basement. Years from now, when I look back on this moment, what music will I hear then?

His eyes hold mine, and I feel a flutter that starts in my throat and moves across my collarbone and chest. "I like you, Lara Jean. I liked you then and I like you even more now. I know you and Kavinsky just broke up, and you're still sad, but I just want to make it unequivocally clear."

"Um . . . okay," I whisper. His words—they come clearly;

they don't miss in either direction. Not even a trace of a stutter. Just—unequivocally clear.

"Okay, then. Let's win you a wish." He takes out his phone and pulls up Google Maps. "I looked up Gen's address before I came over here. I think you're right—we should take our time, assess the situation. Not go in half-cocked."

"Mm-hm." I'm in a sort of dream state; it's hard to concentrate. John Ambrose McClaren wants to make it unequivocally clear.

I snap out of it when Kitty jostles her way back into the living room, balancing a glass of orange soda, the tub of red pepper hummus, and a bag of pita chips. She makes her way over to the couch and plonks down right between us. Holding out the bag, she asks, "Do you guys want some?"

"Sure," John says, taking a chip. "Hey, I hear you're pretty good at schemes. Is that true?"

Warily she says, "What makes you say that?"

"You're the one who sent out Lara Jean's letters, aren't you?" Kitty nods. "Then I'd say you're pretty good at schemes."

"I mean, yeah. I guess."

"Awesome. We need your help."

Kitty's ideas are a bit too extreme—like slashing Genevieve's tires, or throwing a stink bomb in her house to smoke her out, but John writes down every one of Kitty's suggestions, which does not go unnoticed by Kitty. Very little does.

# 46

*THE NEXT MORNING, KITTY IS DAWDLING OVER* her peanut butter toast, and from behind his newspaper, Daddy says, "You're going to miss the bus if you don't hurry."

She merely shrugs and takes her time going upstairs to get her book bag. I'm sure she thinks she can just catch a ride with me if she misses the bus, but I'm running late too. I overslept and then I couldn't find my favorite jeans so I had to settle for my second favorite.

As I'm rinsing my cereal bowl, I look out the window and see Kitty's school bus drive by. "You missed the bus!" I yell upstairs.

No reply.

I stuff my lunch in my bag and call out, "If you're coming with me, you'd better hustle! Bye, Daddy!"

I'm putting on my shoes by the front door when Kitty shoots right past me and out the door, book bag bouncing against her shoulder. I follow after her and close the door behind me. And there, across the street, leaning against his black Audi, is Peter. He grins broadly at Kitty, and I stand there just completely blindsided. My first thought is, *Is he here to see me?* No, couldn't be. My second thought is, *Could this be a trap?* My eyes dart around, looking for any sign of

Genevieve. There is none, and I feel guilty for thinking he could ever be that cruel.

Kitty waves madly and runs up to him. "Hi!"

"Ready to go, kid?" he asks her.

"Yup." She turns back to look at me. "Lara Jean, you can come with us. I'll sit in your lap."

Peter is looking at his phone, and what little hope I had that maybe he partly came to see me is dashed. "No, that's okay," I say. "There's only room for two."

He opens the passenger-side door for her, and Kitty scrambles in. "Go fast," she tells him.

He barely spares me a glance before they're gone. Well. I suppose that's that, then.

"What kind of cake are you making me?" Kitty sits on a stool and watches me. I'm baking the cake tonight so it's all set for tomorrow's party. I've got it in my head that Kitty's slumber party has to be just the best night ever, partly because the party is so belated and should therefore be worth the wait, and partly because ten is a big year in a girl's life. Kitty may not have a mom, but she will have a spectacular birthday sleepover if I've got anything to do with it.

"I told you, it's a surprise." I dump my premeasured flour into a mixing bowl. "So how was your day?"

"Good. I got an A-minus on my math quiz."

"Oh, yay! Anything else cool happen?"

Kitty shrugs her shoulders. "I think Ms. Bertoli

accidentally farted when she was taking attendance. Everybody laughed."

Baking powder, salt. "Cool, cool. Did, um, Peter drive you straight to school, or did you stop somewhere along the way?"

"He took me to get donuts."

I bite my lip. "That's nice. Did he say anything?"

"About what?"

"I don't know. Life."

Kitty rolls her eyes. "He didn't say anything about you, if that's what you're wondering about."

This stings. "I wasn't wondering about that at all," I lie.

Kitty and I have the whole sleepover planned down to a T. Zombie makeovers. Photo booth with props. Nail art.

I chose Kitty's cake with utmost care. It's chocolate with raspberry jam and white chocolate frosting. I've made three different kinds of dips. Sour cream and onion, red pepper hummus, and cold spinach dip. Crudités. Pigs in a blanket. Salty caramel popcorn for the movie. Lime sherbet punch, the kind you pour ginger ale over. I even scrounged up an old glass punch bowl in the attic, which will also be perfect for the USO theme party. For breakfast in the morning I'm making chocolate chip pancakes. I know all of these details are important to Kitty, too. Already she's mentioned to me that at Brielle's birthday, her mom made strawberry smoothies for their snack, and who could forget how Alicia Bernard's mom made crepes when she's mentioning it all the time?

Daddy's banished to his room for the night, which he looks relieved about—but not before I made him drag down the little vintage chest of drawers I have in my room. I artfully arrange my collection of nightgowns and pj's and footie long underwear, plus fuzzy slippers. Between Kitty, Margot, and me, we have a lot of fuzzy slippers.

Everyone changes into pajamas right away, giggling and screaming and fighting over who gets what.

I am wearing a pale pink peignoir set I got from a thrift store brand-new with the tags still on. I feel like Doris Day in *The Pajama Game*. The only thing I'm missing are furry slippers with a kitten heel. I tried to convince Kitty that we should have an old movie night, but she shot that idea down right away. To be funny, I put my hair in rollers. I offer to put the girls' hair in rollers too, but everyone shrieks and says no.

They're so loud I keep having to say, "Girls, girls!"

Halfway into the mani session I notice that Kitty is hanging back. I thought she'd be in her element, belle of the birthday ball, but she's ill at ease and playing with Jamie.

When all the girls run upstairs to my room to do the mud packs I've prepared, I grab Kitty's elbow. "Are you having fun?" I ask. She nods and tries to dart away, but I give her stern eyes. "Sister swear?"

Kitty hesitates. "Shanae's gotten really good friends with Sophie," she says, her eyes welling up. "Like better friends than me and her. Did you see how they did matching manicures? They didn't ask me if I wanted to do matching manicures."

"I don't think they meant to leave you out," I say.

She shrugs her bony shoulders.

I put my arm around her, and she just stands there stiffly, so I push her head down on my shoulder. "It can be tough with best friendships. You're both growing and changing, and it's hard to grow and change at the same rate."

Her head pops up, and I push it back down on my shoulder. "Is that what happened with you and Genevieve?" she asks.

"Honestly, I don't know what happened with me and Genevieve. She moved away, and we were still friends, and then we weren't." I realize belatedly that it's not the most comforting thing to say to someone who's feeling left out by her friends. "But I'm sure that will never happen to you."

Kitty lets out a defeated little sigh. "Why can't things just stay the same as before?"

"Then nothing would ever change and you wouldn't grow up; you would have stayed nine forever and never have turned ten."

She wipes her nose with the back of her arm. "I might not mind that."

"Then you'd never get to drive, or go to college, or buy a house and adopt a bunch of dogs. I know you want to do all that stuff. You have an adventurous spirit, and being a kid can get in the way of that, because you have to get other people's permission. When you're older, you can do what you want and you won't have to ask anybody."

Sighing she says, "Yeah, that's true."

I smooth her hair away from her forehead. "Want me to put on a movie for you guys?"

"A horror one?"

"Sure."

She's perking up, going into bargaining mode like the business lady she is. "It has to be rated R. No kid stuff."

"Fine, but if you guys get scared, you aren't sleeping with me in my room. Last time you guys kept me up all night. And if any parents call to complain, I'm telling them you guys snuck the movie on your own."

"No problem."

I watch her fly up the stairs. Impossible as she is, I like Kitty just as she is. I wouldn't have minded if she'd stayed nine forever. Kitty's cares are still manageable; they can fit in the palm of my hand. I like that she still depends on me for things. Her cares and her needs make me forget my own. I like that I am needed, that I am beholden to some-body. This breakup with Peter, it's not as big as Katherine Song Covey turning ten. She has sprung up like a weed, without a mother, just two sisters and a dad. That is no small feat. That's something extraordinary.

But ten, wow. Ten isn't a little girl anymore. It's right in between. The thought of her getting older, outgrowing her toys, her art set . . . it makes me feel a bit melancholy. Growing up really is bittersweet.

My phone buzzes, and it's a pitiful text from Daddy:

```
Is it safe to come downstairs? I'm so
thirsty.

Coast is clear.

Roger that.
```

# 47

FOLLOWING GENEVIEVE AROUND IS A
strangely familiar feeling. Nothing little observations come
flooding back. It's a heady combination of the things I used
to know about her and the things I don't. She goes through
the drive-thru at Wendy's, and without even looking, I know
what's in the bag. Small Frosty, small fries to dip, six-piece
chicken nuggets, also to dip.

John and I follow Genevieve around town for a bit, but
we lose her at a stoplight so we just head over to Belleview.
There's a USO party planning meeting I have to get to. With
the party so close, we're all doubling our efforts to have everything ready in time. Belleview has become my solace, my safe
place throughout all this. In part because Genevieve doesn't
know about it, so she can't tag me out, but also because it's
the one place I won't run into her and Peter, free to do whatever they want together now that he's single again.

It starts snowing at the beginning of our meeting.
Everyone crowds around the windows to look, shaking their
heads and saying, "Snow in April! Can you believe it?" and
then we go back to work on USO decorations. John helps
with the banner.

By the time we're done, there are a few inches of snow
on the ground, and the snow has turned to ice. "Johnny,

you can't drive in this weather. I absolutely forbid it," Stormy says.

"Grandma, it'll be fine," John says. "I'm a good driver."

Stormy delivers a stinging smack on his arm. "I told you never to call me Grandma! Just Stormy. The answer is no. I'm putting my foot down. The both of you will stay at Belleview tonight. It's far too dangerous." She sends me a stern look. "Lara Jean, you call your father right now and tell him I won't allow you out in this weather."

"He can come get us," I suggest.

"And have that poor widower get into a car accident on the way here? No. I won't have it. Give me your phone. I'll call him myself."

"But—there's school tomorrow," I say.

"Cancelled," Stormy says with a smile. "They just announced it on the TV."

I protest, "I don't have any of my things! No toothbrush, or pajamas, or anything!"

She puts her arm around me. "Lie back and let Stormy take care of everything. Don't you worry your pretty little head."

So that is how it came to be that John Ambrose McClaren and I are spending the night together at a retirement home.

A snowstorm in April is a magical thing. Even if it is because of climate change. A few pink flowers have already sprouted in the gardens outside Stormy's living room window, and snow is shaking down on it hard, the way Kitty shakes powdered sugar on pancakes—fast and a lot. Soon you can't even see the pink of the flowers; it's all just covered in white.

We're playing checkers in Stormy's living room, the big kind of checkers you can buy at Cracker Barrel. John has beaten me twice and he keeps asking me if I'm hustling him. I'm coy about it, but the answer is no, he's just better than me at checkers. Stormy serves us piña coladas that she mixes in her blender with "just a splash of rum to warm us up," and she microwaves frozen spanakopita that neither of us touches. Bing Crosby is playing on her stereo. By nine thirty Stormy is yawning and saying she'll need her beauty sleep soon. John and I exchange a look—it's still so early, and I don't know the last time I went to bed before midnight.

Stormy insists I stay with her and John stay with Mr. Morales in his spare bedroom. I can tell John isn't crazy about this idea, because he asks, "Can't I just sleep on your floor?"

I'm surprised when Stormy shakes her head. "I hardly think Lara Jean's father would appreciate that!"

"I really don't think my dad would mind, Stormy," I say. "I could call him if you want."

But the answer is a firm and resounding no: John must bunk with Mr. Morales. For a lady who's always telling me to be wild and have adventures and bring the condom, she's far more old-fashioned than I thought.

Stormy hands John a face towel and a pair of foam earplugs. "Mr. Morales snores," she tells him as she kisses him good night.

John raises an eyebrow at her. "How do you know?"

"Wouldn't you like to know!" She shimmies off into the kitchen like the grand dame she truly is.

In a low voice John says to me, "You know what? I really, really wouldn't."

I bite the cushiony part of my cheek to keep from laughing.

"Keep your phone on vibrate," John says before he goes out the door. "I'll text you."

I hear the sound of Stormy snoring and the whispery sound of icy snowflakes hitting the windowsill. I keep getting twisted up in Stormy's sleeping bag, twisted and hot and wishing Stormy didn't have the heat turned up so high. Old people are always complaining about how cold it is at Belleview, how the heat is "piss-poor," as Danny in the Azalea building says. Feels plenty hot to me. Stormy's peach high-neck satin nightgown she insisted I wear isn't helping matters. I'm lying on my side, playing Candy Crush on my phone, wondering when John will hurry up and text me.

Wanna play in the snow?

I text back right away:

YES! It's really hot in here.

Meet me in the hallway in two min?

K.

I stand up so fast in my sleeping bag I nearly trip. I use my phone to find my coat, my boots. Stormy is snoring away. I can't find my scarf, but I don't want to keep John waiting, so I run out without it.

He's already in the hallway waiting for me. His hair is sticking up in the back, and on that basis alone I think I could fall in love with him if I let myself. When he sees me, he holds his arms out and sings, "Do you want to build a snowman?" and I burst out laughing so hard John says, "Shh, you're going to wake up the residents!" which only makes me laugh harder. "It's only ten thirty!"

We run down the long carpeted hallway, both of us laughing as quietly as we can. But the more you try to laugh quietly, the harder it is to stop. "I can't stop laughing," I gasp as we run through the sliding doors and to the courtyard.

We're both out of breath; we both stop short.

The ground is blanketed in thick white snow, thick as sheep's wool. It's so beautiful and hushed, my heart almost hurts with the pleasure of it. I'm so happy in this moment, and I realize it's because I haven't thought of Peter once. I turn to look at John, and he's already looking at me with a half smile on his face. It gives me a nervous flutter in my chest.

I spin around in a circle and sing, "Do you want to build a snowman?" And then we're both giggling again.

"You're going to get us kicked out of here," he warns.

I grab his hands and make him spin around with me as fast as I can. "Quit acting like you really belong in a nursing home, old man!" I yell.

He drops my hands and we both stumble. Then he grabs a fistful of snow off the ground and starts to pack it into a ball. "Old man, huh? I'll show you an old man!"

I dart away from him, slipping and sliding in the snow. "Don't you dare, John Ambrose McClaren!"

He chases after me, laughing and breathing hard. He manages to grab me around the waist and raises his arm like he's going to put the snowball down my back, but at the last second he releases me. His eyes go wide. "Oh my God. Are you wearing my grandma's nightgown under your coat?"

Giggling, I say, "Wanna see? It's really racy." I start to unzip my coat. "Wait, turn around first."

Shaking his head, John says, "This is weird," but he obeys. As soon as his back is turned, I snatch a handful of snow, form it into a ball, and put it in my coat pocket.

"Okay, turn around."

John turns, and I lob the snowball directly at his head. It hits him in the eye. "Ouch!" he yelps, wiping it with his coat sleeve.

I gasp and move toward him. "Oh my God. I'm so sorry. Are you okay—"

John's already scooping up more snow and lunging toward me. And so begins our snowball fight. We chase each other around, and I get in another great hit square in his back. We call a truce when I nearly slip and fall on my butt. Luckily, John catches me just in time. He doesn't let go right away. We stare at each other for a second, his arm around my waist. There's a snowflake on his eyelashes. He says, "If I didn't know you were still hung up on Kavinsky, I would kiss you right now."

I shiver. Up until Peter, the most romantic thing that ever happened to me was with John Ambrose McClaren, in the rain, with the soccer balls. Now this. How strange that I've never even dated John, and he's in two of my most romantic moments.

John releases me. "You're freezing. Let's go back inside."

We go to the parlor on Stormy's floor to sit and thaw out. There's only one reading light on, so it's dim and quiet. All the residents are in their apartments for the night, it seems. It feels strange to be here without Stormy and everyone, like being at school at night. We sit on the fancy French-style couch, and I take off my boots so my feet can get warm. I wriggle my toes to get the feeling back.

"Too bad we can't start a fire," John says, stretching his arms and looking at the fireplace.

"Yeah, it's fake," I say. "There must be some sort of nursing-home law about fireplaces, I bet. . . ." My voice trails off as I see Stormy, in her silky kimono, tiptoeing out of her apartment and down the hall. To Mr. Morales's apartment. Oh my God.

"What?" John asks, and I slap my hand over his mouth. I duck down low in my seat and slide all the way off the couch to the floor. I pull him down next to me. We stay down until I hear the door click closed. He whispers, "What is it? What did you see?"

Sitting up, I whisper back, "I don't know if you want to know."

"Dear God. What? Just tell me."

"I saw Stormy in her red kimono, sneaking into Mr. Morales's apartment."

John chokes. "Oh my God. That's . . ."

I give him sympathetic eyes. "I know. Sorry."

Shaking his head, he leans back against the couch, his legs stretched out long in front of him. "Wow. This is rich. My great-grandmother has a way more active sex life than I do."

I can't resist asking, "So then . . . I guess, have you not had sex with that many girls?" Hastily I say, "Sorry, I'm a very inquisitive person." I scratch my cheek. "Some might say nosy. You don't have to answer if you don't want to."

"No, I'll answer. I've never had sex with anybody."

"What!" I can't believe it. How can that be?

"Why are you so shocked?"

"I don't know, I guess I thought all guys were doing it."

"Well, I've only had one girlfriend, and she was religious, so we never did it, which was fine. Anyway, trust me, not all guys are having sex. I'd say the majority aren't." John pauses. "What about you?"

"I've never done it either," I say.

He frowns, confused. "Wait, I thought you and Kavinsky . . ."

"No. Why would you think that?" Oh. The video. I swallow. I thought maybe he was the one person who hadn't seen it. "So you've seen the hot tub video, huh."

John hesitates and then, says, "Yeah. I didn't know it was you at first, not until after the time capsule party when I figured out you guys were together. Some guy showed it to me in homeroom, but I didn't look at it that closely."

"We were just kissing," I say, ducking my head. "I wish you hadn't seen it."

"Why? Honestly, it doesn't matter to me at all."

"I guess I liked the thought of you looking at me a certain kind of way. I feel like people see me differently now, but you still thought of me as the old Lara Jean. Do you know what I mean?"

"That *is* how I see you," John says. "You're still the same to me. I'll always see you that way, Lara Jean."

His words, the way he is looking at me—it makes me feel warm inside, golden, all the way to my frozen toes. I want him to kiss me. I want to see if it's different from Peter, if it will make the hurt recede. Make me forget him, just for a while. But maybe he senses it—that Peter is somehow here with us, in my thoughts, that it wouldn't just be about him and me— because John doesn't make a move.

Instead he asks a question. "Why do you always call me by my full name?"

"I don't know. I guess that's how I think of you in my head."

"Oh, so you're saying you think about me a lot?"

I laugh. "No, I'm saying that when I think about you, which isn't very often, that's how I think of you. On the first day of school, I always have to explain to teachers that Lara Jean is my first name and not just Lara. And then, do you remember how Mr. Chudney started calling you John Ambrose because of that? 'Mr. John Ambrose.'"

In a fake hoity-toity English accent, John says, "Mr. John Ambrose McClaren the Third, madam."

I giggle. I've never met a third before. "Are you really?"

"Yeah. It's annoying. My dad's a junior, so he's JJ, but my extended family still calls me Little John." He grimaces. "I'd much rather be John Ambrose than Little John. Sounds like a rapper or that guy from *Robin Hood*."

"Your family's so fancy." I only ever saw John's mom when she was picking him up. She looked younger than the other mothers, she had John's same milky skin, and her hair was longer than the other moms', straw-colored.

"No. My family isn't fancy at all. My mom made Jell-O salad last night for dessert. And, like, my dad only has steak cooked well-done. We only ever take vacations we can drive to."

"I thought your family was kind of . . . well, rich." I feel immediate shame for saying "rich." It's tacky to talk about other people's money.

"My dad's really cheap. His construction company is pretty successful, but he prides himself on being a self-made man. He didn't go to college; neither did my grandparents. My sisters were the first in our family."

"I didn't know that about you," I say. All these new things I'm learning about John Ambrose McClaren!

"Now it's your turn to tell me something I don't know about you," John says.

I laugh. "You already know more than most people. My love letter made sure of that."

The next morning, I sneeze as I'm putting on my coat, and Stormy raises one pencil-drawn eyebrow at me. "Catch a cold playing in the snow last night with Johnny?"

I squirm. I'd hoped she wouldn't bring it up. The last thing I want to do is discuss her midnight rendezvous with Mr. Morales! We watched Stormy go back to her apartment and then waited half an hour before John went back to Mr. Morales's. Weakly, I say, "Sorry we snuck out. It was so early, and we couldn't fall asleep, so we thought we'd play in the snow."

Stormy waves a hand. "It's exactly what I hoped would happen." She winks at me. "That's why I made Johnny stay with Mr. Morales, of course. What's the fun in anything if there aren't a few roadblocks to spice things up?"

In awe, I say, "You're so crafty!"

"Thank you, darling." She's quite pleased with herself. "You know, he'd make a great first husband, my Johnny. So, did you French him, at least?"

My face burns. "No!"

"You can tell me, honey."

"Stormy, we didn't kiss, and even if we had, I wouldn't discuss it with you."

Stormy's nose goes thin and haughty. "Well, isn't that so very selfish of you!"

"I have to go, Stormy. My dad's waiting for me out front. See you!"

As I hurry out the door, she calls out, "Don't you worry, I'll get it out of Johnny! See you both at the party, Lara Jean!"

When I step outside, the sun is shining bright and much of the snow has already melted away. It's almost like last night was a dream.

# 48

*THE NIGHT BEFORE THE USO PARTY, I CALL*
Chris on speakerphone as I'm rolling a log of shortbread
dough in sage sugar. "Chris, can I borrow your Rosie the
Riveter poster?"

"You can have it but what do you want it for?"

"For the 1940s USO party I'm throwing at Belleview
tomorrow—"

"Stop, I'm bored. God, all you ever talk about is Belleview!"

"It's my job!"

"Ooh, should I get a job?"

I roll my eyes. Every conversation we have turns back to
Chris and the concerns of Chris. "Hey, speaking of fun jobs
for you, what do you think about being a cigar girl for the
party? You could wear a cute outfit with a little hat."

"Real cigars?"

"No, chocolate ones. Cigars are bad for old people."

"Will there be booze?"

I'm about to say yes, but only for the residents, but I think
better of it. "I don't think so. It could be a dangerous combination with their medications and their walkers."

"When is it again?"

"Tomorrow!"

"Oh, sorry. I can't give up a Friday night for this. Something better will definitely come up on a Friday. A Tuesday, maybe. Can you change it to next Tuesday?"

"No! Can you just please bring the poster to school tomorrow?"

"Yeah, but you have to text me with a reminder."

"'Kay." I blow my hair out of my face and start slicing the cookie roll. I still have to chop carrots and celery for the crudités and also pipe my meringues. I'm doing red-white-and-blue-striped meringue kisses, and I'm nervous about the colors blending together. Oh well. If they do, then people will just have to live with purple meringue kisses. There are worse things. Speaking of worse things . . . "Have you heard anything from Gen? I've been so careful, but it seems like she's barely playing." There's silence on the other end.

"She's probably too busy doing sex voodoo on Peter," I say, half-hoping Chris will chime in. She's always the first in line to rip on Gen.

But she doesn't. All she says is "I've gotta go—my mom's bitching at me to take out the dog."

"Don't forget the poster!"

# 49

AFTER SCHOOL KITTY AND I SET UP CAMP IN the kitchen, where there's the best light. I bring down my speakers and play the Andrews Sisters to get us in the right spirit. Kitty puts down a towel and lays out all my makeup, bobby pins, hair spray.

I hold up a packet of individual false eyelashes. "Where'd you get these from?"

"Brielle stole them from her sister and she gave me a pack."

"Kitty!"

"She won't notice. She has tons!"

"You can't just take people's stuff."

"I didn't take it—Brielle did. Anyway, I can't give it back now. Do you want me to put them on you or not?"

I hesitate. "Do you even know how?"

"Yeah, I've watched her sister put them on plenty of times." Kitty takes the eyelashes out of my hand. "If you don't want me to use them on you, fine. I'll save them for myself."

"Well . . . all right then. But no more stealing." I frown. "Hey, do you guys ever take my stuff?" Come to think of it, I haven't seen my cat-ears knit beanie in months.

"Shh, no more talking," she says.

The hair is what takes the longest. Kitty and I have watched countless hair tutorials to figure out the logistics of the victory rolls. There's a lot of teasing and hair spray and hair rollers involved. And bobby pins. Lots of bobby pins.

I stare at myself in the mirror. "Don't you think my hair looks a little . . . severe?"

"What do you mean, 'severe'?"

"It kind of looks like I have a cinnamon bun on top of my head."

Kitty thrusts the iPad in my face. "Yeah, so does this girl's. That's the look. It's got to be authentic. If we water down the look, it won't be true to the theme, and nobody will know what you're supposed to be." I'm nodding slowly; she has a point. "Besides, I'm going over to Ms. Rothschild's for a Jamie training session. I don't have time to start all over again."

For my lipstick, we achieve the perfect shade of cherry red by blending two different reds—one brick and one fire engine—with a hot pink powder to set it. I look like I kissed a cherry pie.

I'm blotting my lips when Kitty asks, "Is that pretty boy John Amber McAndrews picking you up, or are you meeting him at the nursing home?"

I wave my tissue in her face warningly. "He's picking me up, and you'd better be nice. Also he's not a pretty boy."

"He's a pretty boy compared to Peter," Kitty says.

"Let's be honest. They're both pretty. It's not like Peter has a tattoo or huge muscles. In fact he's very vain." We never passed a window or a glass door Peter didn't check himself out in.

"Well, is John vain?"

"No, I don't think so."

"Hmph."

"Kitty, stop making this a competition of John versus Peter. It doesn't matter who's prettier."

Kitty keeps going like she didn't hear me. "Peter has a much nicer car. What does Johnny boy drive, a boring SUV? Who cares about an SUV? All they do is guzzle gas."

"To be fair, I think it's a hybrid."

"You sure like to defend him."

"He's my friend!"

"Well, Peter's mine," she says.

Getting dressed is an intricate process, and I enjoy each step. It's all about anticipation, hope for the night. Slowly I put on the seamed stockings so I don't get a run in them. It takes me forever to get the seams straight down the backs of my legs. Then the dress—navy with white sprigs and little holly berries and floaty cap sleeves. Last the shoes. Clunky red heels with a bow at the toe and an ankle strap.

Put all together, it goes great, and I have to admit that Kitty was right about the victory roll on top of my head. Anything less wouldn't be enough.

On my way out Daddy makes a big fuss over how great I look, and he takes about a million photos, which he promptly texts Margot. She immediately video-chats us so she can see for herself. "Make sure you get a picture of you and Stormy together," Margot says. "I want to see what sexy getup she's wearing."

"It's actually not that sexy," I say. "She sewed it herself, off a 1940s dress pattern."

"I'm sure she'll find a way to bring the sexy," Margot says. "What's John McClaren wearing?"

"I have no idea. He says it's a surprise."

"Hmm," she says. It's a very suggestive *hmm*, which I ignore.

Daddy's taking one last shot of me on the front porch when Ms. Rothschild comes over. "You look amazing, Lara Jean," she says.

"She does, doesn't she?" Daddy says fondly.

"God, I love the forties," she says.

"Have you seen the Ken Burns documentary *The War*?" Daddy asks her. "If you have any interest in World War Two, it's a must-see."

"You should watch it together," Kitty pipes up, and Ms. Rothschild shoots her a warning look.

"Do you have it on DVD?" she asks Daddy. Kitty is aglow with excitement.

"Sure, you can borrow it anytime," Daddy says, oblivious as ever, and Kitty scowls, and then her mouth falls open.

I turn to see what she's looking at, and it's a red convertible

Mustang driving down our street, top down—with John McClaren at the wheel.

My jaw drops at the sight of him. He is in full uniform: tan dress shirt with tan tie, tan slacks, tan belt and hat. His hair is parted to the side. He looks dashing, like a real soldier. He grins at me and waves. "Whoa," I breathe.

"Whoa is right," Ms. Rothschild says, googly-eyed beside me. Daddy and his Ken Burns DVD are forgotten; we are all staring at John in this uniform, in this car. It's like I dreamed him up. He parks the car in front of the house, and all of us rush up to it.

"Whose car is this?" Kitty demands.

"It's my dad's," John says. "I borrowed it. I had to promise to park really far away from any other car, though, so I hope your shoes are comfortable, Lara Jean—" He breaks off and looks me up and down. "Wow. You look amazing." He gestures at my cinnamon bun. "I mean, your hair looks so . . . real."

"It is real!" I touch it gingerly, I'm suddenly feeling self-conscious about my cinnamon-bun head and red lipstick.

"I know—I mean, it looks authentic."

"So do you," I say.

"Can I sit in it?" Kitty butts in, her hand on the passenger-side door.

"Sure," John says. He climbs out of the car. "But don't you want to get in the driver's seat?"

Kitty nods quickly. Ms. Rothschild gets in too, and Daddy takes a picture of them together. Kitty poses with one arm casually draped over the steering wheel.

John and I stand off to the side, and I ask him, "Where did you ever get that uniform?"

"I ordered it off of eBay." He frowns. "Am I wearing the hat right? Do you think it's too small for my head?"

"No way. I think it looks exactly the way it's supposed to look." I'm touched that he went to the trouble of ordering a uniform for this. I can't think of many boys who would do that. "Stormy is going to flip out when she sees you."

He studies my face. "What about you? Do you like it?"

I flush. "I do. I think you look . . . super."

It turns out that Margot is, as ever, right. Stormy has shortened the hem on the dress; it's well above the knee. "I've still got the gams," she gloats, twirling. "My best feature, from all the horseback riding I did as a girl." She's showing a little cleavage, too.

A silver-haired man who rode over in the van from Ferncliff is making appreciative eyes at her, and Stormy is pretending not to notice, all the while batting her lashes and preening with one hand on her hip. He must be the handsome man Stormy mentioned to me.

I take a picture of her at the piano and send it directly to Margot, who texts back a smiling emoji and two thumbs up.

I'm setting up the American flag centerpiece, watching John lug a table closer to the center of the room at Stormy's direction, when Alicia sidles up beside me, and then we're both watching him. "You should date him."

"Alicia, I told you, I just got out of a relationship," I whisper back. I can't take my eyes off him in that uniform with that side part.

"Well, get into a new one. Life is short." For once, Alicia and Stormy are on the same page.

Stormy is now straightening John's tie, his little hat. She even licks her finger and tries to smooth his hair, but he ducks away. Our eyes meet, and he makes a frantic face like, *Help me.*

"Save him," Alicia says. "I'll finish the table. My internment camp display is already done." She's set that up by the doors, so it's the first thing you see when you walk in.

I hurry over to John and Stormy. Stormy beams at me. "Doesn't she look like an absolute *doll?*" She swans off.

With a straight face John says, "Lara Jean, you're an absolute *doll.*"

I giggle and touch the top of my head. "A cinnamon roll–headed doll."

People are starting to mill in, even though it isn't seven yet. I've observed that old people, as a rule, tend to show up early for things. I still have to set up the music. Stormy says that when hosting a party, music is absolutely the first order of business, because it sets the mood the second your guest walks in. I can feel my nerves starting to pulse. There's still so much to do. "I'd better finish setting up."

"Tell me what you need done," John says. "I'm your second-in-command at this shindig. Did people say 'shindig' in the forties?"

I laugh. "Probably!" In a rush I say, "Okay, can you set up my speakers and iPod? They're in the bag by the refreshments table. And can you pick up Mrs. Taylor in 5A? I promised her an escort."

John gives me a salute and runs off. Tingles go up and down my spine like soda water. Tonight will be a night to remember!

We're an hour and a half in, and Crystal Clemons, a lady from Stormy's floor, is leading everyone in a swing-dancing lesson. Of course Stormy is up front, rock-stepping for all she's worth. I'm following along from the refreshments table: one-two, three-four, five-six. Early on I danced with Mr. Morales, but only once, because the women were cutting their eyes at me for taking an eligible, able-bodied man off the circuit. Men are in short supply at old-age homes, so there aren't enough male dance partners, not enough by half. I've heard a few of the women whispering how rude it is for a gentleman not to dance when there are ladies without partners—and looking pointedly at poor John.

John is standing at the other end of the table, drinking Coke and nodding his head to the beat. I've been so busy running around, we've hardly had a chance to talk. I lean over the table and call out, "Having fun?"

He nods. Then, quite suddenly, he bangs his glass down on the table, so hard the table shakes and I jump. "All right," he says. "It's do or die. D-day."

"What?"

"Let's dance," John says.

Shyly I say, "We don't have to if you don't want to, John."

"No, I want to. I didn't take swing-dancing lessons from Stormy for nothing."

I widen my eyes. "When did you take swing dance lessons from Stormy?"

"Don't worry about it," he says. "Just dance with me."

"Well . . . do you have any war bonds left?" I joke.

John fishes one out of his pants pocket and slaps it on the refreshments table. Then he grabs my hand and marches me to the center of the dance floor, like a soldier heading off to the battlefield. He's all grim concentration. He signals to Mr. Morales, who is manning the music because he's the only one who can figure out my phone. Glenn Miller's "In the Mood" comes blaring out of the speakers.

John gives me a determined nod. "Let's do this."

And then we're dancing. Rock-step, side, together, side, repeat. Rock-step, one-two-three, one-two-three. We step on each other's feet about a million times, but he's swinging me around—twirl, twirl—and our faces are flushed and we're both laughing. When the song is over, he pulls me in and then throws me back out one last time. Everyone is clapping. Mr. Morales screams, "To the young ones!"

John picks me up and lifts me into the air like we're ice dancers, and the crowd erupts. I'm smiling so hard my face feels like it could break.

After, John helps me take down all the decorations and pack everything up. He goes out to the parking lot with the two big boxes, and I stay behind to say good-bye to everyone and make sure we have everything. I still feel sort of a high from the night. The party went so well, and Janette was so pleased. She came up and squeezed my shoulders and said, "I'm proud of you, Lara Jean." And then the dance with John . . . Thirteen-year-old me would have *died*. Sixteen-year-old me is floating down the nursing-home hallway, and it's like I'm in a dream.

I'm floating out the front entrance when I see Genevieve and Peter walking up, her arm linked in his, and it's like we're in a time machine and the past year never happened. *We* never happened.

They're coming closer. Now they are about ten feet away, and I am frozen to this spot. Is there no way out of this? Out of this humiliation, and out of losing yet again? I got so caught up in the USO party and John that I forgot all about the game. What are my options here? If I turn and run back into the nursing home, she'll just wait in the parking lot for me all night. Just like that, I am a rabbit under her paw again. Just like that, she wins.

And then it's too late. They've spotted me. Peter drops Genevieve's arm.

"What are you doing here?" he asks me. "And what's with all the makeup?" He gestures at my eyes, my lips.

My cheeks burn. I ignore the comment about my makeup and just say, "I work here, remember? I know why you're here, Genevieve. Peter, thanks a lot for helping her take me out. You're a real stand-up guy."

"Covey, I didn't come here to help her tag you out. I

didn't even know you'd be here. I told you, I don't give a shit about this game!" He turns to Genevieve. Accusingly he says, "You said you needed to pick something up from your grandma's friend."

"I do," she says. "This is just an amazing coincidence. I guess I win, huh?"

She's so smug, so sure of herself and her victory over me. "You haven't tagged me yet." Should I just make a run for it back inside? Stormy would let me spend the night if I needed to.

Just then, John's red Mustang convertible comes roaring up through the parking lot. "Hey, guys," he says, and Peter's and Gen's mouths drop. It's only then that I think of how strange we must look together, John in his World War II uniform with his jaunty little hat, me with my victory roll and my red lipstick.

Peter eyes him. "What are *you* doing here?"

Blithely John says, "My great-grandmother lives here. Stormy. You may have heard of her. She's a friend of Lara Jean's."

"I'm sure he wouldn't remember," I say.

Peter frowns at me, and I know he doesn't. It's just like him not to. "What's with the outfits?" he says, his voice gruff.

"USO party," John says. "Very exclusive. VIPs only—sorry, guys." Then he tips his hat at him, which I can tell makes Peter mad, which in turn makes me glad.

"What the hell is a USO party?" Peter asks me.

John stretches his arm out onto the passenger seat luxuriously. "It's from World War Two."

"I wasn't asking you; I was asking her," Peter snaps. He looks at me, his eyes hard. "Is this a *date*? Are you on a *date* with him? And who the hell's car is this?"

Before I can answer, Genevieve makes a move toward me, which I dodge. I run behind the pillar. "Don't be such a baby, Lara Jean," she says. "Just accept that you lose and I win!"

I peek from behind the pillar, and John is giving me a look—a look that says, *Get in*. Quickly I nod. Then he throws open the passenger door, and I run for it, as fast as I can. I've barely got the door closed before he's driving off, Peter and Gen in our dust.

I turn back to look. Peter is staring after us, his mouth open. He's jealous, and I'm glad. "Thanks for the save," I say, still trying to catch my breath. My heart is pounding in my chest so hard.

John is looking straight ahead, a broad smile on his face. "Anytime."

We stop at a stoplight, and he turns his head and looks at me, and then we're looking at each other, laughing like crazy, and I'm breathless again.

"Did you see the looks on their faces?" John gasps, dropping his head on the steering wheel.

"It was classic!"

"Like a movie!" He grins at me, jubilant, blue eyes alight.

"Just like a movie," I agree, leaning my head back against the seat and opening my eyes wide up at the moon, so wide it hurts. I'm in a red Mustang convertible sitting next to a boy in uniform, and the night air feels like cool satin on my skin, and all the stars are out, and I'm happy. The way John is still grinning to himself, I know he is too. We got to play make-believe for the night. Forget Peter and Genevieve. The light turns green, and I throw my arms in the air. "Go fast, Johnny!" I shout, and he guns it and I let out a shriek.

We zoom around for a bit, and at the next stoplight he slows and puts his arm around me, pulling me closer to his side. "Isn't this how they did it in the fifties?" he asks, one hand on the steering wheel and the other around my shoulders.

My heart rate picks back up again. "Well, technically we're dressed for the forties—" and then he kisses me. His lips are warm and firm against mine, and my eyes flutter shut.

When he pulls away just a fraction, he looks down at me and says, half serious, half not, "Better than the first time?"

I'm dazed. He's got some of my lipstick on his face now. I reach up and wipe his mouth. The light turns green; we don't move; he's still looking at me. Someone honks a horn behind us. "The light's green."

He doesn't make a move; he's still looking at me. "Answer first."

"Better." John pushes his foot on the gas, and we're moving again. I'm still breathless. Into the wind I shout, "One day I want to see you make a Model UN speech!"

John laughs. "What? Why?"

"I think it would be something to see. I bet you'd be . . . grand. You know, out of all of us, I think you've changed the most."

"How?"

"You used to be sort of quiet. In your own head. Now you're so confident."

"I still get nervous, Lara Jean." John has a cowlick, a little piece of hair that won't stay down; it is stubborn. It's this piece more than anything else that makes my heart squeeze.

# 50

AFTER JOHN DROPS ME OFF AT HOME, I RUN
across the street to pick up Kitty from Ms. Rothschild's. And
she invites me in for a cup of tea. Kitty is asleep on the
couch with the TV on low in the background. We settle on
the other couch with our cups of Lady Grey, and she asks
me how the party went. Maybe it's because I'm still on a
high from the night, or maybe it's the bobby pins so tight on
my head that I feel woozy, or it could be the way her eyes
light up with genuine interest as I begin to talk, but I tell her
everything. The dance with John, how everyone cheered,
Peter and Genevieve, even the kiss.

She starts fanning herself when I tell about the kiss.
"When that boy drove up in that uniform—ooh, girl." She
whistles. "It made me feel like a dirty old lady, because I
knew him when he was little. But *dear God* he is handsome!"

I giggle as I pull the bobby pins from the top of my head.
She leans forward and helps me along. My cinnamon bun
unravels, and my scalp tingles with relief. Is this what it's like
to have a mother? Late-night boy talk over tea?

Ms. Rothschild's voice gets low and confidential. "Here's
the thing. My one piece of advice to you. You have to let
yourself be fully present in every moment. Just be awake for

it, do you know what I mean? Go all in and wring every last drop out of the experience."

"So do you not have any regrets, then? Because you always went all in?" I'm thinking of her divorce, how it was the talk of the neighborhood.

"Oh God, no. I have regrets." She laughs a husky laugh, the sexy kind that only smokers or people with colds get to have. "I don't know why I'm sitting here trying to give you advice. I'm a single divorcée and I'm forty. Two. Forty-two. What do I know about anything? That's a rhetorical question, by the way." She lets out a sigh filled with longing. "I miss cigarettes so much."

"Kitty will check your breath," I warn, and she laughs that husky laugh again.

"I'm afraid to cross that girl."

"'Though she be but little, she is fierce,'" I intone. "You're wise to be afraid, Ms. Rothschild."

"Oh my God, Lara Jean, will you please just call me Trina? I mean, I know I'm old, but I'm not *that* old."

I hesitate. "Okay. Trina . . . do you like my dad?"

She goes a little red. "Um. Yeah, I think he's a great guy."

"To date?"

"Well, he's not my usual type. And also he hasn't shown any particular interest in me, either, so, ha-ha!"

"I'm sure you know Kitty's been trying to set you two up. Which, if that's unwelcome, I can definitely make her stop." I correct myself. "I can definitely try to make her stop. But I think she might be onto something. I think you and my dad could be good together. He loves to cook, and he likes to build fires, and he doesn't mind shopping because he brings a book. And you, you seem fun, and spontaneous and just really . . . light."

She smiles at me. "I'm a mess is what I am."

"Messiness can be good, especially for someone like my dad. It's worth a date, at least, don't you think? What's the harm in just seeing?"

"Dating neighbors is tricky. What if it doesn't work out and then we're stuck living across the street from each other?"

"That's a tiny inconsequential risk compared to what could be gained. If it doesn't work out, you wave politely when you see each other and then you keep on walking. No big deal. And I know I'm biased, but my dad is really worth it. He's the best."

"Oh, I know it. I see you girls and I think, God, any man who could raise those girls is something special. I've never seen a man so devoted to his family. You three are the pearls in his crown, you know? And that's how it should be. A girl's relationship with her father is the most important male relationship of her life."

"What about a girl's relationship with her mother?"

Ms. Rothschild tilts her head, contemplating. "Yeah, I would say a girl's relationship with her mom is the most important female relationship. Her mom or her sisters. You're lucky to have two of them. I know you know this already, better than most people, but your parents won't always be there. If it happens the way it's supposed to, they'll go first. But your sisters are yours for life."

"Do you have one?"

She nods, a hint of a smile forming on her tanned face. "I have a big sister. Jeanie. We didn't get along as well as you girls do, but as we get older, she looks more and more like our mom. And so when I'm missing my mom a lot, I go visit Jeanie and I get to see my mom's face again." She wrinkles her nose. "Does that sound creepy?"

"No. I think it sounds . . . lovely." I hesitate. "Sometimes when I hear Margot's voice—like, she's downstairs, and she calls us down to hurry up and get in the car, or she says that dinner's ready—sometimes she sounds so much like my mom, it tricks me. Just for a second." Tears spring to my eyes.

Ms. Rothschild has tears in her eyes too. "I don't think a girl ever gets over losing her mom. I'm an adult and it's completely normal and expected for my mom to be dead, but I still feel orphaned sometimes." She smiles at me. "But that's just inescapable, right? When you lose someone and it still hurts, that's when you know the love was real."

I wipe my eyes. With Peter and me, was the love real? Because it does hurt, it does. But maybe that's just part of it. Sniffling, I ask, "So, just to make sure, if my dad asks you out, you'll say yes?"

She roars with laughter, then claps her hand over her mouth when Kitty stirs on the couch. "Now I see where Kitty gets it from."

"Trina, you didn't answer the question."

"The answer is yes."

I smile to myself. Yes.

By the time I wash off all my makeup and get into my pajamas, it's nearly three in the morning. I'm not tired, though. What I really want to do is talk to Margot, go over every single detail of the night. Scotland is five hours ahead, which means it's almost eight a.m. over there. She's an early riser, so I figure it's worth a shot.

I catch her as she's getting ready to go have breakfast. She sets her computer on her dresser so we can talk as she puts on sunscreen and mascara and lip balm.

I tell her about the party, about Peter and Genevieve's appearance, and most importantly the kiss with John. "Margot, I think I could be a person who is in love with more than one person at a time." I might even be a girl that falls in love twelve *hundred* times. I get a sudden picture in my head of myself as a bee, sipping nectar from a daisy to a rose to a lily. Each boy sweet in his own way.

"You?" She stops putting her hair in a ponytail and taps her finger to the screen. "Lara Jean, I think you half-fall in love with every person you meet. It's part of your charm. You're in love with love."

This may be true. Perhaps I am in love with love! That doesn't seem like such a bad way to be.

# 51

OUR TOWN'S SPRING FAIR IS TOMORROW,
and Kitty has promised the PTA a cake for the cake walk
on my behalf. At a cake walk, music plays while kids walk
around a circle of numbers, like musical chairs. When the
music stops, a number is picked at random, and the kid standing in front of the corresponding number gets the cake. This
was always my favorite carnival game, of course, because I
liked looking at all of the homemade cakes and also for the
sheer luck of it. Certainly, the kids crowd around the cake
table and earmark the cake they most want and try to walk
slowly when they come upon the number, but beyond that
there isn't much to it. It's a game that does not require any
skill or know-how: You literally just walk around a circle to
old-timey music. Sure, you could go to the bakery and pick
out the exact cake you want, but there is a thrill in not being
sure what you'll end up with.

My cake will be chocolate, because kids and people in
general prefer chocolate to any other flavor. The frosting is
where I'll get fancy. Possibly salted caramel, or passion fruit,
or maybe a mocha whip. I've been toying with the idea of
doing an ombré cake, where the frosting goes from dark to
light. I have a feeling my cake will be in demand.

When I picked up Kitty from Shanae's house this

morning, I asked her mom what cake she was baking for the cake walk, because Mrs. Rodgers is vice president of the elementary school PTA. She heaved a sigh and said, "I'll be baking whatever Duncan Hines I can find in my pantry. Either that or Food Lion." Then she asked me what I was baking and I told her, and she said, "I'm voting you Teen Mom of the Year," which made me laugh and also further spurred me to bake the best cake so everyone knows what Kitty's working with. I never mentioned this to Daddy or Margot, but in middle school my English teacher sponsored a mother-daughter tea in honor of Mother's Day. It was after school, an optional thing, but I really wanted to go and have the tea sandwiches and scones she said she was bringing. It was just for mothers and daughters, though. I suppose I could have asked Grandma to come— Margot did that a few times for miscellaneous events—but it wouldn't have been the same. And I don't think it's the kind of thing that would bother Kitty, but it's still something I think about.

The cake walk is in the elementary school's music room. I've volunteered to be in charge of the walking music, and I've made a playlist with all sugar-related songs. Of course "Sugar, Sugar" by the Archies, "Sugar Shack," "Sugar Town," "I Can't Help Myself (Sugar Pie, Honey Bunch)." When I walk into the music room, Peter's mom and another mom are setting up the cakes. I falter, unsure of what to do.

She says, "Hello, Lara Jean," but her smile doesn't quite

reach her eyes, and it gives me a sinking feeling in my stomach. It's a relief when she leaves.

There's a decent crowd all day, with some people playing more than once for the cake of their dreams. I keep steering people toward my caramel cake, which is still in rotation. There's a German chocolate cake that has people entranced, which I'm pretty sure is store-bought, but there's no accounting for taste. I've never been a fan of German chocolate cake myself, because who wants wet coconut flakes? Shudder.

Kitty's been running around with her friends, and she's deigned to help me out at the cake walk for an hour when Peter walks in with his little brother, Owen. "Pour Some Sugar on Me" is playing. Kitty goes over to say hello, while I busy myself looking at my phone as she's showing them the cakes. I've got my head down, pretend-texting, when Peter comes up beside me.

"Which cake is yours? The coconut one?"

My head snaps up. "I would never buy a grocery-store cake for this."

"I was joking, Covey. Yours is the caramel one. I can tell by the way you frosted it so fancy." He stops talking and shoves his hands in his pockets. "So, just so you know, I didn't go to the nursing home with Gen to help her tag you out."

I shrug. "For all I know you've already texted her and told her I'm here, so."

"I told you, I don't give a shit about this game. I think it's dumb."

"Well, I don't. I'm still planning on winning." I put on the next song for the cake walk, and all the kids run into position. "So are you and Genevieve back together?"

He makes a rude sound. "What do you care?"

Again I shrug. "I knew you'd be back with her eventually."

Peter smarts at this. He turns like he's going to leave, but then he stops. Rubbing the back of his neck, he says, "You never answered my question about McClaren. Was that a date?"

"What do *you* care?"

His nostrils flare. "I fucking care because you were my girlfriend up until a few weeks ago. I don't even remember why we broke up."

"If you can't remember, then I don't know what to say to you."

"Just tell the truth. Don't dick me around." His voice cracks on the word "dick." Any other time we would have laughed about it. I wish we could now. "What's going on with you and McClaren?"

There's a lump in my throat that's making it hard to talk all of a sudden. "Nothing." Just a kiss. "We're friends. He's been helping me with the game."

"How convenient. First he's writing you letters, now he's driving you around town and hanging out with you at a nursing home."

"You said you didn't care about the letters."

"Well, I guess I did."

"Then maybe you should have said so." Kitty's looking

over at us, her forehead pinched. "I don't walk to talk about this anymore. I'm here to work."

Peter eyes me. "Have you kissed him?"

Do I tell the truth? Do I have to? "Yes. Once."

He blinks. "So you're telling me I've been living the life of a celibate person ever since we started this stupid game— before, even—and meanwhile you're fooling around with McClaren?"

"We're broken up, Peter. Meanwhile, when we were actually *together*, you were with Genevieve—"

He throws his head back and yells, "I didn't kiss her!" Some of the adults turn and look at us.

"You had your arms around her," I whisper-yell. "You were *holding* her!"

"I was *comforting* her. God! She was crying! I told you! Did you do it to get back at me?" Peter wants me to say yes. He wants it to have been about him. But I wasn't thinking about Peter when I kissed John. I kissed him because I wanted to.

"No."

The muscle in his jaw twitches. "When we broke up, you said you wanted to be someone's number one girl, but look at you. You don't want to have a number one guy." He gestures rudely at the cake table. "You want to have your cake and eat it too."

His words sting just the way he intends them to. "I hate that saying. What does it even mean? Of course I want to have my cake and eat it too—otherwise what's the point of having cake?"

He frowns at me. "That's not what I'm talking about and you know it."

The song finishes then, and the kids come over to claim their cakes. Kitty and Owen, too. "Let's go," Owen says to Peter. He's got my caramel cake.

Peter glances down at him and then back at me, his eyes hard. "I don't want that one."

"That's the one you told me to get!"

"Well, I don't want it anymore. Put it back and get the Funfetti down there at the end."

"You can't have it," Kitty tells him. "That's not how a cake walk works. You take the cake with the number you were standing on."

Peter's mouth falls open in shock. "Aw, come on, kid."

Kitty moves closer to me. "Nope."

After Peter and his brother leave, I hug Kitty from behind. She was on my side after all. Song girls stick together.

# 52

KITTY WANTED TO STAY LONGER AT THE FAIR, so it's just me driving alone when I spot Genevieve's car on the road. And just like that, I'm following her. It's time to take this girl down.

She's still daring. The way she zips through traffic lights, I almost lose her a few times. *I'm not a good enough driver for this,* I want to scream at her.

We finally end up at an office building, one I recognize as her dad's. She goes inside, and I park in the same strip mall, but not too close. I turn off the engine and recline my seat back so she can't see me.

Ten minutes pass, and nothing. I don't even know why she'd be at her dad's office on a weekend. Maybe she's helping her dad's secretary? I might be stuck here for a while. But I will wait forever if need be. I will win, no matter what. I don't even care about the prize. I just want the win.

I'm about to doze off when two people come out of the building—her dad, in a suit and a camel coat, and a girl. I duck low in my seat. At first I think it's Genevieve, but this girl is taller. I squint. I recognize her. She was Margot's year; I think they were in Key Club together. Anna Hicks. They walk out to the parking lot together; he walks her to her car. She's fumbling for her keys. He grabs her arm and turns her face to his. And then they're kissing. Passionately. Tongue. Hands everywhere.

Oh my God. She's Margot's age. Just eighteen. Genevieve's dad is kissing her like she's a grown woman. He's a dad. She's somebody's daughter.

I feel sick inside. How could he do this to Genevieve's mom? To Gen? Does she know? Is this the hard thing she's been going through? If my dad ever did such a thing, I could never look at him the same way. I don't know that I could look at my *life* the same way. It would be such a betrayal, not just of our family, but of himself, of who he is as a person.

I don't want to see any more. I keep my head down until they both drive out of the parking lot, and I'm about to start my car too when Genevieve walks out, her arms crossed, shoulders bent.

Oh dear God. She's spotted me. Her eyes are narrow; she's heading straight for me. I want to drive away, but I can't. She's standing right in front of me, angrily motioning for me to roll down the window. So I do, but it's hard to look her in the eyes.

She snaps out, "Did you see?"

Weakly I say, "No. I didn't see anything . . ."

Genevieve's face goes red; she knows I'm lying. For a second I am terrified she is going to cry, or hit me. I wish she would just hit me. "Go ahead," she manages. "Tag me out. That's what you came here for." I shake my head, and then she grabs my hands off the steering wheel and slaps them on her collarbone. "There. You win, Lara Jean. Game over."

And then she runs to her car.

There's a Korean word my grandma taught me. It's called *jung*. It's the connection between two people that can't be severed, even when love turns to hate. You still have those old feelings for them; you can't ever completely shake them loose of you; you will always have tenderness in your heart for them. I think this must be some part of what I feel for Genevieve. Jung is why I can't hate her. We're tied.

And jung is why Peter can't let her go. They're tied too. If my dad did what her dad did, wouldn't I reach out to the one person who never turned me away? Who was always there, who loved me more than anyone? Peter is that person for Genevieve. How can I begrudge her that?

# 53

*WE'RE IN THE KITCHEN CLEANING UP AFTER* pancake breakfast when Daddy says, "I believe another one of the Song girls has a birthday coming up." He sings, "You are sixteen, going on seventeen . . ." I feel a strong surge of love for him, my dad who I am so lucky to have.

"What song are you singing?" Kitty interrupts.

I take Kitty's hands and spin her around the kitchen with me. "I am sixteen, going on seventeen; I know that I'm naive. Fellows I meet may tell me I'm sweet; willingly I believe."

Daddy throws his dish towel over his shoulder and marches in place. In a deep voice he baritones, "You need someone older and wiser telling you what to do . . ."

"This song is sexist," Kitty says as I dip her.

"Indeed it is," Daddy agrees, swatting her with the towel. "And the boy in question was not, in fact, older and wiser. He was a Nazi in training."

Kitty skitters away from both of us. "What are you guys even talking about?"

"It's from *The Sound of Music*," I say.

"You mean that movie about the nun? Never seen it."

"How have you seen *The Sopranos* but not *The Sound of Music*?"

Alarmed, Daddy says, "Kitty's been watching *The Sopranos*?"

"Just the commercials," Kitty quickly says.

I go on singing to myself, spinning in a circle like Liesl at the gazebo. "I am sixteen going on seventeen, innocent as a rose. . . . Fellows I meet may tell me I'm sweet, and willingly I believe. . . ."

"Why would you just willingly believe some random fellows you don't even know?"

"It's the song, Kitty, not me! God!" I stop spinning. "Liesl *was* kind of a ninny, though. I mean, it was basically her fault they almost got captured by the Nazis."

"I would venture to say it was Captain von Trapp's fault," Daddy says. "Rolfe was a kid himself—he was going to let them go, but then Georg had to antagonize him." He shakes his head. "Georg von Trapp, he had quite the ego. Hey, we should do a *Sound of Music* night!"

"Sure," I say.

"This movie sounds terrible," Kitty says. "What kind of name is Georg?"

We ignore her. Daddy says, "Tonight? I'll make tacos al pastor!"

"I can't," I say. "I'm going over to Belleview."

"What about you, Kitty?" Daddy asks.

"Sophie's mom is teaching us how to make latke cakes," Kitty says. "Did you know that you put applesauce on top of them and it's delicious?"

Daddy's shoulders slump. "Yes, I did know that. I'm going to have to start booking you guys a month in advance."

"Or you could invite Ms. Rothschild over," Kitty

suggests. "Her weekends are pretty lonely too."

He gives her a funny look. "I'm sure she has plenty she'd rather do than watch *The Sound of Music* with her neighbor."

Brightly I say, "Don't forget the tacos al pastor! Those are a draw, too. And you, of course. You're a draw."

"You're definitely a draw," Kitty pipes up.

"Guys," Daddy begins.

"Wait," I say. "Let me just say one thing. You should be going on some dates, Daddy."

"I go on dates!"

"You've gone on, like, two dates ever," I say, and he falls silent. "Why not ask Ms. Rothschild out? She's cute, she has a good job, Kitty loves her. And she lives really close by."

"See, that's exactly why I shouldn't ask her out," Daddy says. "You should never date a neighbor or a coworker, because then you'll have to keep seeing them if things don't work out."

Kitty asks, "You mean like that quote 'Don't shit where you eat'?" When Daddy frowns, Kitty quickly corrects herself. "I mean 'Don't poop where you eat.' That's what you mean, right, Daddy?"

"Yes, I suppose that's what I mean, but Kitty, I don't like you using cuss words."

Contritely she says, "I'm sorry. But I still think you should give Ms. Rothschild a chance. If it doesn't work out, it doesn't work out."

"Well, I'd hate to see you get your hopes up," Daddy says.

"That's life," Kitty says. "Things don't always work out. Look at Lara Jean and Peter."

I give her a dirty look. "Gee, thanks a lot."

"I'm just trying to make a point," she says. Kitty goes over to Daddy and puts her arms around his waist. This kid is really pulling out all the stops. "Just think about it, Daddy. Tacos. Nuns. Nazis. And Ms. Rothschild."

He sighs. "I'm sure she has plans."

"She told me if you asked her out, she'd say yes," I blurt out.

Daddy startles. "She did? Are you sure?"

"Positive."

"Well . . . then maybe I will ask her out. For a coffee, or a drink. *The Sound of Music* is a bit long for a first date."

Kitty and I both whoop and high-five each other.

# 54

*BIRTHDAY BREAKFAST AT THE DINER WAS A* bit of a tradition with Margot and Josh and me. If my birthday was on a weekday, we'd wake up early and go before school. I'd order blueberry pancakes, and Margot would put a candle in them, and they'd sing.

The day of my seventeenth birthday, Josh sends me a *Happy Bday* text, but I get that we won't be going to the diner. He has a girlfriend now, and it would be weird, especially with no Margot. The text is enough.

For breakfast Daddy makes chorizo scrambled eggs, and Kitty's made me a big card with pictures of Jamie pasted all over it. Margot video-chats me to wish me happy birthday and to tell me my present should be arriving that afternoon or the next.

At school Chris and Lucas put a candle in the donuts they got out of the vending machine and they sing me "Happy Birthday" in the hallway. Chris gives me a new lipstick: red for when I want to be bad, she says. Peter doesn't say anything to me in chemistry class; I doubt he knows it's my birthday, and besides, what could I even expect him to say after the way things ended between us? Still, it's a nice day, uneventful in its niceness.

But then, as I'm leaving school, I see John parked out front.

He's standing in front of his car; he hasn't seen me yet. In this bright afternoon light, the sun warms John's blond head like a halo, and suddenly I'm struck with the visceral memory of loving him from afar, studiously, ardently. I so admired his slender hands, the slope of his cheekbones. Once upon a time I knew his face by heart. I had him memorized.

My steps quicken. "Hi!" I say, waving. "How are you here right now? Don't have you school today?"

"I left early," he says.

"You? John Ambrose McClaren cut school?"

He laughs. "I brought you something." John pulls a box out of his coat pocket and thrusts it at me. "Here."

I take it from him, it's heavy and substantial in my palm. "Should I . . . should I open it right now?"

"If you want."

I can feel his eyes on me as I rip off the paper, open the white box. He's anxious. I ready a smile on my face so he'll know I like it, no matter what it is. Just the fact that he thought to buy me a present is so . . . dear.

Nestled in white tissue paper is a snow globe the size of an orange, with a brass bottom. A boy and girl are ice-skating inside. She's wearing a red sweater; she has on earmuffs. She's making a figure eight, and he's admiring her. It's a moment caught in amber. One perfect moment, preserved under glass. Just like that night it snowed in April.

"I love it," I say, and I do, so much. Only a person who really knew me could give me this gift. To feel so known, so understood. It's such a wonderful feeling, I could cry.

*JENNY HAN*

It's something I'll keep forever. This moment, and this snow globe.

I get on my tiptoes and hug him, and he wraps his arms around me tight and then tighter. "Happy birthday, Lara Jean."

I'm about to get into his car when I see Peter striding over to us. "Hold up a second," he says, a pleasant half smile on his face.

Warily I say, "Hey."

"Hey, Kavinsky," John says.

Peter gives him a nod. "I didn't get a chance to say happy birthday, Covey."

"But—you saw me in chem class . . . ," I say.

"Well, you left in a hurry. I have something for you. Open up your hands." He takes the snow globe out of my hand and gives it to John. "Here, can you hold this?"

I look from Peter to John. Now I'm nervous.

"Hold your hands out," Peter prompts. I look at John one more time before I obey, and Peter pulls something out of his pocket and drops it into my palms. My heart locket. "It's yours."

Slowly I say, "I thought you returned the necklace to your mom's store."

"Nope. Wouldn't look right on another girl."

I blink. "Peter, I can't accept this." I try to give it back, but he shakes his head; he won't take it. "Peter, please."

"No. When I get you back, I'm gonna put that necklace back around your neck and pin you." He tries to hold my eyes with his own. "Like the 1950s. Remember, Lara Jean?"

I open my mouth and then close it. "I don't think pin means what you think it means," I tell him, holding the necklace out to him. "Please, just take it."

"Tell me what your wish is," he urges. "Wish for anything, and I'll give it to you, Lara Jean. All you have to do is ask."

I feel dizzy. All around us, people are exiting the building, walking to their cars. John is standing beside me, and Peter is looking at me like we're the only two people here. Anywhere.

It's John's voice that makes me break away. "What are you *doing*, Kavinsky?" John says, shaking his head. "This is pathetic. You treated her like garbage and now you decide you want her back?"

"Stay out of it, Sundance Kid," Peter snaps. To me he says softly, "You promised you wouldn't break my heart. In the contract you said you wouldn't, but you did, Covey."

I've never heard him sound so sincere, so heartfelt. "I'm sorry," I say, my voice whisper-thin. "I just can't."

I don't look back at Peter as I get into the car, but his necklace is still dangling from my fist. At the last second I turn around, but we're too far away; I can't see if Peter's still there or not. My heart is racing. What would I regret losing more? The reality of Peter or the dream of John? Who can't I live without?

I think back to John's hand on mine. Lying next to him

in the snow. The way his eyes looked even bluer when he laughed. I don't want to give that up. I don't want to give up Peter, either. There are so many things to love about them both. Peter's boyish confidence, his sunny outlook on life, the way he is so kind to Kitty. The way my heart flips over every time I see his car pull up in front of my house.

We drive in silence for a few minutes, and then, looking straight ahead, John says, "Did I even have a shot?"

"I could fall in love with you so easily," I whisper. "I'm halfway there already." His Adam's apple bobs in his throat. "You're so perfect in my memory, and you're perfect now. It's like I dreamed you into being. Of all the boys, you're the one I would pick."

"But?"

"But . . . I still love Peter. I can't help it. He got here first and he . . . he just won't leave."

He sighs a defeated kind of sigh that hurts my heart. "Goddamn it, Kavinsky."

"I'm sorry. I like you, too, John, I really do. I wish . . . I wish we got to go to that eighth grade formal."

And then John Ambrose McClaren says one last thing, a thing that makes my heart swell. "I don't think it was our time then. I guess it isn't now, either." John looks over at me, his gaze steady. "But one day maybe it will be."

# 55

*I'M IN THE GIRLS' BATHROOM, RETYING A BOW* around my ponytail, when Genevieve walks in. My mouth goes dry. She freezes, and then she turns on her heel to go inside a stall. When I say, "You and I are always meeting in the bathroom," she doesn't reply. "Gen . . . I'm sorry for the other day."

Genevieve whirls around and advances on me. "I don't want your apology." She grabs my arm. "But if you tell one single person, I swear to God—"

"I wouldn't!" I cry out. "I won't! I would never do that."

She releases my arm. "Because you feel sorry for me, right?" Genevieve laughs bitterly. "You're such a little phony. Your whole sugary sweet routine makes me sick, you know that? You've got everyone fooled, but I know who you really are."

The venom in her voice stuns me. "What did I ever do to you? Why do you hate me so much?"

"Oh my God. Stop. Quit acting like you don't know. You need to own the shit you did to me."

"Wait a minute," I say. "What *I* did to *you*? You're the one who put a sexy video of me on the Internet! You don't get to change the story because you feel like it. I'm Éponine; you're Cosette! Don't make me out to be the Cosette!"

Her lip curls. "What the fuck are you even talking about?"

"*Les Mis!*"

"I don't watch musicals." She turns like she's going to leave, and then she stops and says, "I saw you guys that day in seventh grade. I saw you kiss him."

*She was there?*

She sees my surprise; she revels in it. "I left my jacket down there, and when I went back to get it, I saw the two of you kissing on the couch. You broke the most basic rule of girl code, Lara Jean. Somehow in your mind you've made me out to be the villain. But what you should know is I wasn't being a bitch just for the sake of being a bitch. You deserved it."

My head is spinning. "If you knew, why did you keep being my friend? You didn't stop being my friend until later."

Genevieve shrugs. "Because I liked throwing it in your face. I had him and you didn't. Believe me, we weren't friends anymore from that moment on."

It's odd that out of all the things she's ever said to me, this hurts the most. "Just so you know, I didn't kiss him. He kissed me. I didn't even think of him that way, not before that kiss."

Then she says, "The only reason he even kissed you that day was because I wouldn't. You were second choice." She runs her hand through her hair. "If you had admitted it back then, I might have forgiven you. Might have. But you never did."

I swallow. "I wanted to. But it was my first kiss, and it was with the wrong guy, and I knew he didn't like me."

It all makes sense. Why she went to such lengths to keep me and Peter apart. Leaning on him, making him prove she was still his first choice. It's no excuse for all the things she's done, but I see my part in it now. I should've told her about the kiss right away, way back in seventh grade. I knew how much she liked him.

"I'm sorry, Genevieve. I truly am. If I could take it back, I would." Her eyebrow twitches, and I know she's not unmoved. Impulsively I say, "We were friends once. Can we—do you think we can ever be friends again?"

She looks at me with such complete and utter disdain, like I'm a child who's asked for the moon. "Grow up, Lara Jean."

In a lot of ways, I feel like I have.

# 56

*I'M LYING DOWN ON MY BACK IN THE TREE* house, looking out the window. The moon is carved so thin, it's a thumbnail clipping in the sky. Tomorrow, no more tree house. I've barely thought about this place, and now that it's disappearing, I'm sad. It's like all childhood toys, I suppose. It doesn't become important until you don't have it anymore. But it's more than just a tree house. It's good-bye, and it feels like the end of everything.

As I sit up, I see it, purple string poking out of a floorboard, sprouting forth like a blade of grass. I tug on the end and it pulls free. It's Genevieve's friendship bracelet, the one I gave to her.

*Believe me, we weren't friends anymore from that moment on.*

That isn't true. We still had sleepovers, birthdays; she still cried to me the time she thought her parents were getting divorced. She couldn't have hated me that whole time. I won't believe it. This friendship bracelet proves it.

Because it's what she put in the time capsule, her most treasured thing, just like it was mine. And then, at the party, she took it out, she hid it; she didn't want me to see. But now I know. I was important to her then too. We were true friends once. Tears spring to my eyes. Good-bye, Genevieve, good-bye middle school years, good-bye tree house and everything that was important to me that one hot summer.

People come in and out of your life. For a time they are your world; they are everything. And then one day they're not. There's no telling how long you will have them near. A year ago I could not have imagined that Josh would no longer be a constant for me. I couldn't have conceived of how hard it would be to not see Margot every day, how lost I would feel without her—or how easily Josh could slip away, without me even realizing. It's the good-byes that are hard.

"Covey?" Peter's voice calls up to me from outside, down below in the dark.

I sit up. "I'm here."

He climbs up the ladder quickly, ducking so his head doesn't hit the ceiling. He crawls over to the tree-house wall opposite from me, so we are sitting on either side. "They're bulldozing the tree house tomorrow," I tell him.

"Oh, yeah?"

"Yeah. They're going to put up a gazebo. You know, like in *The Sound of Music*?"

Peter squints one eye at me. "Why did you call me over here, Lara Jean? I know it wasn't to talk about *The Sound of Music*."

"I know about Genevieve. Her secret, I mean."

He leans his back against the tree-house wall, and his head drops back with a slight thud. "Her dad's an asshole. He's cheated on her mom before. Just never with someone so young." He speaks in a rush, like it's a relief to finally say the words out loud. "When things got really bad with her parents, Gen would find ways to hurt herself. I had to be the one to protect her. That was my job. Sometimes it scared me, but I liked being, I don't know . . . needed." Then he sighs and says, "I know she can be manipulative—I've always known that. In some ways it was easier for me to default back to what I knew. I think maybe I was scared."

My breath catches. "Of what?"

"Of disappointing you." Peter looks away. "I know sex is a big deal to you. I didn't want to mess it up. You're so innocent, Lara Jean. And I have all this shit in my past."

I want to say, *I never cared about your past.* But that isn't true. It's only then that I realize: Peter wasn't the one who needed to get over Genevieve. It was me. All this time with Peter, I've been comparing myself to her, all the ways I don't measure up. All the ways our relationship pales next to theirs. I'm the one who couldn't let her go. I'm the one who didn't give us a chance.

Suddenly he asks, "What do you wish for, Lara Jean? Now that you've won. Congrats, by the way. You did it."

I feel a rush of emotion in my chest. "I wish that things could go back to the way they were between us. That you could be you and I could be me, and we'd have fun with each other, and it would be a really sweet first romance that I'll remember my whole life." I feel like I'm blushing as I say this last bit, but I'm glad I did, because it makes Peter's eyes go soft and caramelly at me for just a second, and I have to look away.

"Don't talk like it's doomed already."

"I don't mean to. The first isn't necessarily the last, but it will always be the first, and that's special. Firsts are special."

"You're not first," Peter says. "But you're the most special to me, because you're the girl I love, Lara Jean."

*Love.* He said "love." I feel dizzy. I am a girl who is loved, by a boy, and not just her sisters and father and dog. A boy with beautiful eyebrows and a sleight of hand. "I've been going crazy without you." He scrubs the back of his head. "Can't we just—"

"You're saying I drive you crazy too?" I interrupt.

He groans. "I'm saying you drive me more crazy than any girl I've ever met."

I crawl toward him, and I reach out and trace my finger along his eyebrow that feels like silk. I say, "In the contract we said we wouldn't break each other's hearts. What if we do it again?"

Fiercely he says, "What if we do? If we're so guarded, it's not going to be anything. Let's do it fucking for real, Lara Jean. Let's go all in. No more contract. No more safety net. You can break my heart. Do whatever you want with it."

I put my hand to his chest, over his heart. I can feel it beating. I let my hand fall away. His heart is mine, just mine. I believe it now. Mine to protect and care for, mine to break.

So much of love is chance. There's something scary and wonderful about that. If Kitty had never sent those letters, if I hadn't gone to the hot tub that night, it might've been him and Gen. But she did send those letters, and I did go out there. It could have happened lots of ways. But this is the way it happened. This is the path we took. *This* is our story.

I know now that I don't want to love or be loved in half measures. I want it all, and to have it all, you have to risk it all.

So I take Peter's hand; I put it on my heart. I tell him, "You have to take good care of this, because it's yours."

He looks at me in such a way that I know for sure—he's never looked at another girl quite like this.

And then I'm in his arms, and we're hugging and kissing, and we're both shaking, because we both know—this is the night we become real.

"Real isn't how you are made," said the Skin Horse.
"It's a thing that happens to you."

"Does it hurt?" asked the Rabbit.

"Sometimes," said the Skin Horse, for he was always truthful.
"When you are Real you don't mind being hurt."

—MARGERY WILLIAMS

# Acknowledgments

With most heartfelt thanks to my editor Zareen Jaffery, who I could not have written this book without. Thanks also to Justin Chanda, my publisher and dear friend, and Anne Zafian, Mekisha Telfer, Katy Hershberger, Chrissy Noh, Lucy Cummins, Lucille Rettino, Christina Pecorale, Rio Cortez, Michelle Fadlalla Leo, Candace Greene, and Sooji Kim. It's been ten years now at S&S and I'm more in love with you now than ever. Thank you also to the S&S Canada team for your steadfast support of me and my books.

All my love and admiration to my incredible agent, Emily van Beek, Molly Jaffa, and the whole Folio team—you are so very appreciated. Thank you also to Elena Yip, my part-time gal Friday.

To Siobhan Vivian, my partner in writing, in crime, and all things. I couldn't do it without you. Adele Griffin, one of my most favorite people in all the world—you always find the pulse of every story. Morgan Matson, here's to that night in London!

And finally, to my readers—all of my love, always.

*Jenny*

## About the Author

Jenny Han is the author of the *New York Times* bestselling books *To All the Boys I've Loved Before* and the Summer I Turned Pretty trilogy. She has also written two middle-grade novels, *Shug* and *Clara Lee and the Apple Pie Dream*. She co-wrote the Burn for Burn trilogy with Siobhan Vivian. Jenny lives in Brooklyn, New York. Visit her at dearjennyhan.com.